"A princess," he repeated numbly.

Lucas pulled his eyebrows into a scowl and swallowed his astonishment. "Well, now. I guess that explains a few things," he said gruffly. "The tabloid photographer. The bodyguard. The kidnap attempt. The alias."

She regarded him solemnly. "You said I'd cause you trouble and now you're thinking you were right, aren't you, Lucas?"

Her true identity would take a bit of digesting, but he knew that now was not the time to make an issue of her royal bloodlines. The look in her eyes told him she was worried about his reaction, that her feelings were hanging on her sleeve.

"I was thinking I'd never kissed a princess before today." He pulled her gently into his arms. "And that I'd like very much to do it again."

Happy New Year, Harlequin Intrigue Reader!

Harlequin Intrigue's New Year's Resolution is to bring you another twelve months of thrilling romantic suspense. Check out this month's selections.

Debra Webb continues her ongoing COLBY AGENCY series with *The Bodyguard's Baby* (#597). Nick Foster finally finds missing Laura Proctor alive and well—and a mother! Now with her child in the hands of a kidnapper and the baby's paternity still in question, could Nick protect Laura and save the baby that might very well be his?

We're happy to have author Laura Gordon back in the saddle again with *Royal Protector* (#598). When incognito princess Lexie Dale comes to a small Colorado ranch, danger and international intrigue follow her. As sheriff, Lucas Garrett has a duty to protect the princess from all harm for her country. But as a man, he wants Lexie for himself....

Our new ON THE EDGE program explores situations where fear and passion collide. In *Woman Most Wanted* (#599) by Harper Allen, FBI Agent Matt D'Angelo has a hard time believing Jenna Moon's story. But under his twenty-four-hour-a-day protection, Matt can't deny the attraction between them—or the fact that she is truly in danger. But now that he knows the truth, would anyone believe *him*?

In order to find Brooke Snowden's identical twin's attacker, she would have to become her. Living with her false identity gave Brooke new insights into her estranged sister's life—and the man in it. Officer Jack Chessman vowed to protect Brooke while they sought a potential killer. But was Brooke merely playing a role with him, or was she falling in love with him—as he was with her? Don't miss *Alyssa Again* (#600) by Sylvie Kurtz.

Wishing you a prosperous 2001 from all of us at Harlequin Intrigue!

Sincerely,

Denise O'Sullivan
Associate Senior Editor
Harlequin Intrigue

ROYAL PROTECTOR

LAURA GORDON

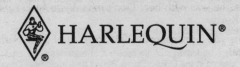

HARLEQUIN®

TORONTO • NEW YORK • LONDON
AMSTERDAM • PARIS • SYDNEY • HAMBURG
STOCKHOLM • ATHENS • TOKYO • MILAN • MADRID
PRAGUE • WARSAW • BUDAPEST • AUCKLAND

ISBN 0-373-22598-9

ROYAL PROTECTOR

This edition published by arrangement with Harlequin Books S.A.

® and TM are trademarks of the publisher. Trademarks indicated with ® are registered in the United States Patent and Trademark Office, the Canadian Trade Marks Office and in other countries.

Visit us at www.eHarlequin.com

Printed in U.S.A.

ABOUT THE AUTHOR

Laura Gordon is a western Colorado author with a penchant for romantic suspense. She is the author of eleven novels. Her greatest joy comes in creating characters who face extraordinary challenges and discover that the magic of their once-in-a-lifetime-love is worth the risk.

When not tied to her desk by deadlines, Laura likes nothing better than hiking the high-country trails of the magnificent mountains near her home. Readers may write Laura Gordon at P.O. Box 55192, Grand Junction, CO 81505.

Books by Laura Gordon

HARLEQUIN INTRIGUE
220—DOUBLE BLACK DIAMOND
255—SCARLET SEASON
282—DOMINOES
316—FULL MOON RISING
345—LETHAL LOVER
387—SPENCER'S SHADOW*
396—SPENCER'S BRIDE*
491—SPENCER'S SECRET*
501—A COWBOY'S HONOR
598—ROYAL PROTECTOR

*The Spencer Brothers

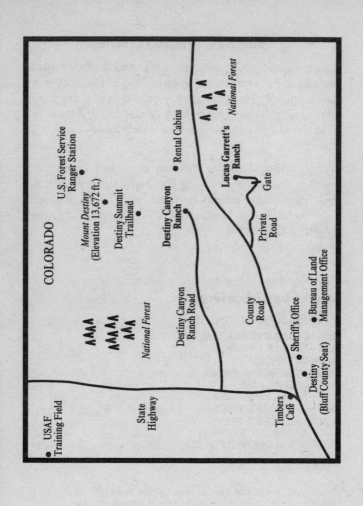

CAST OF CHARACTERS

Lexie Dale—A lovely lady with a secret too deadly to keep.

Lucas Garrett—A lawman and a cowboy determined to protect his home, his family and the woman he loves.

Mo Garrett—With a heart of gold, her home was caught in the crossfire.

Hugh Miller—The victim of a seemingly senseless crime.

Simon Peterson—FBI agent with an attitude.

Tucker Oates—His penchant for gossip proved dangerous.

Will Garrett—Patriarch of a family in turmoil.

Paul Browning—His attention to detail could catch a killer.

Seth Rockwell—Dead witnesses tell no lies.

Inez Estes—This witness has a hot tip for the killer.

Lady Margaret Roche—A blueblood out of place in the West and loving every minute.

Fulton Bobek—The court jester or a man with a vendetta?

Eli Ferguson—A long, tall Texan with an attitude and a badge.

To Tracy.
A real-life princess of grace.

Acknowledgments:

Thanks to Officer Lonnie Chavez of the Grand Junction, Colorado, Police Department for cheerfully and carefully answering my many law enforcement and jurisdiction questions. Thanks, also, to Lynda Sue Cooper for pointing me in the right direction. Special thanks to Kay Bergstrom for her friendship and for always being her inimitable self.

And, finally, my most heartfelt thanks to my editor, Angela Catalano, without whose kindness and compassion this book could not have been written.

Prologue

With the ease of a practiced predator, the sniper moved into position above the trail. Looming pines and rust-colored boulders the size of compact cars afforded him cover, as well as an unobstructed view of his prey. Below, two riders, a man and a woman, came toward him, steadily moving closer to the dark fate he had planned for them.

As he'd been told, the woman rode ahead of her male companion by some fifty yards. She rode well, he couldn't help noticing, with her pretty blond head held high and her slim body moving in perfect sync with the sleek bay mare. More importantly for his purposes, she rode relaxed, unaware of the danger waiting for her.

The sniper allowed himself a brief smile. So far, so good. Everything had gone according to plan, just the way he liked it. No surprises. But then, that was the advantage of a double-cross. The predator always knew what to expect when his victims willingly assisted in their own demise.

Like shooting fish in a barrel. He eased the butt of the rifle against his shoulder and peered through the scope, prepared to take the next crucial step toward a destiny that had been denied him for too long. With a less sophisticated weapon, the rifle's report might have carried a half mile, echoing against the red canyon walls. But his silencer was state-of-the-art.

Confidently, he squeezed the trigger. The ensuing pop barely rated a twitch of one velvety ear from the white-tailed doe and her speckled fawn grazing nearby.

Even as the stricken man fell backward out of the saddle, the assassin knew his shot had found its mark. His victim would be dead before he hit the ground.

Chapter One

Lulled by the rhythmic motions of her well-trained mount and the pristine beauty of a perfect mountain afternoon, Lexie's mind only half-registered the soft popping sound. But with the next heartbeat, her mind made the deadly connection and Lexie knew what she'd heard: a gunshot muffled by a silencer. Someone had fired on them!

"Hugh!" She called out to her companion as she jerked the reins to the right and wheeled around. As Lexie watched in horror, Hugh Miller fell backward in slow motion from the saddle.

Icy fingers of terror closed around her heart as she dug her heels into the mare's sides and raced back to Hugh. Fighting her unbridled fear, she prayed he wasn't dead.

Dismounting at a run, she flung herself to the earth beside him. He lay facedown, and she struggled to turn him over. The grass beneath his head was sticky and wet. *Please don't let him die! Please!*

She rolled him over onto his back. His eyes stared blankly and Lexie gasped. Crimson blood poured from a wound directly in the center of his forehead.

"No!" she sobbed. But even as she denied the awful truth, she knew the worst had happened.

Again.

Stumbling, she rose to her feet and groped for her horse's

reins. Instinct told her to mount up and outrun the danger that made the skin at the back of her neck tingle. But it was too late.

By the time she saw the man wearing the black ski mask, he was already upon her. Numbed by the suddenness of the attack, her arms and legs, and even her mind, seemed temporarily paralyzed. With a hold that was viciously unbreakable, he held her from behind, pinning her arms against her sides. The cloth he pressed over her nose and mouth smothered her cries for help and choked off her airways.

As the acrid smell of some unknown chemical burned her nostrils and blazed a path to her lungs, stinging tears filled her eyes. Her heart convulsed in terror.

Oh God, I don't want to die! Not like this.

With suddenly awakened resolve, Lexie fought for survival with a determination she hadn't known she possessed. Kicking and jerking she battled against the faceless, nameless foe.

When her elbow connected with her attacker's stomach, she heard the sound of his startled gasp and she seized the momentary advantage. Twisting with all her might, she tried again to drive her elbow into his midsection. But this time he anticipated the move and caught her arm and wrenched it painfully behind her back. Lexie's heart sank as the slim opening for possible escape disappeared.

"Help me! Somebody, please help me!" Her pleas were hopelessly muffled as her tormentor pressed the chemically-soaked cloth even harder over her mouth and nose. The acrid-smelling fumes were rapidly working their lethal magic. Every cell in Lexie's body screamed for oxygen.

Sprawled, facedown on the rocky ground beside Hugh Miller, she felt the weight of her attacker's knee in the middle of her back. Helplessly pinned and suffocating, Lexie felt her tenuous hold on consciousness slipping.

She could do nothing as he tied her wrists and secured

the gag even tighter across her nose and mouth. With what little strength she had left, Lexie arched her back and tried to free herself of her attacker's crushing weight.

"Settle down," a cold, hard voice hissed just behind her ear. "Just let it happen. It'll all be over soon."

Lexie's head ached, and her heart beat frantically. The stark reality of her helplessness brought fresh tears to her eyes as she slipped nearer the edge of unconsciousness.

From a distance, she thought she heard someone calling her name. An engine raced. A dog barked. Obviously, the chemical's vapors were not only stealing her strength, but robbing her ability to think straight.

When the world began to spin, she thought she might be sick. Her eyelids fluttered closed and, try as she might, she could not reopen them.

The ensuing darkness that closed over her brought with it a strange mix of stark fear and blessed relief. The worst was over, she told herself. She felt herself sinking slowly, slowly down into a place where there was no light and no sensation, except for the achingly familiar sound of a child crying out from the depths of her darkest memories.

ATTENTION ALL UNITS in the vicinity of mile marker 391 and Destiny Canyon Ranch Road. Reports of a shooting. One unconfirmed fatality. Other injuries reported, but also unconfirmed. Shooter's identity unknown. Officers advised to approach the area with extreme caution.

Even before the dispatcher finished her call, Sheriff Lucas Garrett cranked the steering wheel hard to the left and sent the white SUV with the Bluff County sheriff's seal emblazoned on the doors into a skidding U-turn.

With his free hand he reached for the handheld radio on the seat beside him. "Sylvia, this is Sheriff Garrett. I'm less than five minutes from the scene. Fill me in."

Despite the early summer air rushing through the open

window, it chilled him to think of his family's high-country ranch as a crime scene.

"It happened in the hills, Sheriff. Five miles out on Summit Trail."

Immediately, an image of the narrow, winding trail that led to the summit of Mount Destiny formed in Lucas's mind. He'd ridden that trail on horseback and hiked it on foot countless times, but it had never seemed ominous in any way until now.

"Who made the call?" he asked. "Was it Cal?" Or had it been his older sister, Maureen—or Mo, as everyone had always called her.

"No, sir. It was Virgil."

Virgil Blackburn had been the foreman at Destiny Canyon Ranch for as long as Lucas could remember. "Did Virgil say what had happened? Do you have any idea who was…hurt?"

"No, sir," Sylvia came back quickly. "He just said a man had been shot. Killed. And that a woman had been injured. He said he was calling from an extension in the barn. He hung up while I was dispatching emergency medical."

"Try calling the house," Lucas ordered.

"I already did, Sheriff. Right after Virgil hung up. But no one answered. I'll try again and get back to you."

Lucas thanked his dispatcher and with a mounting feeling of dread, he tossed the radio onto the seat beside him and tried to concentrate on his driving.

As the speedometer inched past ninety, his eyes remained riveted on the road. His thoughts, however, were firmly fixed on his family, on Pop and Cal and Mo. The loved ones who still resided on the ranch where he'd grown into manhood, where some of his sweetest memories lived on, as well.

Despite the lawman's logic that told him not to jump to

conclusions, Lucas couldn't shake the words *fatality* and *injuries* from his mind.

Why hadn't Cal made the call? Where was Mo? And why hadn't anyone picked up the phone when Sylvia called back? Those questions and a dozen more, equally disconcerting, nagged him as he raced down the highway toward the unknown.

When he was within a mile of the ranch turnoff, he grabbed his radio again. "Unit 4, come in."

Deputy Eli Ferguson responded immediately.

"What's your location, Eli?" Lucas asked.

"Westbound at 376."

"Any sign of an ambulance?"

"They're right behind me, Lucas." His usually calm west Texas twang sounded tight and tense. "I'll stay with them and escort them all the way in."

Eli signed off and two more deputies checked in. Lucas could hear the edge in his men's voices. He knew they were all thinking the same thing: The call to Destiny Canyon Ranch could mean one of his own family members had been shot. A call that involved a loved one was every cop's worst nightmare.

And Sheriff Lucas Garrett was no exception.

IN A CLOUD OF DUST, Lucas roared up in front of the sprawling ranch house where various members of the Garrett clan had lived for going on fifty years.

Cal was waiting at the edge of the yard, and Lucas couldn't remember ever being more pleased to see anyone than he was to see the man who had always been more like a brother than a nephew. Like all the Garrett men, Cal was a big man, tall and broad-shouldered. He crossed the gravel driveway in four long strides and met Lucas as he was getting out of the SUV.

"I'm glad you're here," Cal said.

"Where's Mo? Is she all right?"

"She's inside."

"What about Pop? Where is he? Are you sure Mo's okay?" Lucas fired off his questions in rapid succession as he charged across the drive, with Cal close beside him.

"They're fine. Everyone's fine," Cal said. At the gate that opened into the yard, he put a hand to Lucas's shoulder. "Slow down and listen to me, will you? Everyone's fine. The family wasn't involved."

Lucas stood staring at his nephew, almost afraid to allow himself the relief that flooded him. "Thank God." He felt the gentle pressure as Cal squeezed his shoulder in agreement. "So, what did happen? Sylvia said a man had been shot."

"He was one of Mo's guests." Cal pulled his battered straw Stetson from his head, ran a hand through his dark hair and sighed. "And he's dead. Poor bastard never knew what hit him. The woman was riding with him. She was attacked and hogtied. Somebody tried to drug her, but she seems to be all right, now."

Both men turned to see Eli Ferguson and the ambulance pulling into the drive. Cal motioned the paramedics through the gate and across the yard toward the front door.

"Tell us what you know, Cal," Lucas said when Eli had joined them on the porch.

"They were about five miles out on Summit Trail, on their way back after spending the night camped out on the mountain."

"Any sign of the shooter?"

Cal shook his head. "No. He was long gone by the time I got up there. I left a couple of my ranch hands to stay with the body until you could get here." Cal went on to address Lucas's concerns before he could voice them. "Don't worry. They're both armed and I told them to watch their backs and not to disturb any tracks that might still be there."

"I'll need horses for half a dozen men," Lucas said. It wouldn't be easy tracking the killer through the miles of National Forest that bordered the ranch, but it would be nearly impossible on foot.

Cal nodded. "No problem."

Lucas started back toward his vehicle and both men followed. As he walked, he gave Deputy Ferguson his orders. "Stay here and get a preliminary statement from the woman. I'll want to question her myself, later. But right now I need to get up on the mountain. Call the officer at the Mount Destiny ranger station and apprise him of the situation. Tell him to keep his eyes open and his back covered."

Once Lucas got to the crime scene, he'd set a perimeter and establish a command post. Afterward, he'd send his deputies—six, not counting the man he planned to assign to guard duty at the ranch house—into the mountains to try to track the killer. If they were lucky, they'd pick up a trail before nightfall.

"Helluva deal," Cal said as he followed Lucas back to his vehicle. "A man comes here for a vacation and gets shot out of the saddle in broad damn daylight." He sighed and shook his head. "Who'd have thought something like this could happen here?"

"What can you tell me about the dead man, Cal?"

"Name's Miller. Hugh Miller. He checked in on Tuesday after booking a cabin for a month."

"What about his wife? Have you talked to her?"

"No. And she's not his wife. Her name's Lexie Dale. She checked in on Tuesday, as well, but she's staying in her own separate cabin."

"Miller's significant other?"

"I wouldn't know," Cal said.

Lucas wasn't surprised that his cousin had so little information about the couple. Cal had given Mo's guest operation a wide berth from day one. As long as the tourists who stayed in the four small hunting cabins at the edge of the ranch property stayed clear of his cattle and his hay fields, Cal could almost tolerate them.

"There's a good chance Mo knows more about both of them," Cal said. "You know how she is."

Lucas had to smile. Yes, he knew exactly how his older sister went out of her way to make each guest feel as if they were a member of the Garrett family. And when it came to singles, she could be a shameless matchmaker. Although never married, Mo considered herself an expert on relationships. If anyone could give Lucas the lowdown on the relationship between Hugh Miller and Lexie Dale, it was Mo.

"Cal, what do you make of this shooting?" Lucas asked as he pulled open the door and slid behind the wheel. "Do you think it could have been an accident?"

"Doubtful. There's a bullet hole between the man's eyes that looks damn deliberate to me."

"Sounds like our shooter is better than a fair marksman."

Cal frowned. "God only knows what he had planned for Miss Dale. She was unconscious when Mo found her."

A single fact stuck in Lucas's mind and chilled his blood. "Are you telling me Mo was there?"

Cal nodded. "And lucky for Miss Dale, she was. That worthless pup of Mo's wandered off again this morning. She and Tucker Oates were driving around in the Jeep, looking for the dog when they heard somebody yelling for help."

Cal and Lucas exchanged a resigned glance. Both of them wished Mo would be more cautious, but they knew she had a heart as big as all outdoors and would never turn her back on a stray of either the two-legged or four-legged variety.

"Then what?"

"The noise from the Jeep must have scared off the attacker," Cal went on. "They found Hugh Miller dead at the side of the trail. Not far from his body, Lexie Dale was tied up and unconscious."

"She was drugged?"

"Looks like whoever killed Hugh Miller meant to carry her off with him," Cal said.

"And Mo interrupted him right in the middle of his crime." His own sister could have easily become the killer's next victim, Lucas thought grimly. If he'd needed further incentive to bring the killer in, he'd just found it.

He put the SUV in gear. "Did you see anything that might give us an idea who did it?"

"No. But, then, I didn't do much looking around. I didn't want to destroy any evidence."

Lucas nodded and started to pull away when an afterthought struck him. "Tell Mo not to worry. If she needs me to help out with Pop, I'll be around later." It had been six months since Will Garrett's stroke. During that time, the family had formed a protective circle around the ailing patriarch, hoping to make his recovery as peaceful and complete as possible.

Cal said he would deliver the message and Lucas gunned the engine and raced out of the ranch yard and past the stables toward the trail that wound seven miles to the summit of Mt. Destiny.

Despite the disturbing reality that a man had been murdered on Garrett property, Lucas experienced immeasurable relief knowing his family was safe. As he bumped along the trail headed for the crime scene, however, the reality of what had happened took shape in his lawman's brain: A man had been shot to death and a woman attacked. A killer was still on the loose.

It was the kind of crime he might have expected on the city streets where he'd spent five years becoming the kind of lawman qualified to become Bluff County Sheriff.

At age thirty-two, with nearly ten years law enforcement experience under his belt, Lucas Garrett could hardly be called naive, and yet the crime that had taken place today—a seemingly cold-blooded and calculated murder and an attempted abduction—still shocked him. Not because of its brutality, but because it had happened here, on the land that had been his family's home for a generation.

His family and this ranch meant the world to him. Weaned on high-country air and the Garrett heritage of hard work, self-respect and dedication to duty, Lucas took seriously his role as Will Garrett's son. His place within the family defined him as surely as his badge, and protecting those closest to him was even more important than his career.

For a man like Lucas Garrett, the crime that had occurred this morning was almost a personal affront. Things like this just did not happen in Bluff County. Not on his watch, anyway. And sure as hell not on his own doorstep.

THREE HOURS LATER, the effects of the chemical that had rendered Lexie senseless seemed to have finally dissipated. Except for a small bruise over her eye and a metallic taste at the back of her throat that not even Mo Garrett's coffee could dispel, Lexie felt almost human again.

Bit by bit, with Mo's help, she'd been able to piece together the bizarre events of the afternoon, events that had cost a man his life and landed her flat on her back on a couch in the main house at the ranch where she'd rented a cabin for what she'd hoped would be a peaceful month-long vacation.

So much for that fantasy, she thought.

While the paramedics were checking her out, tending to her minor cuts and bruises, a deputy sheriff had taken her statement and then asked Lexie to remain where she was until the sheriff could interview her himself. He also informed her that she was not to leave the main house, where uniformed deputies had been placed on guard.

Lexie had listened politely to the deputy and assured him of her cooperation. But even as she'd given her statement, Lexie knew talking to the local authorities was a waste of everyone's time.

What happened this morning went way beyond anything the Bluff County sheriff's department had the resources or the ability to handle—not that she didn't wish they could. If only it could be so easy....

But Lexie knew better than to even hope. Nothing in her life had ever been that easy, that simple. Or even normal, for that matter. And now, in light of this latest tragedy, it seemed it never would.

If a killer had found her here, in this remote corner of the Colorado Rockies, then there was no safety anywhere. No normalcy. No hope for the peaceful anonymity she'd tried so long to attain. After all her efforts to prove her father wrong, in the end it seemed that maybe he was right. Maybe a simple day-to-day existence really was impossible for someone born to a family whose mere existence made headlines.

As it had countless times over the course of her twenty-eight years, the unfairness of her situation frustrated and angered her. If she lived to be one hundred and two she'd never understand why an accident of birth should hold such power over one's life. Or why the lives of everyone with whom she came in contact seemed to be so negatively impacted. It all seemed so unfair—unfair and obscene—to think a man's life counted for nothing.

Once the wheels of her father's publicity machine started grinding, the events of today would no longer be a matter of *who* had been murdered this afternoon on that mountain trail, but *why*. The humanity of Hugh Miller would be lost in the gears of political damage control, sensationalism and spin.

Shuddering at the thought of the turmoil the next few days and weeks would inevitably bring, Lexie realized the time had come to get herself together and make some decisions. And the most immediate decision had to do with how she was going to handle the local sheriff, what she would and would not tell him about what she suspected was the motive for Miller's murder and the attempt to abduct her. It *had* been a kidnapping attempt. Of that, she was certain.

But before she could decide anything, she had to get to a phone. And fast. If news of Hugh Miller's murder reached her father secondhand there would be hell to pay. Of course, there would be hell to pay, anyway, she thought grimly.

For as far back as she could remember, her longing for independence and her determination to live her own life her way had put her at direct odds with her powerful father. An incident like this would only refuel that conflict and reinforce her father's position that she should be brought back immediately into the family fold, under his control. And coming as it had on the heels of the debacle at Marycrest Prep, Lexie didn't know if she had the strength to stand up to him again.

Although she dreaded making the call and facing the inevitable confrontation, Lexie knew she couldn't put it off any longer. With a resigned sigh, she swung her legs over the edge of the couch and sat up. Immediately a wave of dizziness pushed her back down.

The middle-aged woman in the chair across from Lexie

set aside the book she'd been reading. A frown pulled her pale mouth downward.

"I wouldn't try to get up too fast, Lexie. You know what the paramedics said, that the effects of the drug might still be working their way out of your system." She refilled a water glass from the pitcher on the table beside her and handed it to the grateful Lexie.

"You know, I still think it would have been a good idea to let the paramedics take you to the hospital to be thoroughly checked out."

There was no way Lexie could tell Mo Garrett that in all probability she would be examined by the world's foremost physicians some time in the next twenty-four hours. A woman like Mo would, no doubt, find that claim incredible. Everything about Lexie's hostess and unlikely rescuer, from the silver-gray braid that hung down the middle of her back to her well-worn moccasins and faded blue jeans, reflected her utter lack of pretense.

"The paramedics said my vital signs were normal," Lexie reminded Mo. "And I *am* feeling much better. *Really*," she reiterated, hoping to make up for the lack of conviction in her voice.

The older woman tipped her head to one side and studied Lexie skeptically. "Well…maybe so. But I'll still feel better once Doc Rogers gets here." Mo rose from her chair to pace across the room and stand peering out one of the two large bay windows that dominated the west wall. "He ought to have arrived by now. I left the message with his secretary an hour ago."

"I'm surprised he makes house calls," Lexie said.

"Doc Rogers spends more time running around than in his office. He not only has a general practice, but he's the county coroner. I guess he got tied up at the crime scene."

Lexie filed away that piece of information. She needed to be careful what she said around the doctor. It bothered her that she had to watch her every word. But such was the reality of her life—a life she'd spent shunning the spotlight and yet despite all her precautions, all the scheming and planning, here she was center stage again.

Would it ever be any different? she wondered miserably. Or was she doomed to a life of unsuccessfully playing a game of hide-and-seek with first one pursuer and then another?

A sudden realization of the self-pitying nature of her thoughts brought Lexie up short. A horrible tragedy had occurred. A man was dead. A life had been lost for the sake of preserving hers.

Again.

Knowing she'd caused another man's death brought guilt crashing down on her from all sides. If only she hadn't insisted on spending the night on the mountain. If only she hadn't come to Colorado, in the first place. If only she'd recognized the disaster brewing at Marycrest Prep.

If only Hugh Miller hadn't died.

Before the depressing thoughts could overwhelm her, she forced herself to deal with the next unpleasant task. "I wonder if it would be possible to use your phone?"

"Of course," Mo said. "But are you sure you're up to it? You're still awfully pale."

Lexie saw Mo's gaze taking in her disheveled appearance and she ran a hand through her tangled, shoulder-length hair. "I must look a mess."

Mo's smile was genuine. "Honey, on our best day there aren't many of us who look as good as you do now."

Lexie dismissed the compliment with a quick, "Thanks. And now, if you could just direct me to the phone..." She started to rise again and was surprised and distressed to find her knees still rubbery.

As if sensing her distress, Mo moved back to the couch

and sat down beside her. "Listen, honey. Why don't I make that call for you. Is it your family? Your mom and dad?"

The older woman's kindness touched Lexie. From the moment of her arrival everyone at Destiny Canyon Ranch had treated her like...well, like royalty. And no one had been more thoughtful and welcoming than Mo Garrett, herself.

"It's just my father," Lexie explained. "My mother died when I was very young." That bit of personal information slipped out unexpectedly, leaving Lexie to wonder why she'd revealed even that much about herself to someone who was, for all intents, still a virtual stranger.

"Anyway," she went on quickly, "I think it would be better if I talked to my father myself." And that, Lexie thought ruefully, was the understatement of the year.

"There's a phone in the hallway, and one on the wall in the kitchen. My niece, Jolie, has been after me to buy one of those cordless things, but I just haven't seen the need—until now, that is. Guess we must seem pretty old-fashioned to you. I suppose everyone in Atlanta has a cordless phone."

With an inward groan, Lexie recalled making up the address in Atlanta when she'd called to make her reservations. The lie had been fabricated on impulse. At the time, she'd just wanted to cover her tracks. Obviously, she hadn't covered them well enough.

Looking back, she realized the lie hadn't really been necessary. Even if Boston's social news story of the year had somehow made it this far west, she doubted Mo Garrett would have been interested enough to read it.

The lie about coming from Atlanta now seemed silly, especially when in only a matter of hours all her lies would be revealed. Besides, the truth about her fictitious Atlanta address would be a minor aside when compared to the truth about her identity, and the awful truth behind why Hugh Miller had been murdered.

Suddenly, Lexie felt utterly heartsick and desperately alone. In an uncharacteristic and unexpected surge of unchecked emotion, a tear slipped from the corner of her eye and trickled down her cheek.

"Are you sure I can't make that call for you?" Mo asked again.

Lexie shook her head and swiped at the pools of moisture gathering in her eyes. "Thanks, but no. I think it would be better if he heard about what has happened from me." With her emotions so close to the surface, she wondered if she had the strength to deal with the inevitable confrontation that would follow. Wouldn't it be better to wait until she felt stronger, more in control?

Besides, how could she give her father an accurate report of her physical condition before a real doctor had examined her? Upon further assessment of the situation, it seemed to Lexie not only preferable, but prudent to delay the conversation.

"You know, maybe you're right. Maybe I should wait to call my father until after the doctor checks me out."

Mo's smile was understanding. "Any father would want to know if something like this had happened to his daughter. But I have a feeling that whenever you call, he'll just be so relieved to know you're safe it won't matter that you've waited to contact him."

"You don't know my father," Lexie muttered almost to herself.

"No. But I'm sure your well-being is all he cares about."

There was no way Lexie could respond to Mo's observation. It would be nice to think that every father had only his children's best interests at heart, but in her own case,

Lexie knew better. In fact, she'd never had any illusions about her place on her father's list of priorities.

Of course he cared about her personal safety, but the precious family name, an unblemished public image and positive public perception mattered more. Far more. And that was precisely why the call to him could wait, she told herself resolutely.

With a sigh, Lexie leaned back against the butter-soft leather cushions and closed her eyes. She figured she must have dozed off, because she felt disoriented when she heard footsteps and Mo talking in a low voice to whomever had entered the room.

"Of course, I'm all right," Mo was saying. "It was all over by the time I got there."

Lexie opened her eyes.

"Lexie, honey," Mo said in a gentle voice she might have used to awaken a sleeping child. "This is my brother, Lucas."

The tall, broad-shouldered cowboy standing beside Mo nodded in her direction. "Miss Dale."

The whiteness of his western-cut shirt was a dramatic contrast to hair so dark the sun streaming through the window behind him picked up blue highlights. His long legs were encased in dark blue denim. His boots were black, like the Stetson he held in one large, tanned hand.

"Lucas is the sheriff of Bluff County," Mo said.

Lexie realized she was staring hard and inappropriately long, but for the life of her she felt powerless to look away. She'd been in the company of some of the most attractive and eligible bachelors in the world, but if she'd ever set eyes on a more arrestingly handsome man, she couldn't remember when.

And it wasn't merely his impressive physique or the aura of strength that seemed to surround him that captured Lexie's attention. Nor was it the rich darkness of his hair or the strong outline of his chiseled profile that held her full attention and made her forget for that moment why he was here.

It was his eyes. Those blue, blue eyes, the color of a priceless gemstone, with the same stunning clarity and fascinating depth. The kind of eyes that could look right through a woman or touch the deepest corner of her heart.

"I read the statement you gave my deputy, Miss Dale, and I'd like to clarify a few details, if you don't mind." His voice was deep, rough-edged and strangely appealing. It was the kind of voice that left no question who was in charge.

"All right," she said uncertainly. She tried to tell herself her slightly breathless state was a remnant of the ordeal she'd endured this afternoon on the mountain. But deep down, she sensed it had more to do with her unexpected reaction to Mo Garrett's blue-eyed brother.

Chapter Two

"I'll try to keep this brief, Miss Dale. I know you've been through a lot already, today."

Sheriff Garrett seemed not only thoughtful, but competent and articulate, qualities Lexie hadn't expected to find in a small-town sheriff.

"Ready?" he asked.

She took a deep breath as he settled his tall, athletic frame into the winged chair opposite hers and she reminded herself that all she had to do was repeat what she'd told Deputy Ferguson. If she kept her answers short and to the point, perhaps she could get through this interview with her anonymity intact. Now was not the time to allow a case of simple chemistry to muddle her thinking.

With a bit a luck and just the right verbal maneuvering, she could keep the handsome lawman from delving too deeply into Hugh Miller's murder, at least until the proper authorities arrived to take control of the situation.

"Just start at the beginning, Miss Dale," he said. "Tell me exactly what happened, all that you remember."

"As I told your deputy, everything happened so quickly. One minute I was riding along, enjoying the afternoon and the next thing I knew Hugh had been shot. I was attacked by a man wearing a black ski mask." She added, "I'm sorry. There isn't much more to tell."

His smile was understanding. "It isn't unusual for the victim of a violent crime to want to forget the incident. But later, sometimes hours or even days afterward, important details come to mind. I know it's the last thing you want to do, Miss Dale, but I need you to try to remember those details now."

For some reason, she didn't want him calling her by the name she'd assumed for her trip to Colorado. Her lie felt somehow more indicting coming from his lips. "It's just Lexie," she said.

He smiled again. "All right, Lexie it is. And please, feel free to call me Lucas."

But at the moment, she couldn't have said his name if she'd tried. Her mouth had gone too dry to speak. There was just something about the man, a compelling mix of gentleness and strength that affected her in ways she couldn't begin to explain.

"Perhaps you remember more than you realize. Was there anything unusual about his clothing? Did he wear a wristwatch? Maybe you noticed a tattoo?"

"I think he was dressed all in black. There wasn't anything odd, except for the ski mask."

"Did you hear the gunfire?"

"There was only one shot," she said.

"It must have echoed in the canyon."

"No," she said. "There was only a popping noise. He must have used a silencer."

When he made a note, Lexie wondered if she was saying too much. Of course, she wanted the killer to be apprehended, but to encourage this investigation was futile.

"Maybe there was something unusual in the way he talked," Lucas suggested. "You told Deputy Ferguson he spoke to you."

Lexie shook her head. She didn't want to think about the

attack, the physical violation. She didn't want to remember the hissing sound of her attacker's voice in her ear.

"Do you have any idea why someone would want to harm you, Lexie?"

The sudden change in the direction of his questioning caught her off guard. *Darn it!* Why hadn't she called her father when she'd had the chance? If she'd discussed the situation with him or one of his advisors she would have been better prepared to answer loaded questions.

When she realized he was still waiting for her reply, she pushed a hand through her hair self-consciously and swallowed the panicky feeling she knew would be her undoing. Giving her statement to Deputy Ferguson was one thing. Holding up under Lucas Garrett's blue-eyed scrutiny was proving to be quite another.

"You know, on second thought, I'm not really sure I'm up to this, yet." Her gaze shifted to Mo as she entered the room carrying a coffeepot and mugs on a tray.

"I promise, this won't take long," Lucas said before his sister could come to Lexie's rescue for the second time today.

"But I didn't see anything," Lexie reiterated. "I told your deputy and now I'm telling you."

"But you were there."

She shuddered and wrapped her arms around herself, recalling the sight of a stricken Hugh Miller falling from the saddle, remembering the feel of the attacker's rough touch on her skin.

"I know it's difficult. But it's important. We need your help to catch this guy."

Despite her resolve to stall and postpone, Lexie felt drawn to Lucas's sympathetic coaxing. And once she started talking, it only took a few minutes to recount the events of the attack.

As she spoke, she relived the attack that had come out of

nowhere, the arms grabbing her from behind, the smell of the chemical-soaked rag and her subsequent descent into oblivion. "I barely remember your sister helping me into the Jeep," she finished.

"She was out cold when Tucker and I found her," Mo put in. "And other than poor Mr. Miller, there wasn't a sign of anyone else around."

Lucas's expression turned grim and Lexie guessed he was imagining how close his sister had come to becoming a third victim. "There must have been something," he said. "The killer didn't hike down that trail. He must have had a vehicle or a horse."

"Or maybe he planned to use our horses to make his escape," Lexie said. As soon as she spoke, she realized that she was taking a more active part in this investigation than she'd intended.

"But he left those horses behind." Lucas considered for a moment. "Seems to me, Lexie, there was a reason for drugging you and tying your wrists. Can you think of why he might have done that?"

Abduction. Kidnapping. But that was a line of questioning she knew better than to pursue. "I wouldn't even try to second-guess a motive."

Something else occurred to her. "Your men have been on the trail investigating this afternoon. Surely you've found clues indicating whether the killer was on horseback or in a car."

His eyebrows raised, acknowledging her intelligent assumption. "We found tire tracks."

Her correct deduction pleased her, and she permitted herself another question. "Where?"

"Just around the bend in the trail. About a hundred yards from where we found Hugh Miller's body."

"I didn't see a vehicle," she said. "And I didn't hear an engine starting up."

"Let's go back to last night, Lexie," he said. "You spent the night on the mountain. On your way up the trail, did you see anyone else? Another rider? Hikers? Someone in a vehicle, maybe?"

Lexie shook her head. "No. No one."

"What about this morning? Did you see anyone on your way down the trail?"

"No."

"When did you realize Hugh Miller had been shot?"

Lexie hesitated. "I—I'm not sure."

"Was it when you heard gunfire?"

"Yes."

"Let's talk about that muffled pop," he said, consulting his notes. "How did you know it was a silenced gunshot?"

"I'm familiar with firearms," she said defensively. This interrogation was veering onto potentially dangerous ground. "My older brother owns an extensive weapons collection."

She was impressed that Lucas had picked up on that bit of information. Unfortunately, this interview was largely meaningless. Very soon the entire investigation would be removed from the local sheriff's auspices and taken over by a higher authority. The FBI, probably. Or maybe the Federal Marshal's office. She didn't know exactly how these things were handled. But she did know her father, knew he'd demand a full-scale investigation by the country's top law enforcement officials be launched.

She also knew he'd insist the local authorities, which in this case meant Sheriff Lucas Garrett, be removed from the case before the ink had a chance to dry on her statement.

Lexie poured herself a cup of coffee and lifted the mug to her lips. Too bad Lucas Garrett wouldn't have the chance to finish this investigation. He seemed intelligent, thorough and highly motivated to solve the crime.

He added sugar to his own coffee before asking, "How many gunshots were there?"

"I told you before. Only one."

"Are you sure about that?"

Lexie nodded.

"But you didn't see a gun or the shooter?"

"I told you, I didn't see anything."

"Were you and Hugh Miller riding side by side?" he asked.

"Single file," she said. "He was way behind me."

"How far?"

"Maybe fifty yards."

"And when you realized he was shot, what did you do?"

"I rode back to see if I could help him."

As she visualized those moments, she realized that her instinct to help Hugh had probably saved her from abduction. The kidnapper had obviously been waiting for her. His vehicle was parked just beyond the bend in the road.

If she'd gone forward, she would have run right into him. In fact, that had probably been his plan. If she'd stayed frozen in one place, he would only have to carry her limp, drugged body twenty or thirty yards.

But she had returned to help Hugh. When the kidnapper finally overwhelmed her, they were probably over a hundred yards from his getaway car—too far to drag her body before Mo and Tucker Oates approached.

"What is it?" Lucas asked. "What do you remember?"

Though her deduction offered a significant understanding of the murder and kidnap attempt, she didn't believe it was wise to share her thoughts with him. As soon as she mentioned kidnapping, she might as well print her real name in banner letters. "It's nothing," she said. "I was just thinking about Mr. Miller...."

"This is important, Lexie. You're the sole witness to a murder, the last person to see the victim alive."

"Except for the murderer," she said grimly.

"Of course." His eyes narrowed slightly, but the subtle

change in his demeanor was not lost on Lexie. The man was keenly tuned in to her every nuance. Lucas Garrett might only be a local sheriff in a remote and sparsely populated Colorado county, but every instinct told Lexie there was nothing second rate about his investigative skills. He was astute, intuitive and intelligent, an intriguing combination she found deeply attractive. But also dangerous.

She knew she wasn't yet strong enough to match wits with him. Exhaustion crept over her. Her hand shook when she placed her mug on the pine coffee table in front of her.

"She's not up to this, Lucas," Mo said. "Surely you can see that. Why don't you come back later, after she's seen Doc Rogers."

"Maybe you're right." He rose from the chair. "We'll talk again tomorrow morning."

Though Lexie had been hoping this interrogation would end, she felt suddenly abandoned.

Lucas moved to the doorway, but stopped and turned to face her once more. "Could you handle one last question, Lexie?"

"I suppose so."

"What was your relationship to Hugh Miller?"

His stare was unwavering, and she felt pinned where she sat. *Be careful,* an inner voice warned. *Remember what's at stake.* A careless word here, a misquote there and faster than you could say tabloid, the family name would be dragged through every mud hole from here to Paris and back again.

The lessons that had been drilled into her since childhood came back like the words to a familiar nursery rhyme: *Never relinquish control of an interview. Never let your emotions show or speak without thinking. Take your time. Set the pace. Remember, above all, that when you speak, you're speaking for the family.*

Coolly, she returned his gaze. "There was no relationship, Sheriff."

"You checked in to cabin number one on Tuesday afternoon. Within hours, Miller checked in to cabin number two. Did you know each other before you came here?"

She was able to answer with absolute honesty. "I never met Hugh Miller until I came here."

"You were riding together this morning. Last night, you spent the night together on the mountain."

Those were the facts, and she knew how they must look to the outside observer. "It's not what you're thinking."

"Then, why don't you straighten me out?"

"Miller and I left separately for our ride. We both happened to be on Summit Trail at the same time, but we hardly spoke." She confronted him directly, telling the truth. "We slept in separate tents. If you meant to infer that there was some sort of romantic relationship between us, you'd be dead wrong."

"I could've told you that," Mo put in. "Lexie and Mr. Miller were strangers. Anyone could see that."

"I need to hear it from Lexie," Lucas said to his sister.

"Well, excuse me for trying to be helpful." She scowled at him.

"I know," Lucas said. "But now's not the time. I'll be back later. We'll talk more then."

Mo gave her brother a curt nod even as he turned his attention back to Lexie. "A man has been killed, gunned down in cold blood. You, yourself, were attacked and drugged. Whoever perpetrated these crimes is still out there and it's my job to apprehend him. And, like it or not, Lexie, you're the one person who can give me the information I need to do it."

Despite herself, Lexie felt bound by the intensity of words and the heat of his stare. She couldn't have looked the other way if her life had depended upon it.

"Think about it," he said. The front door closed behind

him, but his admonition hung in the air, vibrating in the tense silence he'd left behind.

Think about it, he'd said. And Lexie knew with absolute certainty that from now until the next time she saw the tall, dark, blue-eyed sheriff she would think of little else.

IT WAS ALMOST MIDNIGHT by the time Lucas pulled up in front of his one-story log home and cut the engine. The smell of pine, sharp and strong, came from looming spruce trees at the edges of the yard. On his way to the door, Lucas exhaled a deep breath into the clear night air and did his best to release the tension that was a fact of life for every cop who took his job as seriously as he did.

Earlier, he'd stopped by the house to feed and water his horses. The four purebred Quarter horses that were his pride and joy would be fine for tonight. All that was left was to fix himself something to eat and find a way to turn off his brain so he could get some sleep.

As always, Rocky was waiting on the porch, his ears peaked forward, tail wagging and an expression that in human terms could only be described as a welcoming smile.

"I could have used your help today, old man," Lucas said as he reached down to stroke the three-legged dog's thick tawny coat. Tomorrow he planned to find out if Rocky could pick up the killer's trail—something Lucas and his deputies had so far been unable to do. Other than a couple of dubious footprints and generic-looking tire tracks, they hadn't found any sign of the killer or discovered one useful clue. Lucas had hoped to find a spent shell casing or some other evidence left behind by whomever had murdered Hugh Miller and attacked Lexie Dale.

"Lexie Dale," Lucas grumbled her name aloud as he shoved open the front door, waited for Rocky to slip inside and then slammed it behind him harder than he'd intended.

The woman with the intriguing violet-blue eyes, honey

blond hair and the face of an angel was nothing if not an unmitigated liar. And a lousy one at that, Lucas thought with a frown.

It was bad enough that she was a reluctant witness, but what made the situation especially troublesome for Lucas was the way the she'd gotten under his skin. For some unknown reason, she seemed to have a stranglehold on his imagination, a hold he couldn't shake loose. There was just something about the beautiful and mysterious witness—or non-witness, as she insisted on remaining—that brought Lucas's thoughts back to her, again and again. Even as he'd coordinated the investigation on the mountain tonight, he'd been distracted by thoughts of her. Even as he'd attempted to track a killer, he'd mentally replayed their conversation, memorizing not only her responses, but the classic contours of her face and the slightly breathless sound of her voice.

He couldn't stop thinking about the way she'd looked at him, the way her eyes seemed to plead with him to accept her half-truths and evasions. Although he hadn't really been tempted to ignore his common sense, logic and well-trained instincts, he *had* felt a measure of compassion for what seemed like her desperate need to convince him.

She was holding back information, he told himself as he opened the refrigerator and grabbed a beer. Although he didn't know what kind of information, his gut told him that she might just hold the key to cracking the case wide open.

As a lawman, Lucas had been trained to rely on facts. He didn't put much stock in things like ESP or the supernatural, but he had learned to listen to his instincts, the instincts that gave cops what some called a second pair of eyes. And that second sight, or whatever one called it, was telling him Lexie Dale was a woman in more trouble than she could handle.

Perhaps that was why he couldn't seem to shut down his intense feelings of concern for her and why she seemed to bring out every protective instinct he possessed. Even now, frustrated as he was by the outcome of their interview, he still wondered if she was all right, worried that she might be in danger from whomever or whatever it was that had her scrambling to measure her every response.

But a reluctant witness was better than none at all, he reminded himself again as he twisted the top off the icy beer bottle.

As a cop, his strongest impulse was to drive back to the ranch, drag her out of bed and push her until she broke down and confessed to whatever it was she knew. But as a man, all he wanted to do was protect her, to comfort and console her and vanquish whatever it was that had her running so scared. But how did a man, even a county sheriff with twelve deputies under his direct command, go about protecting a woman who seemed intent on lying to him?

"It's a helluva situation, Rocky," Lucas muttered and pulled open the refrigerator again to withdraw the steak he'd left defrosting that morning on the top shelf.

Since when did he abide a liar, he asked himself, or give a damn what happened to one? He grabbed a skillet from the rack over head, slid it onto the stovetop and tossed the steak into it.

She *was* lying, he told himself as he slathered the T-bone with butter and leaned back against the edge of the countertop to sip his beer without tasting and listen to his dinner sizzling with deaf ears. But why? Who was she trying to protect? Hugh Miller? Her own or the dead man's reputation? Maybe. Or was it possible she was protecting a murderer?

Lucas didn't think so. In fact, he dismissed the idea even as it formed. After all, Lexie herself had been a victim of this afternoon's violence.

But if she wasn't protecting the perpetrator then that left only the victim. Hugh Miller. And if it was Miller she was protecting then that meant she knew a lot more about the dead man than she was telling. But what? What was so important a man had to be protected even to the grave?

And what about their relationship? It was obvious they'd come to Destiny Canyon Ranch together, despite the few hours gap between their check-in times. She'd been adamant about not knowing Miller before, and Lucas thought she was telling the truth. But he was also certain that Miller figured into her life. Were they business associates? It didn't make sense for her to hide a logical connection like that.

Lucas kept coming back to one explanation: In spite of Lexie's denials, she and Hugh Miller must have been lovers. That possibility caused an unwelcome and uncomfortable tightening sensation in his gut. A sensation that told him he had darn well better find a way to stop thinking about Lexie Dale as a woman and start thinking of her as just one more piece in the puzzle that would ultimately solve this case.

So what if Lexie Dale had been in love with Hugh Miller? Did it make a difference? Probably not, unless one of them was married. That would explain the attempted cover-up, and maybe even supply a suspect. Had Hugh Miller been the victim of a jealous wife? If so, Lucas doubted the wife herself had been the shooter. Not unless the woman was a trained markswoman with the stealth of a cougar.

No. Lucas did not seriously believe that Hugh Miller had been killed as the result of a jealous rage. Criminals driven by passion left obvious signs and this killer had left no such trail, not a scrap of evidence to suggest the kind of wild emotion that led to careless mistakes. In fact, by all appearances, it would seem Hugh Miller had been the victim of a professional hit. And that possibility opened the door to more scenarios than Lucas could even begin to sort out tonight.

The smell of scorching meat brought him up short from the growing mountain of questions for which he had no answers. At this point, all he had were the usual questions about the crime and the victim, the kind of questions that usually led to a motive, a suspect and ultimately to an arrest. Motive, means and opportunity, those were the building blocks of any case.

"Business as usual," Lucas told himself.

But if that really was all there was to it, then why did this case seem anything but usual?

The answer was one Lucas didn't want to consider, but couldn't deny. The answer was Lexie Dale. Or more specifically, his own intense reaction to her.

He slid the charred steak onto a plate, grabbed a fork and knife and took his dinner and his unfinished beer into the living room where he sat in a chair by the window without eating for several minutes.

For tonight, he would concentrate on how best to next approach his reluctant witness. She had to have some idea why someone had tried to abduct her. Was she a runaway wife? A rich heiress? A woman plagued by a stalker? She must have some idea. Tomorrow he would push her harder for answers, especially some answers about her relationship with Hugh Miller. He'd already decided that the next time he questioned Lexie it would be at his office. The more formal setting would serve as a reminder to him to keep his bothersome attraction to the woman from interfering with his judgment. With a killer on the loose, he could hardly afford to let chemistry get in the way of his duty.

Tomorrow, armed with the facts from the background check on Hugh Miller that Deputy Ferguson was gathering even now, Lucas would have the kind of leverage he needed to force Lexie to fill in the blanks.

With his resolve restored and firmly in place, he finished his overdone steak, then leaned back in his chair and fell into the deep sleep of a man who'd put in a long, frustrating day.

A cold wet canine nose nudged Lucas awake hours later. "Hey, Rocky," he mumbled as he stretched his back and frowned at the realization that he'd spent the night in his chair. "Thanks for the wake-up call, old man."

It was still dark when Lucas opened the back door to let Rocky out, but the sun had turned the cloudless morning sky a pale white by the time he'd showered and dressed.

As he poured his first cup of coffee, he mentally ticked off the course the investigation would take today. The ongoing search for tracks or any kind of evidence around the murder scene would be his first priority. But of almost equal importance was his next conversation with Lexie Dale.

His mind was so fully focused on the subject of his rumination that when the phone rang, he almost expected to hear her voice.

"Sorry to bother you so early, Lucas," Eli Ferguson apologized, "but I figured you'd want to have this information ASAP."

"No problem, Eli. What's up?"

"We still don't have a positive ID on yesterday's murder victim."

Lucas frowned as he listened to his deputy explain.

"There's no such address as the one listed on the Illinois driver's license he was carrying, and there's no record of anyone by the name of Hugh Miller residing in Cook County."

"What about the vehicle registration in his car?"

"As bogus as the driver's license," Eli declared. "The registration lists the same information as the license and the plates don't match the car's make and model."

"Stolen?"

"Maybe. But they could have been lifted from a junkyard. The plates were traced to a 1968 Chevy that was totaled and junked twenty years ago."

"It seems reasonable to suspect the car is stolen, too."

Lucas frowned. A stolen car was one thing, but going to such lengths to create a false identity added a new and disturbing dimension to what was already a complex case.

"Probably," Eli agreed. "But we can't confirm that until we hear back from the Illinois State Police. I sent the prints off to the Colorado Bureau of Investigation, but it could be two or three weeks before we hear back from them."

Before he'd left for home last night, Lucas had directed Eli to over-night a set of Miller's fingerprints to the CBI headquarters in Denver where they'd be compared to catalogued prints on file.

"Or longer," Lucas grumbled more to himself than to his deputy. All his thoughts focused on Lexie Dale. The woman with the intriguing eyes that hinted at a heart full of secrets.

"Looks like we're a long way from getting a positive identification," Eli said.

"Maybe not as far as you think, Eli," Lucas said before he hung up the phone, reached for his hat and his car keys and headed out the door. Maybe only as far as Destiny Canyon Ranch and one very beautiful witness.

Chapter Three

The hills that ringed the valley around the ranch house seemed to glow with reflected sunshine, but the beauty of the mountain sunrise was lost on Lucas. He was a man on a mission. Outside, the breeze blew cool, but inside the kitchen the air was warm and deliciously thick with the aroma of bacon, coffee and cinnamon.

Mo was standing at the stove with her back to Lucas when he walked in. In spite of the early hour, Tucker Oates was seated at the kitchen table, sipping coffee and poring over the pages of a tabloid newspaper, *The Exposé*.

"Morning, Lucas." He tipped back in his chair and ran his hand over his grizzled jaw. "Since you hadn't been around to interrogate me, I figured I'd stop by here and save you the trouble of tracking me down."

"As if you'd be so hard to find," Mo said sardonically.

"I get around." Tucker hooked his thumbs through the red suspenders he always wore to keep his blue jeans attached to his scrawny frame. "You'd be surprised, Mo."

"Huh! Like anything you could do would surprise me."

"Wait and see." Tucker chuckled to himself. "Someday you might just find out there's more to old Tucker than you've ever allowed."

Mo glanced at Lucas over her shoulder then wiped her

hands on a dishtowel and reached for an earthenware coffee mug on the counter beside her.

"I figured you'd be by early," she said as she filled the mug with steaming brew and held it out to him. "Cal should be down in a minute."

Lucas eyed the pan of fresh, warm cinnamon rolls sitting on a trivet on the countertop.

"Help yourself," Mo said. "I was just getting ready to put the eggs on. What'll it be, one or two?"

"Thanks, but none for me. I just swung by to pick up Miss Dale." He glanced out the window across the expanse of green meadow at the four guest cabins in the distance, situated on the southwest edge of the Garrett property. "I don't suppose she's made an appearance yet this morning?"

Mo shook her head. "Not yet, poor thing. I doubt she's even awake. She was still on the phone, talking to her family when I turned in last night. Seemed real upset, too, not that it's any wonder, given what she's been through. I'm just glad I talked her into staying in the guest room last night."

"She stayed here at the house?"

"I insisted on it!" Mo informed him. "She said she'd be fine in her cabin, but I wouldn't hear of it, not with that maniac still on the loose! You haven't caught him, have you?"

Lucas shook his head.

"Hmm. Well, then I'm glad I made her stay here. Although I don't think she slept much. I got up to check on Pop around two this morning and noticed the light in her room was still on."

Mo offered to warm up his coffee, but Lucas refused. "You could at least sit down and have a cinnamon roll while you're waiting for her."

Mo's cinnamon rolls were legendary, but this morning Lucas wasn't even tempted. It was all he could do to keep from charging up the stairs and dragging Lexie Dale out of bed. "Thanks, but I'll grab something later in town."

"I'll have some of those cinnamon rolls," Tucker volunteered.

"There's another big surprise," Mo said as she placed the pan in the middle of the long, pine table. "I'm surprised you manage to survive on what passes for food down at The Timbers. Why, sometimes I swear I can taste the grease just walking past the front door of that place."

Cal walked into the kitchen and nodded a greeting toward Lucas and Tucker. "What's wrong with The Timbers?" he asked as he reached for a mug and filled it with coffee.

"Yeah," Tucker said as he swallowed a bite of cinnamon roll. "I'm healthy enough, and I eat most all my meals there."

Mo snorted. "Well, I suppose the food at The Timbers is good enough for a man with beef jerky for taste buds and a brain the size of a pinto bean."

"I'd be happy to make some other arrangement," Tucker offered. "You know, Mo, I've always said you were the best cook in Bluff County."

"Not in your wildest dreams." She slammed a cast-iron skillet onto the stovetop and began cracking eggs into it. "You're doggone lucky there's a place like The Timbers for the likes of you. No woman in her right mind would agree to sign on to cook and clean up after you, old man."

Tucker might have responded with a barb of his own, but his mouth was full. He polished off one cinnamon roll and reached for another.

"But it's different for you, Lucas." Mo seized a spatula and attacked the eggs with short quick movements that were almost vicious. "At thirty-two years old, in the prime of your life, you ought to be eating breakfast at home, at your own table, with your wife and kids around you. At your age, most men—"

"And speaking of breakfast," Cal cut in. "I'm half starved."

Mo muttered something unintelligible under her breath and turned back to her cooking.

Lucas drank his coffee and congratulated himself for resisting the urge to remind his sister that she, herself, had never seen fit to marry. More than a dozen years ago, she'd been engaged to the much-maligned Tucker Oates, but it turned out that they were better as bickering companions than as husband and wife. Theirs was a pure love-hate relationship. Below the surface, Mo and Tucker cared deeply for each other, always had, but they couldn't be in the same room for more than five minutes before the verbal dueling began.

That wasn't the kind of relationship Lucas wanted. He knew some might consider him too picky, but he still hadn't met that special someone to whom he wanted to make a lifetime commitment. It wasn't that he had anything against commitment, or marriage, for that matter. On the contrary. If anything, his estimation of the institution was probably unrealistically high. But that was to be expected, he supposed, having been raised by parents who shared the kind of relationship about which love songs were written.

"Well?" Tucker said. "Aren't you going to interrogate me?"

Lucas had already heard Mo's version, and he didn't expect that Tucker had anything new to add. Still, it never hurt to be thorough. "All right. Tell me about yesterday afternoon, Tucker."

"Mo's new pup had run off, and she needed an extra pair of eyes to look for him. So, I volunteered for the job on account of I'm pretty good at finding things. We were driving up on Summit Trail when..."

He droned on. If there was one thing Tucker liked more than Mo's cooking, it was telling a story. No one could spin a yarn like Tucker, with just the right twists and turns. The problem was figuring out where the truth stopped and Tucker's embellishments started.

Half-heartedly, Lucas listened to the complicated tale of how Mo and Tucker found the body of Hugh Miller and rescued Lexie.

"We were almost back to the ranch," Tucker said, "when I realized I'd seen her before."

"Who?" If anyone else had been talking, Lucas would have been all over them with questions, but Tucker's imagination was nearly as big as his appetite. "Are you saying that you've met Lexie before?"

"Well, it isn't that I've met her—not in person, you understand. But she looks so darned familiar. I'd swear I've seen that gal's face before. Didn't I say so, Mo? Right after we found her?"

"You know I don't listen to half of what you babble on about," Mo replied.

"I said 'That young lady is pretty enough to be a movie star.'" He tapped the front page of *The Exposé* where banner headlines screamed about some starlet's latest hairstyle and aliens landing in Central Park. "You all make fun of me for keeping up with the world news, but I'm beginning to think that's where I've seen her, right here in these pages. If I could only remember when..." He began to flip back to the front page.

Lucas shook his head. He wasn't in the mood for this kind of nonsense when there was a murderer at large. "You want me to believe that a woman who's staying in one of Mo's rental cabins is some sort of celebrity?"

"I'd bet good money on it, Lucas," he said, coming to his feet. "I know I've seen a picture of that little gal somewhere."

"Sure," Cal put in. "And maybe she brought a couple of those Central Park aliens with her to Colorado."

Mo chuckled appreciatively. "Or maybe she's one of those miraculous women who's a hundred and fifty years old but doesn't look a day over twenty-five."

"Go ahead and laugh," Tucker said as he grabbed another

cinnamon roll and headed for the kitchen door. "But you know what they say, fact is stranger than fiction, my friends. Just take ol' Tucker's word on that."

Lucas gave little credence to Tucker's declaration, but he had to admit that the idea that a rich and famous woman choosing Destiny Canyon as a vacation spot made more than a little sense. True, there were few amenities, certainly not the hot and cold running servants that a celebrity might require, but the remote mountain location would afford privacy.

If Lexie Dale was famous—or even infamous—maybe that would explain why she'd gone so far out of her way to find this place. And it might also explain the motive behind the abduction attempt. So, who *was* she? And how had she learned about Destiny Canyon Ranch in the first place?

The need to question her nagged at him even harder. He took a last swig of coffee. "Well, I'd better go talk to our guest and find out for myself if there's any truth to what Tucker said."

"You're not going to wake that girl, are you?" Mo asked, her disapproval ringing in every word.

"Only if she's still asleep," he said.

Before Mo could stop him, Lucas strode out the kitchen door and across the pine-paneled great room, toward the wide, hardwood staircase.

At the second-floor landing, he made a right and walked past the door to his father's room to the guest room at the end of the hallway. He raised his hand to knock, when the door behind him opened slowly.

"Mo? Honey, is that you?"

Lucas turned around and walked back to where his father stood in the doorway. "Morning, Pop. How're you feeling today?"

"Not too bad for the shape I'm in."

The specialists had said Will wouldn't make it through another Colorado winter, but Doc Rogers said he wouldn't put it past Will Garrett to live a hundred years just to spite them. Lucas was less optimistic. Ever since his mother died five years ago, his father had been going downhill. Without the love of his life beside him, Will just didn't seem to have the heart to go on.

"Lots of excitement around here yesterday," Will said. "I suppose you've got your hands full with this homicide investigation."

"Seems like," Lucas confirmed. "But I don't want you worrying about it, Pop. Everything's going to be all right. I'm going to catch this guy before anyone else gets hurt."

"I'm not worried," Will said. "I know you're going to do whatever it takes to bring him in. This county is lucky to have you on the case, son. I just hope that sweet little blonde is going to be all right." He cocked his head in the direction of the guest room down the hall.

"Then, you've met Miss Dale?"

"Lexie?" Will smiled and for an instant, his eyes seemed less tired. "Oh yes. Last night, around midnight, I was coming back from the bathroom and stopped to rest a spell on the window seat. She asked if there was anything she could do to help me and I invited her to sit and chat a while."

The small effort of standing seemed to weaken him. Though Lucas wanted to know what Lexie had said, his concern for his father took precedence. "Maybe you should lie back down, Pop."

"No, son. I want to go downstairs. I've been aching all morning to get outside and sit on the porch for a spell. Your mother and I used to do that, you know. It was one of our favorite pastimes. After I retired, Rose and I had the time to sit and enjoy the view. Just looking out at the mountains and talking about all the things we'd done with you kids and the way we'd built this place...well, it was a sweet time, son. It truly was."

Ten years ago, when Will had finally agreed to retire, Lucas had been fully immersed in his career in law-enforcement. Cal had not only had Lucas's blessing, but a measure of gratitude, when he'd agreed to take over the reins of the Garrett ranch. Cal's father, Duncan Garrett, had been Will and Rose's first born son, the older brother Lucas had never known. Duncan's life had already been lost in the jungles of Vietnam almost five years before Rose and Will Garrett's late-in-life son, Lucas, was conceived.

After his father's death and his mother's subsequent abandonment, Cal and his younger sister, Jolie, were raised as Lucas's siblings on the ranch. With three active young children to raise, Rose Garrett depended heavily on her older daughter, Maureen. Lucas sometimes marveled at the degree of dedication Mo had shown the family. But if the sister who was some twenty years his senior ever resented the years she'd spent tending her younger brother and two young cousins, she'd never shown it. In fact, if anything, it seemed the difference in their ages had given them a special closeness. Lucas adored his mother, but in Maureen he'd always felt he had a second mom, an older, wiser loved-one to whom he could come for kindly wisdom and counsel.

"If you can just help me down this last step…" Will said. Lucas offered his arm for support. Lucas waited until his father was comfortably situated on a porch chair with a blanket tucked around his legs, then he asked, "What did you and Lexie talk about, Pop?"

"Oh, a little of this and that. Mostly, we talked about her late grandfather, how she could always turn to him. How she still missed him. How she wished she had someone to talk to now for advice."

"Did she ask for your advice, Pop?

"Well, yes. As a matter of fact, she did. Not outright, in so many words, understand. But I could tell she had a lot on her mind and was just itching to say it."

Lucas shook his head. Was this the same woman who'd guarded her every comment during their interview yesterday?

"And did you give her advice, Pop?"

"Yes, I guess I did." He seemed almost happy as he gazed across the front yard at the sunlit meadow. "She asked me if I thought it was worth the effort for a person to fight for what she wanted, even if it was something that didn't seem like it would ever work out, even if other people disapproved and told her she was dead wrong."

Lucas knew without asking how his father had answered Lexie's question. Will Garrett had never run from a fight in his life. "You told her to stand her ground, of course."

"Damn right, I did." He nodded to himself. "You know, son, I like that little gal. And I can tell she's got something heavy on her mind, something big, a problem she's not sure she can handle on her own." He met his son's gaze. "Maybe you can find a way to help her, Lucas. I got the feeling she could use a friend about now."

Lucas patted his father's shoulder and smiled. "I'll see what I can do, but right now I have to get going, Pop. I need to talk to Lexie."

Will smiled. "You do that, son. You talk to her." His smiled faded. "But don't go pushing her too hard with all your official questions, you hear? She's been through enough."

Again, Lucas stopped short of making his father any promises where Lexie Dale was concerned.

When he returned to the house he reported to Mo that their father was on the porch, then he hurried up the stairs. What was it about Lexie that caused everybody in his family to want to protect her? First, Mo. Now, his father. Maybe Lexie Dale really was an alien, a supernatural being who'd cast an intergalactic spell over all of them.

He knocked twice on her door and waited. When he heard no movement on the other side, he knocked again. This time louder and with more authority. "Miss Dale. Lexie. It's Lucas Garrett." But still there was no answer, no sound at all on the other side of the door.

Finally, Lucas turned the knob and pushed the door open. The room was empty. The bed had been neatly made, almost as if it had never been slept in.

As a number of disturbing scenarios played through his mind, Lucas retraced his steps and pushed out the front door. On the porch, Mo was tending to their father, but Lucas didn't stop to talk or inform them of where he was going.

As he strode across the meadow toward the cabin, he didn't know whether to be relieved or concerned by the sight of Lexie's rented SUV still parked where it had been yesterday in front of her cabin. If she'd walked out of his family's house without a word to Mo, knowing his sister would be concerned by her unexpected absence, then Lexie Dale's behavior could only be called rude and thoughtless.

But what if she hadn't walked out, Lucas thought, what if she'd been taken by force? The thought propelled him even faster across the meadow. When he reached the cabin, he was surprised to see the door that opened into the small two-room cabin standing wide open.

"Lexie!" he called out as he crossed the small yard and walked up onto the porch.

There was no answer, but what he saw as he stood on the threshold stopped him cold. The interior of the cabin looked like a scene from a low-budget horror movie. The small, hand-hewn, knotty pine table and chairs had been overturned. The bedding had been ripped off the bed and the mattress pulled from its pine frame. Each of the six drawers had been pulled from the dresser in the corner and the contents dumped in a heap in the middle of the floor. The clothes strung all over the room were distinctly feminine. Lexie's clothes. But where was Lexie?

Where was the deputy assigned to guard the cabin last night? Had Lexie's change in venue pulled his attention away from the cabin? The questions came to Lucas in rapid succession, but there would be no answers, not until he found Lexie.

With his gun drawn, Lucas moved carefully into the room. When he'd made certain no one was waiting behind the door in ambush, he made his way toward the bathroom.

Past the open door, he saw her. Seated on the floor, surrounded by the chaos of the ransacked room, she seemed almost in a state of shock. The shower curtain sagged behind her, where it had been torn from the rod. All of her belongings had been ruined. Her cosmetics were everywhere, crushed underfoot on the floor, along with a tangle of jewelry and the remains of a broken hair dryer.

"Lexie!"

She turned and looked up at him, seemingly oblivious to the blood trickling from her left hand.

"What the hell happened here?" He moved into the small room and reached down to pull her to her feet. "My God, are you all right?"

She allowed him to pull her to her feet. "I—I'm fine. I just walked in and found it like this."

"You're bleeding." She looked down at the broken pieces of a perfume bottle still in her hand.

"Here." Carefully he took the jagged pieces from her and dropped them onto the floor. She stood without speaking as he wrapped her hand in the lone towel still hanging on a hook over the sink.

The look on her face was haunted and her eyes shone with unshed tears. Lucas put his arm around her and led her out of the cabin and onto the sun-drenched porch.

"What's this all about, Lexie?" he asked her. "Why would someone want to do this to you?"

When she looked up at him, he found he had to steel himself against the abject vulnerability reflected on her face. "It—it's hard to explain," she began. "I—I can't—"

"But you have to," he said softly, firmly. "I can't protect you unless I know what's going on. I can't help you until you trust me. Trust me, Lexie."

She met his gaze with a look that told him she longed to

do exactly that, to place her trust in him and damn the consequences that until this point had her scared silent.

She opened her mouth, but then closed it again without saying anything. The lawman in Lucas sensed she was ready to crack. If he pushed her now she might be able to give him the answers he needed to catch a killer.

But the man in him held back, momentarily overwhelmed by compassion for a woman who he sensed had already been through more than her share of pain. He remembered his father saying she needed a friend. Was it possible to be that friend and still do his duty?

"Come with me, Lexie," he said quietly. "We'll talk in town, at my office."

She hesitated for a moment and looked back at the ravaged mess inside the cabin. "But what about—"

"I'll have my men take over here, and see to your things."

Then he put his arm around her and walked with her across the meadow and into his family's home where he knew, at least for the moment, she'd be safe.

THEY'D SPOKEN LITTLE on the drive into town, and they remained separated by an uneasy silence while Lucas ushered Lexie past Sylvia's desk and into his office. It wasn't that he'd gone soft, he told himself as he directed her to the chair opposite his desk. He did not intend to let her off without another round of solid questioning. But she had been through another ordeal this morning and it seemed only right to give her a little time to recover from the shock of finding her possessions rifled. Besides, giving her time to mull over the seriousness of her situation just might convince her to cooperate.

"Make yourself comfortable," he told her. "Can I get you something? Coffee? Tea? A lawyer?"

"I don't need a lawyer. Not unless you're planning to charge me with something."

Lucas shook his head. "No. But I do need answers, Lexie. And I don't intend to let up until I get them. If you'd feel better with counsel present, now's the time to let me know."

"I don't need a lawyer," she said calmly, in a voice that revealed none of the emotion he'd witnessed less than an hour ago inside the ransacked cabin. "There's nothing more to say. I told you everything yesterday."

"I remember what you said." Lucas leaned back against the edge of his desk and folded his arms across his chest. "All right. Then let's talk about today."

She nodded uncertainly.

"Do you have any idea why someone would ransack your cabin?"

"No."

"Any idea what they might have been looking for?"

Again, she responded with a flat, "No."

"Who was Hugh Miller?"

"What do you mean?"

"I mean, who was he? We know that wasn't his real name. And the address he gave Mo when he checked in was phony, too. Who was he, Lexie?"

When she didn't reply immediately, he pressed her. "His prints have been sent to CBI and it's only a matter of time before they match them with an identity. If you tell me now you'll be saving everyone a lot of trouble."

She rose and moved over to the window where she stood with her back to him. "I only knew him as Hugh Miller."

"Where did he come from?"

"I don't know. I can't tell you anything more about the man."

"Can't or won't?" It took some doing, but Lucas managed to keep his voice even. "Look, Lexie…whatever is keeping you from telling me the truth, it can't be worse than the legal ramifications that could result from your stonewalling."

She turned around to face him with an openly defiant expression. "There's no point in threatening me, Sheriff."

Lucas felt his control slip. An innocent witness afraid to come forward was one thing, but Lexie's constant evasions were making him question just how innocent she really was. "Damn it! A man is dead. Doesn't that mean anything to you?"

"I'm sorry," she said softly. The note of desperation in her voice touched off an unwanted rush of protective instincts inside Lucas. She stood silently for several minutes, then sighed and turned to face him once more. "I know you're trying to help, Lucas. But there's no need. Everything…well, it's just too late."

"Too late for what, Lexie?"

She started for the door. "Could you please arrange for someone to drive me back to the ranch?"

Lucas covered the length of his office in three long strides. "What are you hiding, Lexie? Tell me."

"Let me go."

"Do you know why he was killed?"

"No!" Although he couldn't yet begin to explain why, Lucas sensed a world of pain behind that single word.

"You never knew him as anyone but Hugh Miller?"

"That's right."

Well, at least that's something, Lucas thought. "How about his family? Do you know how to contact them?"

"I don't know anything about his family…or even if he had any."

"Why was he here, Lexie? What did Hugh Miller have to do with you?"

A look of something close to panic flickered across her face and Lucas could feel her shutting down, again.

"Level with me, Lexie. I can help you, but you have to tell me the truth."

"I can't!" When she tried to push past him, he reached for her hand and held her where she stood.

"Let me go! You have no right to detain me."

Her wrist felt warm and fragile. "I'm just trying to help you."

She shook her head and pulled away from his grasp. "I know," she said. "And I appreciate your position. But you don't understand. Things are not what they appear. It's out of your hands. Out of mine! There's nothing anyone can do, now."

"Tell me what that means, Lexie. Why is it too late? What are you involved in?" Even as he asked the questions, Lucas hoped against all reason that she was as innocent as she claimed to be.

"Please," she nearly begged him. "Just take me back to the ranch."

They stood close, so close the faint perfume that was her essence mingled with his every breath, so sweet and distinctly feminine, he could almost taste it.

"I only want the truth," Lucas said. "And I'm not going to stop until I get it."

She walked past him to the window and stood once more gazing out at the mountains in the distance.

He moved across the room to stand close behind her, so close it was hard not to touch. "Tell me what has you running so scared. I promise, I'll do everything in my power to protect you, but you have to trust me."

He watched her shoulders tense and he felt torn. He didn't enjoy pressuring her, but he had a duty to bring in a killer.

And if there was a battle raging inside Lexie Dale, Lucas meant to come out the winner.

"Just tell me the truth," he continued to urge in a low, even voice.

As the moments of taut silence stretched between them, Lucas sensed she wanted to give in. It took every bit of control he possessed, but he allowed her the time she needed to reach her decision. The vow he'd made to her was real. If there was a way to protect her, to help her out of whatever trouble had her scared silent, Lucas would find it. After all, as a cop it was his sworn duty to protect, even if the reaction she sparked inside him was anything but professional.

"Lexie?" he said finally.

She sighed. "There's nothing anyone can do," she said without turning around. Her words were tinged with a sadness Lucas could not ignore.

He placed his hands lightly on her shoulders and turned her gently around to face him. With the tip of his finger, he lifted her chin so that he could look directly into her face. The eyes that stared back at him seemed haunted and the expression on her face was one of uncertainty mixed with loneliness. Lucas felt his heart turn over at the sight of such aching vulnerability, and before either of them realized what was happening, he gathered her into the circle of his arms.

She didn't resist, but seemed, instead, eager to lose herself within the shelter of his embrace. For the space of a few breathless heartbeats the grim circumstances that had caused their paths to cross ceased to exist.

When the phone rang, she pulled back, out of his arms. It rang a second time, before Lucas turned away and reached for it.

"It's Ritter, with the Burea of Land Management," Sylvia's voice announced.

"Tell him I'll get back to him."

"He says he's got to talk to you, Sheriff. One of their trucks was stolen."

"Get the information and tell him I'll send a deputy out to talk to him."

"Want me to dispatch Burt?"

"Yes. Thanks, Sylvia." As he spoke to his secretary his eyes searched Lexie's face, looking for something—anything—that would solve the mystery that was increasingly surrounding her. "Oh, and, Sylvia, please hold all my calls until I let you know otherwise."

He hung up the phone but didn't make a move to close

the distance between them. "Level with me, Lexie. Tell me what you know about the man who called himself Hugh Miller. Begin by telling me why he used a false identity."

She blinked and some of the color left her face.

"You really didn't know, did you?"

She shook her head. "The first time I saw him was here at the ranch."

"But you weren't surprised to meet him. Why, Lexie?"

She stared at him a long moment and Lucas sensed she was close to cracking. Finally, she sighed, moved back to her chair and sat down. "He was a paid bodyguard."

Her admission wasn't really all that surprising. Her obvious distress at having been forced to admit it, however, was. "How long had he been working for you?"

"He wasn't working for me, exactly. My family hired him." Unmistakable anger turned her eyes a darker shade of blue. "Or to be more precise, my *father* hired him. He made all the arrangements."

"What made your father believe you needed the services of a bodyguard?" Lucas studied her face as he waited for her answer and imagined what he'd do to anyone who tried to harm even one hair on her lovely head.

"There was a kidnapping attempt—" She hesitated. "It was a long time ago. When I was a child."

"Tell me about it."

"I don't...remember much. I was very young."

"What *do* you remember?"

"Not much. My mother died years ago. And my father...well, it's never been a subject he's felt inclined to discuss." Something about the way she said the word father made Lucas want to punch the man.

"I'll want to talk to him. To your father."

Her laugh was short, dry and completely without humor. "Oh, believe me, you will. In fact, he's probably tried to reach me this morning at the ranch."

Lucas reached for the phone again. "What's his number?"

She leaned back in her chair. "I don't have it with me, but even if I did, you wouldn't be able to get through."

"Why not?"

She sat forward in her chair. "Because it doesn't work that way."

"What do you mean?"

"I mean, there's no way to get through to him. He's a very...busy man. Lots of meetings. And he travels a lot, too. I wouldn't know how or where to begin looking for him today."

"But you spoke to him yesterday."

She nodded. "Yes. That's why I know he's undoubtedly tried to reach me today."

"If you don't mind my saying, you seem less than happy by the prospect of talking to your father."

She shrugged, but the indifference she seemed to want to portray was undermined by the distinct sadness in her eyes.

"Are you sure there's no way to contact him, now? At his office or at home?"

She gave him a small smile. "Trust me on this one, Lucas. By the time you drive me back to the ranch, His— My father will have left a message instructing me *exactly* when and where to call."

Lucas reached for his hat. "Then let's go."

She nodded and rose to walk ahead of him out of his office, with all the enthusiasm of a woman headed for the gallows.

Chapter Four

In the outer office, Deputy Eli Ferguson reclined in a chair with his long legs stretched out on the desktop in front of him. "Hey, Lucas," he said and came to his feet.

"Am I glad to see you!"

Lucas was fortunate to have such a competent second-in-command. In spite of Eli's few annoying affectations, like wearing his sunglasses indoors and sliding into a west Texas drawl that stretched a single sentence into a lengthy monologue, he was smart and a good leader. Lucas asked Lexie to wait in his office while he turned over the loose threads of the investigation to his deputy.

"I want four more men up on that trail, checking for anything we might have missed yesterday. Also, BLM just reported a stolen truck. It's a long shot, but there could be a connection."

"Could be our shooter needed the truck for his getaway. I'll compare the cast we took of the tire prints on the trail with the BLM vehicles."

"Put out an APB on that truck," Lucas said.

The next task was more complicated. "Last night, someone ransacked Lexie's rental cabin. Send two men over there to check for prints and take photos."

Eli removed his sunglasses and glanced toward the office where Lexie was waiting. "Is she all right?"

"Mo insisted she stay in the guest room at the house." His sister had been correct in assuming there was still a danger. "I don't need to tell you that those cabins are within spitting distance of the ranch house. I sure as hell don't like the idea of something like this happening so near Pop's front door."

"I'll get a full report from the deputy who was supposed to be on patrol last night and have it on your desk by noon."

Lucas nodded. "From now on until this thing is over, I want you to personally oversee the surveillance at Destiny Canyon Ranch."

"Consider it done." Eli slipped the sunglasses back onto the bridge of his nose. "There'll be someone on the premises round-the-clock from now until we bring in the perpetrator. So, where are you headed, Lucas? Back up to the mountain?"

"Later," Lucas replied and inclined his head toward Lexie. "Right now, my first priority is finding out how she fits into this thing." His gut instincts told him that the answers they sought resided somewhere in Lexie Dale's stubborn little head. If he could find a way around her fears, convince her he was not the enemy, there just might be a way to not only apprehend a murderer but keep Lexie safe, as well. "I need you to follow up on the loose ends, so I can be free to act on whatever information I manage to pry out of our witness."

"Did you know that she told Mo she lived in Atlanta, but her driver's license was issued in Boston?" Eli's question gave Lucas another ill-fitting piece of an increasingly scrambled puzzle. Every cop knew it wasn't difficult to falsify information on a driver's license, but Lucas hoped in this case there was some other explanation. "She might have recently moved," Lucas suggested.

"Maybe," Eli allowed.

"It should be easy enough to confirm. In the meantime,

I'll try to get some straight answers of my own." Lowering his voice so that only the two of them could hear, he said, "If Miller was using an alias, maybe she is, too. But let's not assume too much, Eli. We have no evidence that she's involved in any way with the murder. Don't forget, the lady herself was attacked, and that ransacked cabin makes it clear someone is intent on causing her harm. From now until we bring that someone in, my first priority is keeping her safe."

A slow grin spread across Eli's face. "Keeping an eye on such a beautiful target shouldn't be too difficult, but if you need any backup, be sure to let me know."

Lucas suppressed a smile. "I think I can handle that particular duty alone, Deputy, but thanks for the offer."

With the feeling that he'd covered most of the immediate investigative bases, Lucas ushered Lexie out to his SUV After they returned to the ranch and he had that phone conversation with her father, he might have some idea of the motive for the crimes. Typically, a kidnapper wanted a ransom, but he sensed that there was more at stake here than money.

As he drove through town, he noticed a green pickup in the rearview mirror. The vehicle stayed back far enough that Lucas was unable to make out the features of the driver or passenger. But he didn't need to see either man to know the truck was following them.

As HE DROVE, Lexie found it difficult to keep from stealing an occasional sideways glance at the dark-haired man with eyes the color of the clear blue Colorado sky above them. But then, why wouldn't her interest keep returning to him? After all, she'd never met a man like Lucas Garrett. And everything about him fascinated her.

As rugged as the untamed land he called home, the sheriff of Bluff County seemed at first glance to epitomize the stereotype of the quintessential western lawman. But during the past twenty-four hours, Lexie had glimpsed another side of Sheriff Lucas Garrett, a compassionate side. Even when she'd tried his patience, he'd treated her with respect and what seemed to be genuine concern.

While there was no doubt in her mind that Lucas was dedicated to duty, the way he'd held her and tried to allay and soothe her fears told Lexie that in every way that mattered, he was his own man first and an officer of the law second. The kind of man who placed people and their needs above procedure. A man a woman could trust with her life.

And her heart.

Startled by that sudden turn of thought, Lexie shifted in her seat to gaze out her window at the peaks in the distance. "They really are...*awesome*," she said. "Oh, I know, you hear people using that word to describe everything from an ice-cream sundae to a golf score, but these mountains...well, they really do define the word. I can't imagine what it must be like to wake up every morning surrounded by such beauty. You must feel as if you're living in paradise."

"Well, almost."

She turned to him in time to catch his wry smile. At the moment, he seemed strangely preoccupied with something, probably concerned with this investigation. She was glad that she'd finally told him Hugh Miller was her bodyguard. Even if her father was outraged, Lexie preferred being truthful.

"You're blessed, you know. Living in a place like this, with such a terrific family."

He glanced at her, then back to the road, then concentrated on his rearview mirror. "I'm pretty lucky. But what about your family? Your father? That would be Mister *Dale*."

The way he emphasized her fake name caused her to tense slightly, but she shrugged off her apprehensions. "I don't see him much."

"No? How about the other members of the Dale family?"

Lexie shook her head.

"Too bad. Family's a wonderful thing. At least, it can be. Growing up, I didn't realize how much my family meant to me until I left home and spent several years separated from them. We kept in touch, of course, but, still, it's not the same as living nearby."

"Then you don't actually live on the ranch?"

He shook his head. "I enjoy being close, but a man needs his privacy." He glanced in the rearview mirror, again. "And while we're on the subject... Do you mind if we stop by my place on the way?"

"No. Not at all." Delaying the next inevitable conversation with her father was no imposition. And besides, it would be interesting to see the place Lucas Garrett called home.

"One of my mares is due to foal any day now and I want to check on her." He tromped on the gas. They were flying along the two-lane road when he abruptly made another turn, then another onto an unpaved road.

"It's a short cut," he said.

As the SUV bounced over deep ruts and gaping ditches, Lexie held on to her seat for dear life. She'd noticed that Lucas drove fast, but this was ridiculous. He wasn't even paying attention to the twists and turns. Instead, his attention seemed more focused on the rearview mirror.

"Lucas, what's wrong? Why are you going so fast on this horrid little cow path?"

"It's a private road," he said without apology and without slowing down.

Lexie hung on the armrest to keep from jostling out of her seat. "Where are we going?"

"I told you. We're going to my place."

"This is *your* road?"

"Spring runoff tears it up. I'll have it graded later this summer."

If this was how he maintained the approach to his home,

she couldn't imagine what his house looked like. In her experience, men who lived alone were unconcerned with housekeeping standards. Lexie prepared herself for the predictable clutter and sloppy repairs. A rustic cabin, perhaps.

As they ricocheted across the washboard road, her teeth rattled. A rodeo ride on a bucking bronco would have been more comfortable. Suddenly, at the crest of a small rise, he swerved to a complete stop. A thin cloud of dust settled around them, and through the haze Lexie beheld a panorama of rust-colored cliffs surrounding a grassy meadow.

She turned her attention to the man beside her. As he glanced over his shoulder, the sinews in his neck tightened. His large hands gripped the steering wheel. She could easily imagine those hands holding a gun or clenching into fists, but her senses remembered the gentleness when those hands had pulled her into an embrace.

"What is it?" she asked.

"A rattling noise." When he turned to face her, he avoided direct eye contact. "I heard something jostling around in the back."

She wasn't fooled for a minute. His reckless driving and swerving stop had not been without purpose. A rattling noise? Not likely! She made the obvious deduction: Their wild ride was an escape. But what were they escaping from?

His unspoken tension coiled around her like a noose as she mentally took the next logical step. Less than twenty-four hours ago, Hugh Miller died protecting her, and the danger wasn't over yet. The murderer and would-be kidnapper was still at large. Obviously, Lucas had sensed some danger and decided because of her presence to outrun it.

If anything happened to Lucas because of her, Lexie couldn't bear it. He hadn't asked for this job. Unlike all the other bodyguards her father hired, Lucas had not been hired and paid to stand in the way of danger. *Her* danger.

Before she could confront him and demand to know the

truth, he opened the car door. "I should take a look at that back tire."

It did not escape her notice that he took his rifle from the sheath before he left the vehicle. Apprehension descended like a curtain, obscuring her view of this brilliant sunlit afternoon. The everlasting fear was a blight she could no longer accept. Nor could she allow Lucas to shoulder the burden of protecting her.

When he climbed back into the car, his eyes were calm. "Nothing wrong. It must have been something in the road."

"Lucas, I—"

He pointed through the windshield. "Over there, by that bunch of spruce tress. That's my place."

In the distance, she glimpsed the log house with sunlight glinting off the solar panels on the roof. She'd seen this house before on a trail ride and had thought it beautiful, but other concerns loomed foremost in her mind. "Lucas, I think I know why you were driving so fast."

"I'm always in a hurry to get home," he said, evading the topic she wanted to discuss. "So, what do you think of my place? I designed and built it myself."

"I'm impressed." But she had more important issues on her mind. "Lucas, the way you were driving—"

"I'll slow down," he cut in. "But you really have nothing to worry about."

"Are you quite sure?"

"Trust me, Lexie."

While he turned the key in the ignition and cranked the engine, she straightened her shoulders, trying to shed the mantle of fear that weighed her down. Apparently, he thought they were safe. He'd asked her to trust him.

Glancing over at his chiseled profile, she realized that she did, in fact, trust this small-town sheriff. His quiet confidence reassured her. If there had been a threat, he'd dealt with it. For now, at least, they were safe.

For a few moments, she would allow herself the simple pleasure of sharing his obvious pride in his home and his land. "It must be satisfying to build something with your own hands."

"When I finally finished, it was great seeing my plans come together," he said. "But before that happened, there were times when it seemed I'd never get done."

She peeked over her shoulder. There was nothing behind them but wide open spaces. In the midst of open meadowland, his house was well situated for security purposes. The rugged dirt road appeared to be the only approach, and no one could drive across the meadow without being noticed.

Lucas pulled to a stop in front of a sturdy gate, got out, unlocked it and then drove through and stopped to lock it behind them. For much of her life, Lexie had been surrounded by some of the most sophisticated security systems available. Yet the simple fastening of the gate made her feel completely protected. It was as if nothing bad could happen to her while she was with Lucas.

Her tension all but vanished when the long ranch house came into clear view. The stone foundation matched the tall chimney which butted up against a natural rock formation. Pine logs, lightly stained and treated, were burnished gold by the sunlight. The slanted green roof stretched over a wide veranda shaded on one end by a stand of delicate aspen trees.

"Your house fits into this setting like it was meant to be here," she said. "As if it grew from the earth."

He smiled. "I tried not to disturb the natural surroundings," he said. "Some people like bluegrass and perfectly trimmed hedges, but I didn't think I could improve on the natural backyard God had already provided."

Lucas was right. No landscape artist could have improved on the splendor that stretched out in every direction from his front door. The buffalo grass and wildflowers of brilliant scarlet, yellow and blue made a perfect complement to the stone-and-log structure.

Lexie's attention turned to the barn behind the house. It was constructed of the same finished logs as the house and the attached corrals.

"Your place is idyllic," she said.

As soon as Lucas parked and they climbed out of the vehicle, a large, tan dog raced toward them.

"That's Rocky," Lucas said, edging cautiously between her and the animal. "Be careful around him. He's not fond of strangers."

As they moved away from the SUV, Lexie kept a respectful but interested distance from the animal. Growing up, she'd never been permitted to have pets, but she'd always adored kittens and puppies—not that Rocky fell into that cuddly category. He wasn't a particularly attractive creature, either. For starters, he only had three legs. His ears stood up like a German shepherd, but his snout was short—like the pug nose of a boxer who had taken too many blows to the face. Though she knew dogs didn't really have eyebrows, she thought the black spots over each of his eyes seemed like brows etched in a permanent scowl.

Cautiously, Lexie bent down to study the dog, being careful to keep a safe distance. "What breed is he?"

"Pure mongrel," Lucas said fondly. "I don't know how he lost his leg. It happened before I got him."

"But even on three legs, he manages such a proud bearing."

"I know. Sometimes I think he's all ego. I guess Rocky doesn't know he's a mutt. From the day I rescued him from the pound, he's pranced around the place like it was his exclusive property. That's his barn over there, and those are his horses, too."

Lexie took a step closer to the animal. "He seems to be warming up to me."

"Careful, Lexie."

Rocky leaned toward her. A low rumble in his throat underscored Lucas's warning. Lexie didn't move, but began to murmur in soft, reassuring tones to the animal. Inching closer, Rocky tilted his head. Lexie did the same. Something about the diffident, proud manner of this mongrel appealed to her, and when he sniffed his way nearer, she didn't back away.

"Rocky…" Lucas warned in a stern voice.

"It's all right," Lexie assured him. "He's just making sure I'm no threat."

"I don't want you to get hurt, Lexie," Lucas said even as Rocky licked her hand.

She laughed when the big dog nuzzled her leg and whined. "I don't think you have to worry about that." When she reached down to scratch him behind his ears, he licked her chin.

Lucas stared, slack-jawed. "I've never seen him do that before."

"He senses I would never hurt him. Or you," she said. "I love your place, Rocky," she told the dog. "Your house is beautiful."

"Um, excuse me, lady, but despite what the dog might tell you, it's *my* house," Lucas said with a wry smile. "Would you like a tour?"

She whispered to the dog. "Would that be all right with you, Rocky? May I take a tour of your castle?"

The dog licked her again. Lexie laughed and stood up to follow Lucas. "I'll take that as a yes."

With his head held high and his tail waving like a banner, Rocky trotted beside her toward the house.

"I don't believe this," Lucas muttered.

With Rocky close beside her, Lexie followed Lucas from room to room. The house was larger than it looked from the outside, with four spacious bedrooms and a library with floor-to-ceiling shelves lined with books. The gleaming hardwood floors and baseboards gave a feeling of warmth. The furnishings were simple, with clean lines and a distinctly masculine styling.

"Your place is spotless. I'm impressed."

"I can't take credit for that," he said. "I have someone come in once a week and keep things up."

That would explain the pretty bouquet of fresh wildflowers on the kitchen table. "A girlfriend?"

"A housekeeper," he said firmly. "It was Mo's idea that I hire someone. She said it would be a crime to build such a nice house and not keep it up on the inside."

"And she was right," Lexie said.

"I thought so, too." He held open the back door. "I need to check on the horses. Want to come?"

Again, she hunkered down beside the tawny dog. "Is that okay with you, Rocky? Is it all right if we go to the barn?"

Rocky licked her cheek again. When she stroked his rough fur, he wriggled with pleasure.

Lucas interrupted, "Much as I hate to break up this love fest, we really need to get going."

Lexie stood. "After you, Rocky."

The dog went first through the door Lucas was holding. And Lexie followed. In the yard, Rocky paused beside the trough. Hopping up on his hind legs, he pressed down on the pump with his single front paw.

"What's he doing?" Lexie asked.

"It's just one of his tricks," Lucas said. "Usually, he waits for me to water him, but around you, he's acting like some kind of trained circus pup."

As Rocky worked the pump, fresh water spilled from the spout and filled his water dish. Lexie applauded delightedly. "That's wonderful."

"His favorite stunt is ringing the front doorbell when he wants me to let him in."

Lexie laughed and bent down to pet the dog's large head. "What a smart and handsome dog you are, Rocky."

"Oh yeah, a regular Einstein." Lucas smiled. "Rocky's a great mutt, but my horses are my beauties." He opened the barn door and ushered her inside, to reveal scrupulously clean stalls housing six magnificent horses, including one heavily pregnant mare.

"That's Miss Molly," Lucas said proudly. "The soon-to-be mother of the latest in a long line of champions." Lucas went on to give Lexie a brief history of the mare's distinctive lineage.

"She's twelve years old and has already produced three champions."

"Do you race them?"

Lucas shook his head. "No, although some Quarter Horses are bred for speed, mine are specifically bred for confirmation. My animals are champions in the show ring, in halter and performance classes. For me, continuing the classic Quarter Horse confirmation is all important." He walked to the end of the barn where a stunning chestnut-colored stallion stood with ears peaked forward watching them draw nearer. "And that's where he comes in. This is King's Pride Q-282, a direct descendant of King P-234, arguably the greatest Quarter Horse that ever lived. When you look at this animal, you're seeing royalty on four legs."

Although Lexie's family had owned only Arabians, she recognized and appreciated stunning beauty and quality confirmation in all breeds. "He certainly looks regal," she agreed.

The three remaining brood mares in Lucas's stable were equally impressive examples of the best of the breed. Their coats glistened, evidence of a good diet and loving care.

"And over here are my saddle horses," Lucas said as they walked to the far end of the barn. "This is Sonata, she's the youngest of bunch, only three. For her age, she's extremely well-mannered, but still green.''

Lexie stroked the pretty bay mare's velvety muzzle and smiled, appreciating the animal's gentle nature.

"And this is G-Bar, my personal saddle horse," Lucas explained as they moved together to the last stall. "He didn't have the confirmation to stand at stud, but he's the most dependable and surefooted animal on the place, an invaluable asset on a steep mountain trail." Lexie took in the sight of the well-muscled black gelding and found it difficult to believe that G-Bar might not have sired a line of worthy heirs.

"They're all beautiful," Lexie said as they retraced their steps through the center aisle and she looked over each animal again.

"Each one is the product of careful breeding," he said. "In King's case, the bloodline goes all the way back to the beginning of the breed here in North America."

Though she admired Lucas's horses, Lexie wasn't impressed by their heritage. In her life, she'd had too many unpleasant encounters with those who claimed a perfect pedigree. "Don't you think all that attention to breeding is overrated? In the end, isn't it performance and heart that counts most?"

"No one can discount the importance of heart, but good breeding assures the best of both worlds. It's the bloodlines that guarantee quality."

"I would have to disagree," she said. "A princely heritage is no guarantee. Take Richard the Third, for example. He was born a king, but he was also a monster who ordered the death of his own nephews and murdered his way to the throne."

Ignoring her comments, Lucas stood a moment in front of King's Pride. "Just look at him, Lexie. He's one of the finest animals I've ever seen. Don't tell me genetics doesn't determine the final product.''

She leaned against the support beam in the tidy barn with Rocky at her feet. Though she could appreciate Lucas's horses, she preferred his dog—an intelligent mongrel with a personality all his own, who could even fill his own water dish.

Lucas continued, ''I believe everything is a product of what came before. Sometimes, when I look at these horses, I can see all the generations standing behind them.''

''I know what you're saying. But I would argue that it's not the same for human beings,'' she said.

''Sure it is,'' he said as he moved into Miss Molly's stall to check her one more time. ''If you want to know what you're going to be like in twenty years, take a look at your parents.''

She shuddered. For most of her life, she'd fought against her heritage. ''Do you mean to say that we have no choice in our development? That our mother and father dictate who we will become?''

''Of course we have choices. But if I'm half the man my father is, I'll be content.'' He emerged from Molly's stall and closed the gate securely behind him. ''I'm proud of my heritage, of the Garrett name and someday I hope my sons will be equally as proud to carry it on. And speaking of Pop, he said you had a little talk with him last night.''

She nodded, fondly remembering the kind, elderly man who had offered her such wise counsel. ''What a lovely gentleman. He reminds me of my grandfather.''

''You were close?''

''Very. Growing up, I think he was the only person in my family I ever had a real relationship with. He was a good man, wise and funny, like your dad.''

As she watched him tend the horses, Lexie considered her own family name. It was not a blessing but a curse. If she hadn't been born to her parents, she might have had a chance at a normal life. A life without bodyguards and kidnappers and the constant pressure that came with all that attention to breeding.

"What did you and my father talk about?" Lucas asked.

"Priorities," she said. "He helped me clarify some things."

Thanks to Will Garrett, Lexie was on the brink of a decision. She had almost decided—against all logic—that she would take a stand against her father when he tried to whisk her away from this difficult and potentially dangerous situation. Lexie was determined that Hugh Miller's death would not be in vain. She would stay here in Bluff County until his killer had been apprehended and do everything in her power to make sure the man who had given his life for her was not forgotten in the process.

"Let me ask you something," Lucas said with practiced casualness. "Was your grandfather named *Dale?*"

"Actually, he was my maternal grandfather," she said, irritated by Lucas's harping on her name. "All right, Lucas. I can see you're about to make a point. Why don't you go ahead and ask me?"

"Are you using an alias, Lexie?"

She considered for a moment. She could evade his question, but what was the point? Very soon, he would find out anyway. And, besides, she was tired of lying. "Yes," she said.

"Then your name isn't Lexie Dale?"

"No. I'm sorry for the evasions, Lucas, and if you'll give me the chance, I'd like to explain." As she stepped into the sunlight beside the corral, Rocky stiffened beside her. A low rumble came from somewhere deep in his throat.

"What is it, old man?" Lucas asked.

The hair on the dog's back stood up, and he began to bark ferociously at the sound of a car engine in the distance.

Chapter Five

With Rocky barking a frantic alert, Lucas stepped into the sunlight and stared toward the road. The green pickup had already come through the gate. It was headed toward the house. Though it didn't make sense for a murder suspect or a potential kidnapper to drive right up to his doorstep and say howdy, Lucas wasn't taking any chances.

He sensed Lexie moving up beside him. "Get back, Lexie. Stay in the barn until I call you. No matter what happens, don't come out."

"Who is it? Do you recognize them?"

"I don't know who it is, but I don't want to take any chances with your safety. Just stay put until I give you an all clear."

Reluctantly, she turned and walked back into the shadows of the doorway.

He crossed from the barn to his police vehicle, pulled the rifle from the back and waited for the pickup. The man sitting in the passenger seat was no stranger. Lucas shook his head and frowned. What was Tucker Oates up to this time?

As soon as the car parked, Tucker hopped out. Instead of his usual red suspenders and worn jeans, he was dressed in his Sunday best—white shirt with a bolo tie, black vest and clean black trousers that were still too baggy for his scrawny bowed legs.

His step was spry, and his grin spread from ear to ear as he called out, "Hey, Lucas. Where'd you stash that pretty little blonde?"

Tucker's smart and sassy attitude was a direct contrast to the man who slid out from behind the steering wheel. Too sophisticated to show emotion, he was dressed for a stroll down city streets in a shiny gray suit and brick red shirt which was unbuttoned to show off a gold medallion. When he reached back into the car, Lucas tightened his grip on the rifle. But the stranger emerged holding nothing more threatening than a large camera.

"This here is a real important man," Tucker announced with a high-pitched cackle. "You all make fun of me reading my newspapers, but it pays to stay well-informed. Yes sir, it surely does."

The stranger approached. His long brown hair was slicked back in a tight ponytail. "Mr. Oates tells me you're the sheriff of Bluff County, the man I should talk to about the recent murder."

"Mr. Oates has a big mouth."

The stranger took one step too close, and Rocky appeared from nowhere. The shepherd mix had dropped his performing circus pup routine and turned into the snarling watchdog that he was.

"Watch out for that mutt," Tucker warned. "He'll take your leg off on command."

"Call your dog off, Sheriff," the stranger pleaded nervously. "I'm no threat," the stranger said. He had an accent that Lucas couldn't quite identify. "I'm just looking for Lexie."

"Oh? And why's that?" Lucas asked.

Rocky moved toward Tucker, who quickly retreated behind the open car door. "Call him off, Lucas. Dang, you're downright unfriendly this afternoon. How about showing a little hospitality?"

Coolly, Lucas said, "I asked the man a question. Why is he looking for Lexie?"

The stranger demanded, "Is she here?"

Rocky continued his aggressive three-legged assault, holding both men at bay.

"She's famous, Lucas," Tucker squeaked. "I knew it the minute I saw her face. I knew I'd seen that lady before."

Lucas called off his dog. Just possibly there was something to Tucker's claim that Lexie was a celebrity. Finally, Lucas might learn her true identity. But other concerns came first. He confronted the stranger. "You were following me earlier."

"It is my job," he said laconically. With Rocky quiet, his accent was more pronounced but still unidentifiable. Possibly French or Italian. "I am a photographer. My name is Ramon Acardi."

"What do you want with Lexie?"

"I want to shoot her." The corner of his mouth curved into a sneering grin. "With my camera, that is."

Lucas generally tried to keep an open mind until he knew a person, but if this guy had one redeeming quality, Lucas hadn't sensed it. Acardi reminded him of a citified vulture, a carrion creature without an ounce of humanity.

Unfortunately, he had Lucas at a disadvantage because if Tucker's claim was true, Acardi just might have useful information about the beautiful witness.

"What if she doesn't want her picture taken?"

"Of course, she is always reluctant. However, I must say, the curiosity of the world seems more important than her feigned and petty modesty."

"Not in my county," Lucas said. "An individual has a right to privacy. And that includes Lexie."

"And the public has a right to her story."

"Why?"

"Because she is—" Acardi stopped himself. His smugness became more pronounced as he leveled a gaze at Lucas. "You can't pretend you don't know."

Lucas didn't respond.

"And you can't pretend you don't care for her either. It's all over your face."

Lucas had had enough. "I think you'd better take your new friend back to town, Tucker."

Acardi laughed. "No need to be so defensive, Sheriff. No one could blame you. You're not the first man to fall for the lovely Lexie without fully understanding her situation."

"Damn it, Tucker. You've really stepped in it this time," Lucas grumbled.

"Ah, come on, Lucas," Tucker appealed, waving his scrawny arms. "He didn't mean no offense. Listen, Mr. Acardi, the sheriff, here, he doesn't fall for anybody. He's a love-'em-and-leave-'em kind of guy. You can ask his sister about that."

"Not this time," Acardi said with oily certainty.

"Enough," Lucas said. Lexie had told him she was ready to reveal her identity. He didn't need to put up with the likes of Tucker Oates and Acardi to get at the truth. "There's no story here for you, Mr. Acardi. And no pictures, either. Now, I suggest you *gentlemen* get back in that vehicle and head out of here. Now."

"Ah, this is most excellent," Ramon said. "A romance between the small-town sheriff and the reluctant Alexandra. It's perfect."

As he backed toward the pickup, he lifted his camera and snapped a photo of Lucas. In spite of the bright sunlight, a flash exploded. Then another. And another.

"Click that button one more time," Lucas growled, "and you and that piece of equipment will be spending time in the Bluff County jail."

"On what charge?"

"We'll start with trespassing. Now, you've got exactly five seconds to get off my land."

"But, Lucas," Tucker whined, "you'll be famous! Your picture's going to be in *The Exposé,* right up there by the check-out counters at the grocery store."

"One," Lucas said. Casually, he cocked his rifle. "Two...three."

Both men dove into the truck and in seconds gravel sprayed in all directions as they sped toward the gate.

When Acardi got out to open it, he turned and gave Lucas a jaunty salute and shouted, "I shall return."

"And I'll be waiting," Lucas muttered as he slid his rifle back into its case.

He watched the pickup career through the open gate. Apparently, Lexie—whoever she was—rated the attention of the paparazzi. But why? Lucas had never paid much attention to the tabloids, other than an occasional glance while waiting in line at the grocery store. As for movie stars, well, he enjoyed a good film now and then, but he hardly kept up with the latest Hollywood gossip. And he almost never watched television, except for the Broncos games. For all he knew, Lexie could be the latest soap opera queen or supermodel. He'd have no way of knowing, firsthand. But she was pretty enough to be a star, that much he did know.

Maybe too pretty. And maybe he'd let his attraction to her get in the way. Maybe he'd gone easy on her because she'd seemed to be hurting. But maybe that broken wing vulnerability had only been an act. Was she the kind of woman who used her femininity and her beauty to charm men and manipulate situations to her advantage? Had she played him for a fool? Maybe. Maybe not. Either way, this game of hide-and-seek with her identity had gone on long enough.

Lucas turned on his heel and strode into the barn. He wanted answers, and he wanted them now.

"Lexie!" His voice echoed sharply off the stalls and fell into silence. She wasn't here. And neither was Sonata. Seconds later, he discovered the missing saddle.

Lucas cursed under his breath. He'd given Lexie one simple order, and she'd ignored it, fled from the barn. The anger that flared inside him was immediately overwhelmed by concern when he spotted the tracks heading into the hills behind his home.

Damn it, anyway! The woman had taken a huge risk climbing onto the back of a green-broke horse, not to mention the fact that a murderer and would-be kidnapper was still at large.

As soon as she'd recognized Ramon Acardi, Lexie made the decision to flee. The young horse was willing, and in moments the mare had carried her a quarter of a mile beyond the barn, to the banks of a narrow, rippling stream. Amid the stand of white aspen trunks, Lexie had an unobstructed view of the meadow in front of Lucas's home. If Acardi came back, she'd have an enormous head start.

Only a few weeks ago, that sleazy paparazzi had ruined the life she'd created for herself in Boston. He'd destroyed her chance for tenure as an English teacher at the prestigious Marycrest Prep School by causing such a stir she'd been forced to resign. Her heart ached when she recalled the day when her notoriety had forced her to leave in a humiliating maelstrom of publicity. She thought about the students who had been counting on her to help them ready their applications for scholarships in the fall. As it had since the day she'd left, the guilt washed over her. There had to have been another way. Running out on those kids made her feel like a coward. She should have stayed and fought.

But with Acardi leading the latest charge of tabloid attacks on Lexie's private life, she'd had little ground to stand on. When she'd pleaded with the school's administrators to be patient, to just allow the furor to die down, they'd been quick to remind her of the adverse publicity that had attended their decision to hire her in the first place. At the time of her hiring, they'd warned Lexie that they would not allow the Marycrest name to take another media hit. A few days later, when a reporter fell out of a tree outside the campus library, Lexie knew there was no escaping the inevitable. Her famous name had intruded on her life, once more.

The jaws of fame were inescapable, it seemed. The media's appetite voracious. Reporters and photographers like Acardi would always be out there, laying in wait to snap up and devour any semblance of a normal life Lexie tried to build for herself.

Her horse nickered, and Lexie concentrated her gaze on the ranch house, expecting to see the diamond glint of Acardi's long-distance zoom lens.

Instead, she saw Rocky trotting toward her. Lucas, astride the handsome G-Bar, followed the dog. Coming directly across the meadow toward her, he showed an easy command of his graceful steed. Sitting comfortably in the saddle, controlling his mount with the subtle moves of an experienced horseman, he looked like the archetypal cowboy in his black Stetson and fitted jeans pulled tight across his muscular thighs.

Pure mountain sunlight cast him in a golden hue. The sheer grandeur of man and horse against the backdrop of such rugged beauty took her breath away. For a moment, she spun a fantasy of daily life amid such natural splendor. A morning horseback ride through the hills, with her man beside her. An evening walk along a crystalline stream. An afternoon spent picking wildflowers, safe and free, with nothing looming over her shoulder but the shadow of the snowcapped peaks in the distance.

"Lexie," he called out. "Stay where you are."

Despite his command, she eased her horse forward to meet him.

"I told you to wait in the barn," he said when he was within a few feet of her.

"I thought this would be better."

"You thought wrong." He reined his horse in next to hers. His blue eyes blazed with barely suppressed anger. "As it turned out, our visitors were looking for you."

"I know. And I didn't want to see them."

"Then you recognized that man?"

She nodded. "Ramon Acardi," she said. "A tabloid stringer. I despise him."

"I can't say that I blame you. The slimy son of a gun snapped off three pictures of me before I knew what had happened."

Welcome to my world.

Lucas continued, "Forget Acardi. You deliberately disobeyed my order, Lexie."

Affronted, she shot back, "An order you had no right to give!"

"Do I need to remind you that whoever tried to kidnap you hasn't been apprehended, yet? For all you know, you could have been riding out of my barn and straight into a trap."

The thought hadn't occurred to her. Her only concern had been to escape Acardi's camera. "I didn't think," she admitted grudgingly. "It was a foolish thing to do."

"Well, after meeting your Mr. Acardi, I can't say as I blame you for wanting to be as far away from him as possible. But, Lexie, you need to understand that from now until this is over we have to take every precaution. Next time, just do what I tell you without question, and you'll be all right."

If only life could be that simple...

"You have no idea what you're asking, Lucas. There are

times when I'm going to have to make my own decisions, whether you approve or not.''

''Not while you're in my county,'' Lucas said. ''Not with your life at stake. Like it or not, with Hugh Miller gone, you're stuck with the Bluff County sheriff's department for your protection.''

She didn't like it. And she had no intention of putting anyone in the kind of peril that had killed Hugh Miller. ''I'm afraid that's unacceptable.''

''You don't have a choice. Right now, I'm your body-guard, lady.'' He caught hold of her horse's reins. ''Let's get you back to Destiny Canyon Ranch. It's a short ride from here and going cross-country we'll avoid Acardi if he's watching the road. From now on, there'll be a deputy posted on Mo's front porch, round-the-clock.''

She stopped short of reminding him that she'd easily evaded his own surveillance this morning when she'd slipped out of the house and gone to the cabin and found it torn apart. ''Fine.''

Reading her mind, he said, ''And no more running off by yourself, Lexie. Do you understand what I'm saying? You stay put.''

She didn't bother making him a promise she knew she couldn't keep.

''Let's dismount and lead the horses across the creek. Sonata is still kind of spooked about going through water with a rider on her back.''

Lexie slipped out of the saddle to the spring-scented earth. In this magnificent land, there was so much freedom. It went against every instinct to take orders from Lucas or anyone else. She stroked the groomed chestnut coat of her mare. ''I can find my way to the ranch alone,'' she said. ''You must have things to do. A job to attend to.''

''Right now, you're my main priority.'' He swung his long leg over the saddle and joined her on the ground. ''And, in case you've forgotten, keeping you safe from a killer is my job."

"You needn't worry. He won't kill me," she said with bleak certainty. "I'm no use to him dead."

He came up beside her and caught hold of her shoulders. Gently, he turned her toward him. His voice held a low intensity. "Don't say that, Lexie. There are worse things than dying, you know."

Startled, she looked up into his clear blue eyes. Lucas had given voice to what she'd imagined so many times in the past. Was it possible that he might be able to understand her worst fears?

Since childhood, Lexie believed that death itself was gentle relief compared to the guilt she carried daily in her heart. She'd always felt alone in her remorse.

"I haven't always been a small-town sheriff," he told her. "I've seen violence and the aftermath, the pain of the survivors." He released her shoulders and stood close, staring intently into her eyes. "Somebody took a bullet for you. I can't imagine how that must feel, but I know it would be a hard thing to live with."

"He gave his life for me." Just saying the words hurt, and yet she felt comforted by his empathy. "That's why I don't want your pledge of protection, Lucas. I don't want anyone putting his life on the line for me again." She swallowed hard. "If anything happened to you—"

"Nothing will," he said firmly. "I'm good at what I do, lady."

"Two days ago, Hugh Miller would have said the same thing."

"I'm sorry he died," Lucas said. "But he should have recognized that the two of you were riding into the perfect setup for an ambush. I guess he just let his guard down. He didn't know this country. But I do. I've lived here all my life. I know this area like I know the inside of my own house. I've memorized every twig, every rock and flower. Out here on my land, nobody is going to catch me by surprise."

She wanted to believe him. She wanted to lean into the safety of his assurances and feel protected from a world that seemed always to be nipping at her heels. In his gaze, she saw the fierce power of a good, honest man. He knew exactly who he was, where he belonged, how to handle himself. He'd built his place in the world and nothing could shake him from that foundation.

"I've been blessed," he said. "I was born a Garrett, on Garrett land, surrounded by a terrific family. Thanks to my father, the Garrett name is well-established and beloved in this part of the country."

"And you never wanted to be anything or anyone else?"

He smiled. "I doubt there's a man or woman alive who hasn't wondered 'what if.' But overall, no, I can't say that I'd change places with anyone."

She followed him as they led their horses across the small stream. On the other side, he stood staring at her, frowning.

"What is it?"

"You," he said in a low voice. "I'm beginning to think you're a dangerous woman, Lexie."

"Dangerous? Me?"

"Yes, you," he informed her. "When I rode out here, I was mad as hell that you'd put yourself in jeopardy by disobeying my orders. I was ready to turn you over my knee and paddle your behind."

She couldn't help smiling. "Is that the usual punishment for disobeying an order in Bluff County?"

"Sometimes, I think it ought to be." His frown deepened. "Why do I have the feeling you're going to bring me nothing but trouble?" But she saw forgiveness in his eyes and felt the warmth of a new understanding pass between them. She'd made a connection with Sheriff Lucas Garrett.

"I appreciate your trying to help me, Lucas," she said quietly. "I know I haven't made things easy for you."

It was time to tell him the whole truth, and yet she hesitated, reluctant to sever the link forming between them. Any minute, her father's influence would be making itself known. Top investigators, possibly even the FBI, would take over. She'd be torn away from Lucas, forced to deal with her father, to assert herself to gain even the smallest measure of independence.

"Kiss me, Lucas," she said on impulse.

He stared a moment into her eyes, then took a step closer.

"I shouldn't." But when he pulled her into his arms and leaned down and pressed his lips against hers, there was nothing tentative about his kiss. When it ended, she gazed up at him, dazzled by the heat of their shared passion. Although inexperienced at making love, Lexie sensed what had passed between them was unique.

In his arms, she felt swept into another world where the harsh realities of her life ceased to exist. In his arms, there was only here and now, and the wonderful feel of this strong, compassionate, sexy man. Within the protective circle of his embrace, it didn't seem to matter who or what she was. Here and now, she was simply a woman. And she'd never felt more like a woman than when she saw the desire shining in his eyes.

She didn't have to ask him to kiss her again, but when he did, she reveled in the taste of their mingled passion.

"Now," he whispered as he dragged his lips from hers, "tell me, sweet lady. Who are you?"

Chapter Six

Lexie groaned. The moment of utter bliss was over. Too soon, Lucas Garrett would vanish out of her life like a silver moon at dawn. Even if after learning the truth he still wanted to be near her, countless outside forces would make that impossible.

"I want to tell you everything, but—"

He lifted her chin. "You don't trust me."

"Of course, I do."

He seemed to be measuring her words, then slowly he shook his head. "How can you say you trust me when you won't even tell me your real name."

"It isn't you, Lucas. I do trust you. I know you have only my best interests at heart." How could she explain? She caught hold of his hand and squeezed it. "But sometimes there's more to a situation than meets the eye. Just like today, on that wild ride to your house. There was much more going on than you wanted me to know, wasn't there?"

"What do you mean?"

"When you were flying along the back road to your house, you lied to me. You said you were stopping to check out a rattle. As if you could hear anything over all that bumping and jarring."

He had the good grace to look sheepish as he glanced down at the toe of his boot. "You didn't buy that story?"

"Not a word," she said. "You thought we were being followed and that's why we took that detour, right?"

She watched a muscle tighten in his jaw.

"Why didn't you just tell me the truth, that you thought someone was following us?"

"I didn't want to worry or frighten you."

Slightly irritated, she disengaged her hand from his and took a backward step, away from him. "In the last twenty-four hours, I've seen a man shot and killed, someone made an attempt on my own life and my possessions have been rifled through and ruined, but you didn't think I could take knowing someone was tailing us?"

"I saw no need to put you through anymore trauma. I'm the cop, remember? You're the victim."

"But I've survived," she reminded him. "I had no intention of setting myself up for Acardi to ambush me and I took steps to avoid it. I'm stronger than you know, Lucas. And, like you, I have reasons for keeping certain pieces of information to myself."

"Even when that information could help solve a murder?"

"No one wants Hugh's killer caught more than I!" she replied hotly. "And for the record, I always prefer the truth," she snapped. "Look, Lucas, you don't have to treat me like a porcelain doll. I fought my attacker with every ounce of my strength and I've spent a good deal of my life fighting the odds. Believe it or not, I'm a real flesh-and-blood woman."

"So I've noticed." A slow smile tugged at the corner of his full mouth. "And speaking of the truth, don't you think it's about time you told me your name? Your real name?"

"It's Alexandra Dubois." She held her breath, waiting for him to make the connection.

He shrugged, showing no more interest than if she'd said her name was Jane Doe. "Okay, Alexandra Dubois. So, who are you, really? Some kind of celebrity? Is that why Acardi wants so badly to photograph you?''

''I come from a…famous family. But until a few weeks ago, I was just a teacher at a private school in Boston. It's my family name that is well-known…internationally. That's why I use the alias. That's why Acardi wants my picture. I've lived in the United States for almost ten years and despite my father's wishes, I'm just Lexie Dale, school-teacher.'' That was the identity she'd carved out for herself, the identity she hoped to soon regain.

''And that's why your relationship with him is strained, because you choose to lead your own life?''

''Partly.'' For a moment, she struggled internally. She didn't want to tell him more, didn't want to see the inevitable change in his expression. He'd find out soon enough. ''So, now you know my real name and the reason I use an alias. Any other questions?''

''Is it *Miss* Dubois or *Mrs.?*''

A shiver of pure delight went through her and she experienced the kind of thrill that came with the certainty of knowing a man she found wildly attractive desired her, as well. ''I'm not married. Never have been.''

He nodded and smiled and helped her swing up into the saddle once more. Atop the forested hill was a narrow gate in the barbed wire fence. After he opened it, and led his horse through, Lexie followed and they proceeded along the trail single file.

Watching his back, Lexie couldn't guess at his emotions. He seemed to be merely taking care of business, delivering her to the ranch house where she'd make her phone calls and be safely guarded. Had he already forgotten their shared moment of intimacy?

On the other side of the fence, he glanced down at Rocky. ''Home, boy.''

With a farewell yip, the dog trotted back toward Lucas's house.

Astride her mount again, Lexie leaned forward and patted the horse's muscular neck. She glanced over at Lucas and could almost see his mental gears grinding.

"I apologize for lying to you," he said, startling her. "You had the right to know someone was following us."

For Lexie, a woman who had spent her life fighting for respect and control of her own life, his simple apology meant more than he could ever know. "Thank you," she said. "And I'm sorry I waited so long to tell you my name."

"It's a pretty name," he said simply.

She felt warmed by his compliment. The memory of his kiss and the impact of his gentle understanding and respect touched a secret place deep within her. Remarkably, in little more than twenty-four hours, the woman who'd spent a lifetime keeping strangers at bay felt as if she'd formed a relationship bond with this man. It seemed as if an insistent emotional force seemed to be at work, pulling them together, despite the circumstances that threatened to divide them.

And yet, the exciting possibility of their newfound relationship was tinged with sadness. What chance did they have for any kind of real relationship? The kind of relationship any normal man and woman could look forward to building.

"Tell me about being a schoolteacher," he said, interrupting her thoughts.

"I love it, especially when I feel like I make a difference in my students' lives." She rode beside him through a wide clearing. "In the case of this one student, Tina, an eighth grader, I thought I'd really made progress. She was as bright as they come. Her only problem was her attitude."

Lexie went on to tell Lucas about Tina's multi-pierced ears, pierced nostril and tongue. "And I stopped counting the hair color changes a long time ago. Anyway, she was always in trouble, hell-bent to mess up her life."

"A real rebel. A little like you, maybe?" He tossed her a questioning look.

"I admit, I've had moments of rebellion. My father can attest to that. But I never indulged in self-destructive behavior and I try to live up to my responsibilities."

"I can't imagine you doing otherwise," he said. "So, tell me what happened with Tina?"

"Well, in spite of being intelligent, she was failing all her classes, except mine. For some reason, she seemed to want to cooperate with me, so I offered to tutor her in her other subjects after school." Lexie went on to explain how during these sessions the girl had opened up to her. "Tina loved the symbolic language of poetry and she shared some of what she'd written with me." Tina's verses had revealed to Lexie the complicated facets of the young girl's life, including the deep resentment she felt toward what she thought were her affluent family's preconceived expectations for her.

"I actually felt like I was really getting through to her. Her attitude had improved, along with her grades. She'd even invited her family to attend the upcoming open house. It was a big step for her, admitting she needed and wanted their love and approval. I wasn't able to talk with her before I left Boston and now I can't help feeling like I let her down."

"Boston?"

Lexie stopped short, realizing she'd stumbled over her own lie. "That's where I lived until I quit my job."

"But you told Mo—"

"I know. And I've regretted lying to her, ever since."

He frowned and stared past her.

"I know I shouldn't have done it, Lucas, but soon you'll understand why I felt I had to protect myself."

He turned a little in the saddle. "You don't have to explain. I met Acardi, remember?"

They rode in silence for a few minutes, before Lucas said, "Have you spoken to Tina since you left?"

Lexie shook her head. "Sadly, no. I was too worried about—"

"Someone like Acardi tracking you here?"

"Exactly." Unbelievably he seemed to truly understand.

"But now, the arrival of Acardi makes that worry a moot point, doesn't it? There isn't any reason why you can't contact Tina, now. If you explain, I'm sure she'll understand why you had to leave."

Lucas made it all sound so simple. "I'll call her tonight," Lexie said. "Thanks, Lucas."

He smiled at her and then took the lead again as the trail narrowed. "We'll need to go single file for the next quarter mile. The trail is hardly wide enough for one horse."

Lexie had been so busy talking she hadn't noticed the route they were taking. Down the hillside there was a wide arid gully. From here, she could see the peak of Mount Destiny where she'd camped two nights ago. Though she couldn't actually see the trail, she recognized the terrain.

Lucas had mentioned that her murdered bodyguard had taken them through country ideally suited for ambush. Studying the landscape, she had to agree with him. The sniper must have layed in wait behind one of the many rock formations at the edge of the trail. Quietly, she said, "How do you suppose the shooter knew we were coming?"

"Good question." He turned around in the saddle. His gaze surveyed the surrounding territory. "I figure he must have known you were camped up top, and he took the time to scout out the trail coming down ahead of time. Either way, he must have had inside information."

That last bit of conjecture sent a chill down Lexie's spine. "But why didn't he attack during the night while we were sleeping?"

Again, Lucas had an answer. "From the top of the mountain, there's not a decent escape route for a vehicle. He'd have to ride out on horseback. If he was planning to kidnap you, there would have been a greater chance of being seen trying to get you out on horseback.''

Lexie realized again what a stroke of pure luck it had been that Mo and Tucker had been out and about on the trail. If they hadn't come along when they did, the kidnapper's plan would have gone forward without a hitch.

As she followed behind Lucas, she relived the events that had taken place only yesterday. Lost in her thoughts, she barely noticed the warmth of the afternoon sun on her back or the soft mountain breeze in her hair.

When she thought back to the sound of the muffled gunshot that had taken Hugh's life, her heart thudded with renewed fear. The hairs on the back of her neck prickled. What if someone was watching them right now? What if the sniper was taking aim? What if, like Hugh Miller, Lucas was shot?

Nervously, she glanced over her shoulder and peered through the forest of trees. Every shadow seemed alive. Every tree branch and boulder posed a potential threat.

Lexie took a deep breath and forced the thoughts of danger from her mind. If she succumbed to this tension, she'd be paralyzed and ineffective. It was important to use her wits if she had any hope of helping bring the killer to justice.

Her mind began to rearrange the pieces of the puzzle. Lucas had said witnesses often recalled more of what they'd seen hours or even days later. If she concentrated on exactly what had happened yesterday maybe she would remember something that could help identify the killer.

She remembered turning at the sound of the gunshot. Hugh was already falling from the saddle. She'd ridden back to him in terror, dreading the worst and discovering it to be true. He must have been dead before he hit the ground.

The sniper had caught up to her immediately. Aloud, she

wondered, "Do you think there could have been two of them?"

"I wish I could tell you that," Lucas said. "What I do know is that it was a clean, professional hit. No bullet casings left behind and darned few footprints. There were a few broken twigs in the area where the sniper waited. The only other evidence we found were the signs of your struggle where he grabbed you. You must have fought like a wildcat."

"I guess I did." She remembered the metallic smell, the violation of a stranger's hands on her body, the brutality. "I remember thinking I was going to die and it seemed to give me strength."

"Survival instinct," he said. Again, he swiveled around in his saddle and checked out the landscape behind her. "It's the second strongest urge."

"What's the first?"

He only smiled.

"Oh." She felt the color rise to her cheeks. Before he'd kissed her, Lexie might have put up an argument. But the sensations he'd ignited were still burning in the back of her mind. She was eager to taste his lips again. The only thing holding her back was the knowledge that just one more kiss would never be enough.

Lucas scanned the forested hillside above them and the grassy meadow below. He pointed. "Do you see something down there?"

She squinted through the sagebrush and scrub oak. "I don't see anything unusual."

"Let's take a closer look."

He nudged his horse into a fast walk down the trail, then doubled back at an even faster clip. Lexie had to work to keep pace with him, even though Sonata was light-footed and incredibly responsive.

"Are you okay?" Lucas shouted.

''I'm fine.'' She enjoyed the ride, the opportunity for a burst of speed. The power of the well-muscled horse exhilarated her.

Then they came to an abrupt stop.

Lucas dismounted in one fluid motion. At the same time, he pulled his rifle from its sheath on his saddle. ''Stay back,'' he ordered.

Another two-word command? She was much too excited to blindly obey. Cautiously, she inched her mount forward.

Lucas stood beside a dark green tarp stretched out behind some dense undergrowth. She was amazed that he'd noticed the naturally camouflaged tarp from the trail. Apparently, his claim to have memorized every inch of this landscape had been no idle boast.

He looked up at her and frowned. ''This may not be a pretty sight, Lexie. Save yourself a few nightmares and look the other way.''

''Is it a body?''

''I'll know in a minute,'' he said as he eased back the corner of the tarp.

Lexie held her breath and knew instinctively that this time she would do well to obey his command.

LUCAS DROPPED the edge of the tarp. There was nothing he could do for Seth Rockwell; the man had been dead for at least a day, maybe longer. The blood from several gunshot wounds to the chest had already dried to rusty brown stains on Seth's white undershirt.

Lifting his gaze away from the carnage, Lucas scanned the arid gully, rugged sagebrush and patchy buffalo grass. This was Garrett property; his heritage. This mountainous countryside was the place where he'd grown to manhood, but it was more than a mere location. Here, Lucas found his solace, his sense of being. His roots sank deep into this rocky soil. The unnatural violence offended his mind and tore at his heart. He would never again cross this terrain without remembering the sight of Seth Rockwell's murdered body.

"Lucas?"

To his relief, he realized Lexie had heeded his suggestion to back away from the sight of the horror hidden beneath the tarp.

He met her troubled gaze. Astride his handsome mare, Lexie was a beautiful vision. She was vibrant, full of life. Though fine-boned and slender, Lexie had the soul of a tigress. An inner strength lent power to her small, wiry body. Yet, she was completely feminine. Her sunlit blond hair rippled in the breeze. Her delicate chin lifted and set as she prepared herself for more bad news.

"His name was Seth Rockwell," Lucas said.

"A local man?" she asked.

"He worked for the BLM, the Bureau of Land Management." Lucas mounted his horse. "This morning they reported a truck stolen and Seth was the first suspect when he failed to show up for work."

"Who was he, Lucas?"

"I didn't know Seth very well. I'm not sure he was from around here. I think he dated one of the waitresses at The Timbers, for awhile."

In a small voice, she asked, "Do you think his murder was connected to Hugh's death and the kidnap attempt?"

He hated to drop another dead body at her feet and was tempted to sugarcoat the facts, but their conversation about the incident with Acardi made him change his mind. He respected her need to know the truth. "I doubt it's a coincidence that another dead body turned up so near where you were attacked and Hugh Miller was killed. It seems a safe bet Seth Rockwell's murder is connected."

A soft moan escaped her lips. She lifted trembling hands to cover her face, and her shoulders shuddered. "I should never have come here."

He wanted to comfort her, to hold her again and kiss away her fears and remorse and tell her everything would be all right. But now was not the time for gentle caresses. Lucas was not only a man, he was the sheriff. He had another crime scene to deal with, and he needed to get her safely away from the site of the latest killing.

Maneuvering close beside her on his horse, Lucas reached out and touched her arm. "This isn't your fault, Lexie."

She sat erect in the saddle. Her violet blue eyes glistened with unshed tears, but her features were composed.

"There's only one person to blame for a murder," Lucas said. "The perpetrator. The man who aimed the gun and pulled the trigger. It's his guilt. Not yours."

"If not for me, none of this would have happened." Her voice quavered with emotion. "Seth Rockwell would not be dead. Hugh Miller would not be—"

"You want to start spreading the guilt?" he interrupted. "Throw a little my way. I'm the sheriff. I should have kept a better watch."

"How could you? You didn't know."

"Neither did you," he said. "How could you have known you would be the victim of a kidnapping attempt? There wasn't a damn thing you could do to prevent it."

"There have been other attempts," she said. "I should have anticipated the danger to myself and to others. I should have..."

"And lived your life under lock and key, in seclusion, always afraid?" He shook his head. "Honey, you and I know that's no life at all. Isn't that what you've tried to prove to your father? That you can't let others control how you choose to live your life?"

A brightness flashed across her face. Her lips twitched on the verge of a smile which quickly disappeared.

He eyed her curiously. "What?"

"Nothing important," she said. "It's just that…well, no one's ever called me honey."

Lucas couldn't believe it. Honey was a common enough term of endearment. "Never?"

"Not once." She dashed her hand in front of her face. "Oh, Lucas. I'm sorry. I'm so sorry I came here and brought all this trouble down on you and your family's ranch."

He couldn't say that he was happy about the crime wave, but part of Lucas felt good about her arrival and the chance to know her. Deep down, it almost felt like she belonged here, that she was someone he had been destined to know. "Are you all right?"

She nodded.

"Okay. Then we need to get moving. Let's ride."

THEY WERE less than a mile from the ranch house when Lucas kicked his horse into a gallop. He needed to get his deputies working on Seth's murder as quickly as possible. The tarp probably wouldn't take fingerprints, but there had to be other clues. Seth hadn't walked into that area. Where was his vehicle? Was his the stolen truck? And what had he been doing in the area in the first place? This area was not part of BLM's jurisdiction. It was Garrett land.

Lucas wondered if Seth had been onto something. Maybe he'd seen the sniper, or heard the shot. Maybe he'd had some kind of lead or tip that there would be trouble. He decided it would be a good idea to call Seth's office and talk to his co-workers. He also wanted to talk to that waitress at The Timbers, the one who'd supposedly dated Seth.

When they came in sight of the ranch house, Lucas reined his horse to a stop. The usually tranquil scene below looked like it had been transformed into a public parking lot. The pickup that Tucker and Acardi had been driving was parked in the drive, and there were two other unfamiliar vehicles, plus Eli's SUV, Cal's truck, Mo's Jeep and a white stretch limousine.

Even from this distance, he could make out two figures on the porch. One of them was Acardi, shouting and waving his arms. The other was a tall man in a black windbreaker. The distinctive letters on the back read FBI.

He dismounted and directed Lexie to do the same. Together the walked to the far side of the barn where they could not be observed from the house. "What's the FBI doing here?" Lucas wondered aloud.

"They usually handle kidnappings, don't they?" Lexie said as she led her horse into an empty stall.

"I didn't contact them, Lexie."

"No, but I told you I'd spoken to my father yesterday."

"Your father must be very well connected if he has the kind of clout it takes to mobilize the FBI and send them running to this far corner of the country for an attempted abduction."

She merely shrugged, but Lucas had the strong sense that something big was about to hit the fan. For what he hoped she knew was the last time, he asked, "Who *are* you, Alexandra Dubois?"

Her violet blue eyes darkened with sad resignation. She sighed. "I was born and raised in Europe, in a small country called St. Novia. My father is the…king. King Frederick the Fifth."

"A king!" The concept of royalty was as foreign to Lucas as the name of Lexie's birthplace. "So, if your father's the king, that would make you…"

"Princess Alexandra Constance Martina Dubois, Exalted Highness of the Royal Court, Guardian of the Palais, fourth in line of succession to the throne of St. Novia."

IT TOOK A MOMENT for her full title to sink into his brain. "A princess," he repeated numbly.

"Yes," she said, her gaze locked on his expectantly.

Lucas pulled his eyebrows into a scowl and swallowed his astonishment. Lexie had gone to great lengths to hide her identity, and he didn't want to make her feel unduly uncomfortable by gawking. "Well, now. I guess that explains a few things," he said gruffly. "The tabloid photographer. The bodyguard. The kidnap attempt. The alias."

"I'm really not all that important in my own country," she said. "I'm the fourth child, unlikely to ever sit on the throne. Unfortunately, none of my older siblings has married or produced an heir."

Lucas knew next to nothing about European royalty, and less about the rules of succession. "Are you saying if you had a child, that kid would be a prince or princess, and maybe even a king or queen?"

"Yes." She regarded him solemnly. "You said I'd cause you trouble and now you're thinking you were right, aren't you, Lucas?"

Her true identity would take a bit of digesting, but he knew that now was not the time to make an issue of her royal bloodlines. The look in her eyes told him she was worried about his reaction, that her feelings were hanging on her sleeve. "Do you really want to know what I was thinking?"

Tentatively, she nodded.

"I was thinking I'd never kissed a princess before today." He pulled her gently into his arms. "And that I'd very much like to do it again."

The way the color rose to her cheeks when he bent to kiss her only intensified his considerable desire. Her mouth was soft and warm and he lost himself for a moment in their shared passion.

"Lucas," she gasped finally, pulling a few inches away from him. "We have to talk. We have to discuss how we're going to deal with this. I don't think you realize how your world is about to be turned upside down.''

"I can handle it, Lexie. But what about you?" He ran a finger gently across her cheek, savoring the silky feel of her skin.

"I'm used to it," she said bravely. "But I hope when it's all over this won't change the way you think of me."

He lifted her chin with the tip of his finger and planted a light kiss on her still moist lips. "I'll tell you what, Lexie." He grinned. "You may be royalty to the rest of the world, but you're still just *honey* to me."

The gratitude in her eyes caused his heart to turn over. "Thank you, Lucas."

"No problem." *Your highness*, he added to himself.

Chapter Seven

As she walked out of the barn, Lexie practiced the aloof attitude that she'd always thought of as her royal facade. Her posture was ramrod straight. Her chin lifted. Her nostrils flared slightly, as if she smelled something vaguely unpleasant. Her eyelids lowered in an expression of bored disdain.

In early childhood, her older brothers and sister had taught her how to act like a princess in order to intimidate a nanny or connive an extra dessert from the chef. As she grew older, Lexie used the royal facade to fend off boors at state dinners, to keep curiosity seekers at bay when she attended public events and to discourage a number of suitors whose goal in life was to marry a wealthy princess from the small but glamorous principality of St. Novia.

Occasionally, Lexie took advantage of being a member of royalty. She wasn't proud of that fact, but, at times, she just couldn't help herself. It was great fun to mention her title and be whisked to the front of the line. She could always get the best table at a restaurant or obtain tickets to sold-out performances.

But if she'd had the choice, she preferred being plain old Lexie. Perhaps, she'd have looked at things differently had she been first in line for the throne. Maybe then she would have understood what her siblings seemed to take for granted. She'd have studied protocol, statesmanship and economics. But as it was, Lexie had never understood why an accident of birth should make her anyone's better.

Over the years, she had established a "no ceremony" policy. During the few obligatory weeks per year she spent in St. Novia, she visited hospitals and shelters. She quietly supported her favorite charity, which promoted literacy in her homeland. Although the small country that was her birthplace was economically sound and free from strife, in Lexie's opinion literacy and education was the key to keeping it that way.

While her brothers and sister earned dubious reputations as trendsetters throughout Europe and the United States, Lexie eschewed public display. Nevertheless, her presence was sought out. *The Exposé* had dubbed her "The Reluctant Princess," and Ramon Acardi had been the bane of her existence for many years.

"Are you feeling okay, Lexie?" As they walked together to the end of the barn, Lexie realized Lucas was staring at her with frank curiosity.

"I'm fine. Why?"

"Your face seems…changed, like you're angry, or something."

"It's called my royal facade," she said.

"Your royal what?"

"It's a pose, Lucas."

"I get it." He nodded. "When you're being a princess, you're supposed to look like you're about to throw up."

"It's not that bad," she protested.

"Go ahead and do what you have to do." He reached over and kissed her lightly on her royal cheek. "Just let me know when you're ready to be Lexie again."

"Most people wait *on* me. Not *for* me."

"Well, honey. I'm not most people."

"Maybe that's why I like you so much," she admitted. He couldn't know how much she appreciated his disinterested acceptance of her identity, but she also knew that this was only the beginning.

As Princess Alexandra, she'd be under constant scrutiny. Smothered by attention and well-meaning directives, she had to fight for every scrap of privacy. Fervently, she hoped Lucas would still want to call her honey after the onslaught, that he would want to find a way to steal another kiss.

As if he'd read her mind, he said, "Why don't you slip around to the back and go in through the kitchen. That'll delay the uproar at least a few more minutes."

As he strode toward the front, Lexie cut across the yard and slipped through the back door and into Mo's kitchen unobserved.

TUCKER OATES sat at the table, nursing a cup of black coffee while Mo Garrett slid a huge casserole dish into the oven. He glanced up at Lexie and scowled. "I hope you're pleased with yourself, Missy. Acardi was going to pay me a thousand dollars for an exclusive photo of you, but now it's too late."

"That's the story of your life," Mo said as she wiped her hands on the apron she wore over her jeans. "A day late and a dollar short. Serves you right for bringing that slimeball tabloid photographer out here."

"I told you before, I didn't *bring* him here, Mo. I just made a call and asked a simple question," Tucker muttered. "I guess you know, if this had worked out, we all could have been famous."

"Fame won't change you from a jackass to a Thoroughbred." Mo turned to Lexie. "Well, let's hear your story, young lady. I've never met a real-life princess before. What am I supposed to call you, anyway?"

"Lexie," she said. "Just plain old Lexie."

"Good," Mo replied. "I never was one to stand on ceremony."

How refreshing it was to know that Mo was not intimidated by her title, that she intended to treat Lexie in the down-to-earth manner that she had from the start.

"There are a couple of dignitaries from your country in the living room waiting for you. I made them some tea, but they're getting kind of antsy. Maybe you should go talk to them."

Lexie groaned inwardly. She'd noticed the limousine parked in front and assumed that she'd be dealing with someone from St. Novia. At least it wasn't her father. "I apologize, Mo. For all the commotion."

"Nonsense. Surprises make life interesting." She folded her arms below her breasts. "Did Lucas come back with you?"

Lexie nodded. "He said he'd meet me here after he updated Eli on the latest developments in the case." And Lexie could only hope that wouldn't take too long, that Lucas would return to her soon. Although she hardy dared admit it to herself, she knew she would feel immeasurably better with Lucas by her side when she faced her father's emissaries. Despite the obvious difference that threatened to extinguish the glimmers of any possible of a relationship between them, Lexie couldn't still the longing of a hopeful heart.

But perhaps Lucas felt otherwise. Perhaps on second thought, he realized the differences between them were just too varied and vast.

"What developments?" Tucker asked.

"Don't say a word," Mo cautioned her. "Not in front of this gossipy old rooster. Not unless you want it spread all over the county."

"It's not a secret." Lexie felt a frown pinching her eyebrows. "We found a body. Lucas said the man's name was Seth Rockwell."

"Good Lord! I don't think I knew him," Mo said. "Was he a local fellow?"

"Worked for the BLM," Tucker said. "Had something hot and heavy going on with one of the waitresses at The Timbers. Was he...murdered?"

"Yes," Lexie said. "Shot. His body was hidden under a tarp. Lucas said he'd probably been dead a day or more."

"I'm surprised the animals didn't get him," Tucker said.

Lexie shuddered as Tucker pushed back his chair from the table and straightened his bolo tie. "I'm going to check with Lucas and see if there's anything I can do to help. Thanks for the java, Mo."

He gingerly shuffled closer to her. For a moment, it looked like Tucker intended to give Mo a friendly little peck on the cheek, then he thought better of it and headed out the kitchen door.

"I don't know why I put up with that man," Mo said after he'd gone.

Lexie knew. Mo Garrett was a thoroughly generous woman who couldn't turn anyone away. In spite of her teasing manner, she radiated warmth and kindness. "Mo, you've already been so kind to me, but I wonder, could I ask for one more favor?"

"Of course, Lexie. Whatever I can do to help."

"Those people out there, the ones waiting for me in your living room and on your porch are going to advise me to leave Destiny Canyon Ranch. In fact, they're going to want to whisk me away from Colorado altogether. They'll claim I'm not safe here."

"They could be right, Lexie," Mo said. "There have been two murders, already. And someone attacked you."

But Lexie didn't want to run away. "But don't you see, Mo, if someone wants to do me harm, abduct me, or even...kill me, they'll find a way to get to me, whether it's here or someplace else. It doesn't matter where I go. I don't want to hide, anymore. Can't anyone understand that?''

Nor was she willing to allow another bodyguard to put his life in jeopardy trying to protect her. ''I'd like to stay here, at least until this investigation is over.''

''That could be very dangerous for you, Lexie,'' Mo said.

''I know. But I just can't allow myself to become a hostage of fear.'' Lexie repeated the words Lucas had said to her, ''There are worse things than dying, you know.''

Sagely, Mo nodded. ''I think I understand how you feel. I can't imagine feeling boxed in, smothered, even if those trying to protect me were well-meaning.''

''So, if you're willing, here's what I need you to do,'' Lexie said. ''I'd like to stay here, if not in the cabin, in the ranch house. If that's a problem for you, too much of a disruption, I'll find a place in town, but—''

''You're welcome to stay as long as you'd like, Lexie.'' Mo bustled toward her. Gently, she enveloped Lexie in a comforting hug. ''But I won't have you out in that cabin all by yourself. We have plenty of room in the ranch house. You'll stay here. And trust me, Lucas will see to it you're protected.''

Lexie rested her cheek on Mo's ample shoulder. The big woman smelled like vanilla, like fresh-baked cookies. Her arms were strong and protective. The way a mother's arms ought to feel.

Closing her eyelids, Lexie tried to remember her own mother. She'd died when Lexie was ten, and there had never been much physical contact between them. Her mother was a regal woman, every inch a queen, and she never seemed to have the time or inclination for hugs and kisses and childish play. Her latest stepmother, a former super-model, was only a few years older than Lexie herself. Hardly a mother figure.

A familiar sense of longing tugged at Lexie's heart. "Thank you, Mo," she whispered.

"I should be thanking you." Mo held her at arm's length and grinned. "I'll be the envy of Bluff County with a real-life princess staying under my roof."

"Which reminds me," Lexie said. "It's time to deal with the dignitaries from St. Novia."

"I'll back you up, Lexie. Whatever you decide. I don't know how much influence I'll have, but I won't let them bully you into leaving if you don't want to go."

Lexie gave Mo another hug and then taking a moment to put her royal facade carefully in place, she stepped from the kitchen into the living room of the homey ranch house.

With a shudder, she recognized Fulton Bobek, a supercilious young aide to the St. Novia ambassador who maintained an office in Washington, D.C. The other dignitary was the wife of the St. Novian ambassador. Lady Margaret Roche was what some would call a piece of work. With her towering gray hairdo bobbing like the crest of a large-breasted pigeon, she chatted loudly in a high-pitched, nasal squawk.

She had cornered Cal Garrett beside the mantel. Suppressing a chuckle at cowboy Cal's obvious discomfort, Lexie took a deep breath and approached the assembled group.

In clarion tones, Lady Margaret inquired, "Tell me, Mr. Garrett, does a cowpuncher actually strike at the cows? Or is this merely a colorful turn of phrase?"

"Lady Margaret," Lexie interrupted.

"Your Highness!" Lady Margaret cooed, curtsied and inclined her head in an abbreviated show of respect. "I cannot tell you how delighted I am to see you looking so well after your dreadful ordeal."

"I must say, I'm surprised to see you here, Lady Margaret. Tell me, why have you come all this way?" Lexie asked.

Fulton Bobek sidled up beside her, clicked his heels and

bowed from the waist. "Your Highness, if you'll permit me to explain. The moment we heard what had happened, we left at dawn on a private jet, with the express purpose of accompanying you back to the embassy in Washington."

Embassy was not the name Lexie would have assigned to the suite of offices and luxurious living quarters housed on the top floor of a swank D.C. hotel. In most countries, St. Novia's embassies were the same, opulent penthouses, staffed with an army of dedicated servants whose sole purpose was to cater to the whims of the likes of Lady Margaret and her ambassador husband.

"I regret that you made such a hasty and ill-advised trip," Lexie said. "You see, I have no plans to leave Destiny. Not yet, anyway. Not until the murderer and the would-be kidnapper is apprehended."

"Oh, my dear." Margaret fluttered a white lace handkerchief. "But King Frederick was quite emphatic in his instructions."

"You may inform my father of my decision," Lexie said. "On second thought, never mind. I'll tell him myself. In the meantime, I'm terribly sorry you traveled all this way for nothing. I'm afraid my father has inconvenienced you both terribly."

"Frankly, Your Highness," Margaret confided, "Fulton and I consider it an honor to serve His Majesty. And this little trip isn't as inconvenient as you might think. As you know, my husband, the ambassador, has family connections in Colorado, quite near here, I'm told. He insisted I contact them while I'm in the area."

Lexie was fully aware of Lord Edward's ties to the West. In fact, when she'd contacted the ambassador explaining her need to flee the situation in Boston, he'd offered Destiny Canyon Ranch as the ideal destination for a temporary escape from the unwanted media attention. His secretary had provided all the information, including Mo Garrett's phone number.

"They're relatives from his mother's side. No blood connection, I'm glad to say." Lady Margaret had a very unattractive way of talking down her nose whenever she referred to anything or anyone she deemed beneath her dignity. "Though, I must say, why anyone would want to live in this uncivilized part of the country is beyond me."

"I rather like it," Lexie informed her. "I've never seen such natural beauty and, without exception, I've found the people here gracious and genuine, to a fault." Lexie smiled at Cal who eased his long, lanky frame away from the fireplace. "It's a most refreshing change." When Cal returned her smile, she felt a sense of inexplicable friendship. Maybe it was because he looked enough like Lucas to be a brother instead of a nephew.

"I think you ought to let Lucas know you've decided to stick around," Cal said.

"Thank you, Cal, but I believe he already has a pretty good idea of my intentions."

She glanced toward the front door. The porch windows were open to the springtime breezes, and the rumbling noises of male conversation drifted inside.

"Excuse me," Cal said. "I think I hear him out front, now."

The front door had hardly closed behind him when Lady Margaret said, "What a handsome devil, that Cal Garrett! In a somewhat overtly masculine way, I mean. Tell me, my dear, are all the cowpunchers so utterly virile looking?"

Lexie thought of the scrawny Tucker Oates and had to laugh. "No, Margaret. Not all."

It was only the Garrett men—with their jet-black hair and sky-blue eyes—who could take a woman's breath away, even an old prune like Lady Margaret.

"Princess Alexandra," Fulton said, sniffing slightly as he

consulted a solid gold pocket watch, "begging your pardon, but I really would like to get back to town and see if there's someplace to find a decent meal. But before we go, I would advise you to reconsider your decision and return with us to Washington, Your Highness." He took a step toward her. "This is an entirely dangerous situation."

"My decision stands," Lexie said. "When you leave to return to Washington, I'll not be joining you."

Lady Margaret wrung her hands. "But your father—"

"I've made my decision," Lexie reiterated in her most regal tone.

"My husband will be beside himself with worry."

That was hard for Lexie to imagine. Lord Edward Roche was an even-tempered little butterball with a talent for socializing and very little skill at anything else. "Why should Lord Roche be upset? He's known me long enough to know I have a mind of my own. And he's never seemed particularly intimidated by my father."

"This is different," Margaret insisted. "He feels personally responsible for the situation, since it was his suggestion that you come here," she reminded.

"Please thank your husband for me," Lexie said. "This place was exactly the retreat I was looking for."

Lady Margaret gasped. "I don't understand how can you say that, in light of all that's happened."

"It could have happened anywhere. I certainly don't blame Lord Roche or anyone else. And I assure you my father will not hold him responsible, either."

"But Your Highness," Fulton nagged, "if you'd only listen to reason. I would be glad to help you pack and by this time tomorrow—"

"I'm staying," Lexie said, regarding him with imperious scorn. "If you wish to make yourself useful, Fulton, you might see what you can do about getting rid of that photographer, Acardi."

"Surely, you're not suggesting I confront the fellow myself?" Nervously, Fulton eyed the front door. The voices outside on the porch had turned angry. "Dealing with the paparazzi can be most difficult."

The voices outside grew even louder and Lexie caught a glimpse of Acardi peeling out of the drive in his rented vehicle. "Never mind, Fulton. It looks as though Sheriff Garrett has dealt with Acardi and saved you the trouble."

Seconds later, the front door burst open and Lucas charged inside.

Lady Margaret gasped. "Oh my! Another magnificent man!"

The tall FBI agent in the black windbreaker was right behind Lucas. "You don't have a choice, Sheriff," he was saying. "You're not running this show."

"This is my county," Lucas boomed. "My jurisdiction."

"Let's get real, Sheriff. You're out of your league. The FBI has the resources needed to solve this case before it becomes an international incident."

"I can't argue with your advantage in manpower and resources, Peterson. But I know this country, know every trail and back road from here to New Mexico."

"What's to know?" Agent Peterson impatiently raked his fingers through thinning brown hair. His high forehead made his narrow face seem even longer. "We've been here since early this morning and I've got the place pretty well scoped out. We've been all over the scene of the kidnapping."

"There was no kidnapping," Lucas reminded him. "But there was a homicide. And that's my case," Lucas said. "And my department will handle the investigation."

"The FBI is equipped to deal with this kind of abduction—"

"Abduction attempt," Lucas interrupted.

"Excuse me," Lexie said, stepping into the fray.

"Who are you?" the FBI man demanded.

Fulton Bobek clicked his heels together. "Allow me to introduce Princess Alexandra DuBois of St. Novia."

Nonplussed, the FBI man was caught between a bow and a handshake. "Sorry, Miss...I mean, Your Highness. I didn't know, didn't recognize you."

"Your name, please," Lexie demanded.

"Agent Simon Peterson, lead investigator assigned to your case." He gestured to a man in a dark suit and necktie who had quietly entered the room. "And this is Agent Paul Browning."

Though Browning was second in command, he maintained an attitude of calm control as he extended his hand toward Lexie. "Pleased to meet you, Princess Alexandra." He was a well-groomed man, quiet and reserved. The touch of gray at his temples added an air of dignity to his demeanor.

Lexie shook Agent Browning's hand and returned her attention to Simon Peterson. "I couldn't help overhearing your conversation. As Sheriff Garrett pointed out, I have not been kidnapped. Therefore, it seems the FBI's involvement is unnecessary."

"We're here at the request of the State Department," Peterson informed her.

"Absurd," she said with icy disdain. "It is my express wish that Sheriff Garrett remain in charge of this investigation."

"Begging your pardon, ma'am, but I'm afraid what you want is irrelevant. I have my orders."

"If you truly wish to avoid an incident," Lexie warned, "you'd be well-advised to pass on my wishes to your superiors."

"Now, just hold on a minute," Lucas cut in. Anger shimmered around him like sparks from a campfire. His eyes shone with a cool blue flame. "We're wasting time arguing jurisdiction when we should be tracking a killer. My men are out on the mountain right now, Peterson, and I have every intention of joining them." He turned and headed for the door. "I'll keep the FBI informed of my progress."

"Unacceptable," the Peterson replied.

Lucas stopped at the doorway and turned to face the man. "That's the way it's going to be, Peterson. Live with it." He shifted his gaze to Lexie. "Thanks for the vote of confidence, Princess Honey, but I don't need anyone to fight my battles for me."

With that, he slapped his Stetson back onto his head and strode out the front door.

The discordant voice of Lady Margaret trembled with affronted dignity. "Well, I never! Princess Honey, indeed!"

Chapter Eight

Lucas, along with a team of his deputies, worked at the Rockwell murder scene until long after dark. The next morning, as he pulled into the drive in front of the Garrett ranch house, he was still mad enough to chew nails. And even angrier to see the limousine that had delivered the St. Novian delegation yesterday parked in the drive, right next to Agent Peterson's rented car.

Chomping back his anger, he reminded himself that it wouldn't pay to lose control again. Coming unglued at the FBI yesterday had been foolish. And he shouldn't have taken his frustration out on Lexie, either.

He'd tried calling her last night, but Mo said she'd gone to bed early. She had left him a message, though, explaining that she hadn't been able to reach her father, but would try again today.

Lucas's sleep had been fitful, thinking about the way he'd left things with Lexie and simmering over Agent Peterson's smug attitude.

The FBI couldn't come in here and take over, damn it! This territory belonged to him and no bunch of stuffed suits from Washington was going to tell him otherwise.

Eli Ferguson was leaning against the fender of his police vehicle when Lucas stepped out of his own vehicle.

The easy-going deputy sauntered over to him. In his west Texas accent, he drawled, "What's going on, Lucas?"

"I want this case solved, Eli. And I want all those folks in there to go back where they came from and leave my county alone!"

Fierce determination sliced through his anger. Not only was Lucas driven by pride and the sincere belief that he could handle this investigation, but he was motivated by the heart. Two cold-blooded murders had taken place in his own backyard. The danger had come too close. How was he supposed to relinquish control to the FBI while a murderer stalked so near to his family? He had to protect them. And he had to protect Lexie.

The thought of her caused a twinge of regret. Again, he regretted the way he'd left things between them yesterday. He should have been more patient, more understanding. No doubt she'd thought her snooty princess attitude—her so-called royal facade—would help him gain an upper hand with the FBI. She hadn't meant to offend him. He knew that now and he regretted hurting her feelings.

"Okay, Lucas. What do you want me to do?" Eli asked.

Still irritable, Lucas growled, "Well, you can start by taking off those damned sunglasses when I'm talking to you. It feels like I'm looking in a mirror."

The glasses came off. Eli tucked them into his uniform shirt pocket. In spite of a laid-back attitude that sometimes bordered on insolent, Eli had always shown the discipline and intelligence of a man who knew better than to argue with his superior officer.

Lucas said, "We need to act fast and be smart. It's only a matter of time before the FBI finds a way to take jurisdiction of this case away from us. Damn it, Eli. This isn't right. I know they're going to screw things up. I don't want this murderer to go free."

"Where do we start?"

So many questions and plans swirled around in his head. He needed all his power of concentration to coordinate the investigation of a double homicide and kidnapping plot.

"I need you to remain stationed here at the ranch house, Eli. I don't trust anybody else to handle the FBI *and* Lexie."

"She's a handful," Eli agreed.

Lucas thought of her, riding beside him. She'd looked so good astride Sonata. And then, she'd put on that princess routine, trying to act like royalty—whatever that meant. A woman like her didn't need a facade. She didn't need to be anything but what she was: beautiful, intelligent, sexy. All the woman anyone could ever want. That last thought shocked him at the same time Eli cleared his throat.

"Here's what I think, Sheriff. Since I'm going to be settled here in one place, I should be the information center for our investigation. I'll keep in touch with Sylvia and keep you apprised of everyone's movements in and out of the ranch."

"Sounds good." Lucas dragged his thoughts away from Lexie. He had an investigation to organize. "I still need to contact Rockwell's next of kin. I don't want his family finding out about his murder secondhand."

"Doc Rogers should have his autopsy report for you sometime tomorrow," Eli said.

"Good. And we still need an identification on Hugh Miller. Do we know anyone over at CBI that can pull some strings and get those fingerprints run faster?"

Eli shook his head.

"I'll tell Sylvia to call and see if she can light a fire under them."

"Is there anything I can do to speed this thing along, Lucas?"

Lucas stopped to think. The hardest part of a complex investigation like this one was keeping track of all the minor details without losing sight of the big picture. One of those details was contained in something Lexie had said yesterday.

She'd wondered if there had been more than one perpetrator involved in the crime. Logistically, it seemed logical that an abduction would be easier to pull off with at least two operatives: One to subdue and contain the victim. Another to pick up the ransom. Assuming that the ransom demand would go to Lexie's father, the king of St. Novia, the second person might have ties to that country.

Which brought up a detail: Lucas didn't even know where to find St. Novia on a map. He needed more information from Lexie...Princess Alexandra. She was an integral part of this investigation. Without her help, he was just a cowboy cop with two very disturbing crime scenes.

"So, if that's all I guess I'll check in with Sylvia and let her know where I'll be," Eli said. "Is there anything else you need, Sheriff?"

"I'll let you know."

The deputy started to push his sunglasses back in place, but hesitated.

"Ah, go on," Lucas said. "They suit you."

Eli smiled and pushed the glasses up onto his face as he sauntered back toward his vehicle to make the call to Sylvia on his police radio. To look at the lanky ex-Texan, nobody would guess he was a highly efficient investigator. But Lucas knew better. Someday, when he retired to concentrate on raising and training horses, he'd feel confident recommending Eli as his replacement.

"Hey, Deputy," he called out to the tall Texan.

Eli turned slowly. "Yeah?"

"Thanks."

"No problem," Eli replied and reached for his radio.

Lucas made his way around the house and entered through the back door. It was time to talk to Lexie, to apologize and ask her to help him fit together more pieces of this puzzle of a case.

As it turned out, Lexie was the first person Lucas saw when he walked through the door. She sat, hunched over the long, pine dining table. In front of her was a plate of bacon and eggs, undoubtedly an offering from Mo who thought any disaster could be solved with a good meal.

A cell phone was gripped in Lexie's hand. Her fingers were clenched so tightly her knuckles were white. When she raised her head and looked up at him, he saw the storm brewing in her eyes.

"No, Father," she said emphatically into the phone. "Yes, that's right. I'm staying," she said. It didn't take a master detective to deduct that Lexie was standing up to her father, defying the man who just happened to be a king. Lucas watched her set her jaw and he couldn't help feeling proud of her.

"Because I'm a witness," she said, "and I may be able to help catch the killer. I won't run away from this, Father. And, yes, I do care how this effects the family." She looked up at Lucas and rolled her eyes.

His heart went out to her. Though he had no concept of what it was to be royalty, he knew how it felt to confront a strong parent. Despite a relationship based on love and mutual respect, Lucas and Will Garrett had butted heads on occasion.

Lexie was still on the phone when Mo walked into the kitchen and asked, "How many of those folks out there do you think I should plan on for dinner tonight?"

"You don't have to feed any of them as far as I'm concerned," Lucas said. "Send them to The Timbers. Maybe they'll all contract food poisoning."

Absently, she dusted her hands on her apron. "Well, that's a fine example of western hospitality. I wouldn't feel right doing that, Lucas. Those investigators all but spent the night here. They're working hard to do their jobs. And I'm guessing the St. Novia bunch is going to hang around at least a couple more days, trying to convince Lexie to see things their way.''

''Are they really pushing her that hard?'' he asked in a low voice.

Mo nodded. ''She's under a lot of pressure, Lucas. And it just doesn't seem fair. She's got a good head on her shoulders and she has the right to make her own decisions.''

Lucas couldn't have agreed more.

''Where'd she get that thing?'' Lucas asked, pointing to the cell phone.

''Agent Peterson loaned it to her when she said she was going to call her father.''

Lucas frowned.

''All right. So, what about dinner?'' Mo asked again.

''Do what you want, sis,'' Lucas said, knowing she would anyway. ''While you're cooking, whip up a batch of crow for Agent Peterson and I'll do what I can to make sure he eats it.''

Lexie ended her phone call with a vicious jab at the disconnect button. She snapped the phone closed, slipped it into her jeans pocket and looked up at him, her eyes still simmering.

''Did I hear you correctly?'' he asked. ''Are you planning to stay here and help with the investigation?''

''Yes.'' There was none of the former hesitance in her manner. Clearly, she intended to stick with her decision come hell, high water or pressure from the St. Novian monarch.

''I'm heading back to the gully where we found Seth Rockwell,'' he said. ''Want to ride with me?''

''I'd love nothing more than a way out of here this morning. Let's go,'' she said, ''before anybody else tries to stop me.''

He turned to Mo. "I need to use your Jeep."

She leaned against the countertop and scowled. "There's not one person in the other room—not Lady Margaret and certainly not the FBI agents—who would approve of you taking Lexie back out on that trail."

"You're probably right about that," Lucas responded.

"And the FBI would like nothing more than to have a good reason to jerk you off this case."

Lucas nodded. "Can't argue with that, either."

Mo dug into the pocket of her jeans and produced a set of keys for her Jeep. As she handed them to him, she whispered. "Be careful, little brother. And take good care of our princess."

In spite of all the pressures raining down on her, Lexie felt free as they drove away from the Garrett ranch house in Mo's battered Jeep. She was defying her father, but more importantly she was following her instincts, facing her problems instead of running from them.

In the driver's seat beside her, Lucas navigated across the rugged off-road terrain with his usual brand of speed and control. Lexie hadn't expected him to be on her side.

Yesterday, when he'd left her standing in the midst of the FBI and the St. Novian delegation, she'd known she'd bruised his pride.

"So, why did you ask me to come with you, Lucas?" she asked.

The brim of his black Stetson obscured his eyes, making his expression almost unreadable.

"I need your help," he said.

Those simple words were all the vindication she needed. Lady Margaret and the ridiculously foppish Fulton wanted to curry favor with her father. The FBI's Agent Peterson no doubt saw a promotion in solving this high profile case.

Their supposed concerns on her behalf were rooted in ulterior motives.

Of all of them, only Lucas cared about her as an individual. He didn't care about the politics, promotions or royal favors. He was interested in her and in solving this case. He knew and wasn't too proud to admit that her input could be valuable. After all, if anyone could give him insight into a kidnapper's motive, it would be her.

Her gaze rested lightly upon him. Of all the people on the planet, this cowboy lawman didn't seem to notice or care that she was a princess, a member of a royal family, the possible heir to a fortune and maybe even a throne.

To him, she'd been a victim of a crime. Then, a witness. For a time, even a suspect. And now, it seemed, he was willing to accept her as an asset to his investigation.

"Thanks," she said softly.

He glanced over at her. "For what?"

"For including me."

"If you can help me catch this guy, I'll be thanking you, honey."

"Tell me how I can help, Lucas. I know I was difficult in the beginning, but I want to help now. I really do."

He brought the Jeep to a halt. Though it seemed they were parking in the middle of nowhere, she knew they were near where Seth Rockwell's body had been discovered.

Lucas turned toward her. He tipped back his hat and gazed directly into her face. Honesty and determination were etched in the chiseled features. "This is my home. I know these lands. I know that sometimes you can turn over a rock and find a rattlesnake. My men can pick up clues that the FBI would walk right past."

She nodded, still unsure of why he thought he needed her.

"I'm a good lawman," he continued. "I know how to put together an investigation and compile the details."

"I don't doubt that," she said. "But I need to know how I can help."

"Investigative procedure is all part of a bigger picture. Taking fingerprints and putting together clues are the individual brush strokes in the final picture. But sometimes I have to step back and see the whole canvas. I've got to look at the overall picture to understand the motive for the crime. And that's where you come in, Lexie. You can help me understand why someone would come after you. Was it money? Power? Political gain?"

She felt a bit overwhelmed by his questions. It was almost as if he expected her to slip inside the mind of the killer and would-be kidnapper. Self-doubt rose up inside her, but she stamped it down, reminding herself of the stakes. A man had given his life for hers. She owed him whatever effort it took to help bring his killer to justice. "I'm going to have to work on that one, Lucas," she said. "Of course, money would be the obvious motive. As far as politically, every leader has his enemies."

"Do you think you could get me a list of names, political enemies, individuals who have threatened your family or have a special vendetta against your father?"

"I'll see what I can do," she promised.

"Also, when we were riding back to the ranch house yesterday you said something about the possibility of two kidnappers. I want to know what made you think of that."

"Timing," she said quickly, having mulled this over last night. "I was too distraught to keep track of the moments passing, but it seemed like my attacker had to have been in two places at once for the abduction attempt to succeed. First, he shot Hugh. Then, he was on top of me. How did he imagine he could pull it off? Wouldn't it have made sense to have someone else in hiding, nearer the trail, waiting to grab me?"

"That seems logical," Lucas agreed.

"One person shoots. The other takes care of me."

"That could have been the plan, but it didn't happen that way or it would have succeeded, wouldn't it?"

She frowned. "You're right."

"I paced off the distance and as near as I can figure it, you were almost directly below the sniper's position when he pulled the trigger. He was only ten or fifteen yards away from you, and he should have been able to slide down, grab your horse's reins and drug you. From there, it was only a short walk around the bend to where his getaway vehicle— probably the stolen BLM truck—was waiting."

She shuddered at his re-creation of the cold hard facts. It was difficult to separate herself from the role of victim and think like a detective.

"But you did something the killer didn't expect," Lucas said. "You rode back to help Hugh Miller."

"I had to see if I could help him in some way," she said. "I knew even from that distance he'd been wounded badly, but I thought maybe I could save him. I couldn't just leave him like that."

"Of course you couldn't. You were concerned above all else that he might die," Lucas said.

Lexie swallowed hard as the image of the stricken man formed again in her mind. "Yes."

"You wanted to help."

"Of course."

"In short," he said, "you didn't act like a princess. You didn't believe your own life was worth more than Hugh Miller's."

"I—I didn't think about that, I only wanted to—"

He reached for her hand. "I know, honey. You wanted to help. But the sniper didn't expect you to behave like that. Your instincts, the instincts that make you a good and decent person, put another's welfare ahead of your own. And those instincts saved your pretty neck."

He reached out and trailed the back of his hand along the line of her jaw. "You're a good woman, Lexie."

His compliment warmed her. She'd always thought of herself as a good person; trustworthy, honorable and independent. In the company of someone like Lucas, she sensed those aspects of her personality could blossom and grow even stronger.

"But my theory is still wrong, isn't it, Lucas? You believe the kidnapper acted alone."

"I'm not sure. But if there had been two of them, they would've carried you off before Mo could interfere." He patted her cheek and withdrew his hand. "But in a way, you're still right."

"All right. Now you've lost me. How can I be right and wrong at the same time?"

"The best plan would have been to have two men on the trail. The shooter was smart and skilled. He used a state-of-the-art weapon, and I don't need to tell you that his marksmanship was excellent. But he should have anticipated your movements and made sure he had a backup, waiting to grab you in case you rode back to help Miller."

"But he didn't," she said.

Lucas nodded, encouraging her participation. "He underestimated you, honey. And now, all we have to figure out is why. Our sniper acted alone and there's a reason for that."

As she saw how her input had helped him form a total picture, Lexie felt gratified. Feeling confident, she ventured another question. "There's a whole wide world of suspects to choose from. How do we narrow the list?"

"That's where motive comes in," Lucas said.

As they'd discussed, the obvious reason was greed. She didn't delude herself by thinking that her father would be heartbroken by her absence, but public pressure would demand he pay whatever the kidnapper demanded.

It wasn't that her father didn't care. He did. But, in truth, he hardly knew her. Their relationship had always been distant. They saw each other only occasionally and exchanged obligatory phone calls. His secretary remembered Lexie's birthday and always made sure an appropriate present was mailed.

The SUVs in the distance distracted Lexie from her ruminations.

Two Ford Explorers were headed across the open country toward them. Lucas climbed out of the Jeep to meet his deputies. "Keep thinking about motives, Lexie. I need to talk with my men about the direction the search will take today and then we'll discuss the situation further."

While Lucas put his men to work, she stayed in Mo's Jeep, keeping her distance from the crime scene, watching Lucas. He was a natural-born leader, directing his deputies in their widening search for evidence. He was also—as Lady Margaret had noticed—a magnificent specimen of a man.

When he turned to see her watching him, Lexie ducked her head and told herself she hadn't come out here to admire Lucas Garrett's physical attributes. Her sole purpose for staying in Destiny was to help bring Hugh's killer to justice.

Lucas had said she should try to concentrate on motive. She climbed out of the Jeep and walked toward a shady spot under a lacy Aspen tree, leaned her back against the trunk and tried to think. But as she thought back to all she knew about the political situation in St. Novia, she came to realize that she was woefully out of touch with her homeland. The only two people she kept in contact with were her father's secretary and the woman who ran the St. Novia Literacy Program.

With a sigh, she tried to get comfortable, and felt something in her pocket jab her. The cell phone! She'd inadvertently walked off with Agent Peterson's cell phone.

"Thanks, Agent Peterson," she murmured aloud. As long as she had the means and the opportunity, she decided she

Play **LUCKY HEARTS** for this...

exciting FREE gift!
This surprise mystery gift could be yours free

when you play **LUCKY HEARTS!**
...then continue your lucky streak with a sweetheart of a deal!

1. Play Lucky Hearts as instructed on the opposite page.

2. Send back this card and you'll receive 2 brand-new Harlequin Intrigue® novels. These books have a cover price of $4.25 each in the U.S. and $4.99 each in Canada, but they are yours to keep absolutely free.

3. There's no catch! You're under no obligation to buy anything. We charge nothing— ZERO—for your first shipment. And you don't have to make any minimum number of purchases—not even one!

4. The fact is thousands of readers enjoy receiving their books by mail from the Harlequin Reader Service®. They enjoy the convenience of home delivery...they like getting the best new novels at discount prices, BEFORE they're available in stores...and they love their *Heart to Heart* subscriber newsletter featuring author news, horoscopes, recipes, book reviews and much more!

5. We hope that after receiving your free books you'll want to remain a subscriber. But the choice is yours—to continue or cancel, any time at all! So why not take us up on our invitation, with no risk of any kind. You'll be glad you did!

© 1996 HARLEQUIN ENTERPRISES LTD. ® and ™ are
trademarks owned by Harlequin Enterprises Ltd.

Visit us online at

www.eHarlequin.com

▲ DETACH AND MAIL CARD TODAY! ▼

The Harlequin Reader Service®—Here's how it works:

Accepting your 2 free books and gift places you under no obligation to buy anything. You may keep the books and gift and return the shipping statement marked "cancel." If you do not cancel, about a month later we'll send you 4 additional novels and bill you just $3.57 each in the U.S., or $3.96 each in Canada, plus 25¢ shipping & handling per book and applicable taxes if any.* That's the complete price and — compared to cover prices of $4.25 each in the U.S. and $4.99 each in Canada — it's quite a bargain! You may cancel at any time, but if you choose to continue, every month we'll send you 4 more books, which you may either purchase at the discount price or return to us and cancel your subscription.

*Terms and prices subject to change without notice. Sales tax applicable in N.Y. Canadian residents will be charged applicable provincial taxes and GST.

might as well do a bit of investigative work, here and now. With her legs stretched out in front of her and her back against the white bark of the Aspen tree, Lexie began placing telephone calls to St. Novia.

After a half an hour of inquiry with two different contacts, Lexie was rewarded with three names. The first two individuals, both political enemies of her father's, were easily eliminated as suspects, once she discovered they were both in jail. But the third name could not be dismissed. The name of Ian Solé.

Solé, according to the information she'd gleaned from a helpful aide in her father's office, was a mercenary, a notorious freelance killer for hire. No one knew from what country he hailed, but it was believed he wasn't a citizen of St. Novia. His crimes, however, had touched countless European nations, as well as the United States. The notorious criminal had been linked to countless contract killings, bank robberies and heists of national treasures. But the fact that chilled Lexie to the bone was the information that linked Solé to the kidnapping of a wealthy heiress in France.

Still stunned by the disturbing facts she'd learned from her father's aide, Lexie tried to absorb the horrific possibility that an international mercenary might have tracked her all the way to Colorado.

But before she could begin to come to grips with that fact, the approach of another vehicle interrupted her. The nondescript sedan bounced wildly over the unpaved terrain. When the car parked beside Mo's Jeep and the two FBI agents got out, Lexie mentally echoed Lucas's sentiment that these guys had no business prowling around on Garrett land. These city slickers didn't even know what kind of car to take off-road.

While Agent Peterson strode toward Lucas, Agent Browning walked in her direction. As he approached, she rose to her feet and held out the cell phone toward him.

"Sorry," she said innocently. "I seem to have accidentally walked away with Agent Peterson's phone. Would you see he gets it back?"

"Sure. No problem."

He slipped the high-tech instrument into his suit coat pocket. Lexie knew Agent Paul Browning was not in charge of the FBI's activities in Bluff County, but something told her he was the more mature and capable of the two federal investigators.

"You know, of course, that you shouldn't be out here," he said. "As long as the killer is still on the loose, it's not safe."

She gestured toward the investigation scene where Agent Peterson and Lucas were standing toe-to-toe in intense conversation. "I think I'm safe with half a dozen lawmen within shouting distance."

"Then, you're not worried about snipers."

"Not particularly." She really didn't believe that anyone wanted to kill her. Her only value was to garner a literal king's ransom.

"What about tabloid photographers with long-distance lenses?"

"Ouch," she said, glancing nervously around her. "I'd forgotten all about that." If for no other reason than to protect her family and the Garrett's privacy, maybe it wasn't such a good idea for her to be out in the open. "Thanks for the reminder."

He stood quietly beside her, seemingly waiting for orders from Peterson. Lexie appreciated Browning's silence. Unlike his overbearing partner, Paul Browning seemed quiet, reserved and even thoughtful.

Finally, he said, "I've done a bit of research on your country."

"Really?"

"Yes. It sounds like a wonderful place. I'd love to visit sometime. It seems so…idyllic."

"I suppose so," she said. "At times, I think my country must seem unreal to the rest of the world, like a setting for a fairy tale."

"Exactly."

"But it's not true, Agent Browning. St. Novia isn't a fairyland. We have all the problems of any modern civilization—crime, poverty, illiteracy…"

"Professional killers?" he asked.

She glanced sharply at him. His comment was too well-timed to be a coincidence. "Why do I get the feeling my phone calls home weren't completely private?"

Without admitting that he'd been listening in, he said, "We're the FBI, Your Highness. We have to know what's being said over our own phone lines."

"I would only ask that the information you overheard not be leaked to the press."

"Of course." Lexie didn't know why, but she believed him.

"Lexie—do you mind if I call you Lexie?"

"Not at all."

"Ian Solé is dangerous and cunning criminal. From the beginning, I suspected he was a likely suspect in the killing of Hugh Miller and the attempt to kidnap you. He's the main reason the FBI is interested in this case. We've been tracking him for years, to no avail."

"Do you know for a fact that he's in the United States?"

"I'm not at liberty to disclose that information, Lexie."

"I suppose this killer is under some sort of surveillance?"

"Again, I can only say I'm not at liberty to—"

"Fine," she snapped. Apparently, the FBI had been well aware of Solé's existence and his movements, also aware that he might be a threat to her. But they hadn't arrested the man, yet, or moved in to stop him from killing Hugh Miller.

No doubt, he was part of some larger plot, a plot that meant more to the agency or some other political power than a fourth string princess—even when her bodyguard had been killed in cold blood. "I will never understand the way politics work," she said bitterly. "But if you know where this man is, you have to stop him."

"The FBI is the finest law enforcement agency in the world," Browning said.

Lexie's laugh was completely humorless. "Agent Browning, don't try to confuse me with spin. You forget who you're talking to. If anyone knows how to effectively evade a difficult question, it's a member of royalty." And with that, she turned in her most regal fashion and left him staring after her.

She noticed Lucas was leaving the scene of the investigation, Agent Peterson trailing behind him. Lexie met him at Mo's Jeep.

"Princess Alexandra, please wait." Browning handed her a card. "I didn't mean to offend you. Please, I want to help. This phone number rings through to my pager. I know you've decided to work with the sheriff, but if you ever need my services, please, don't hesitate to call."

Though she slipped his card into her pocket, Lexie doubted she'd ever make that call.

Lucas helped her into the Jeep and with Agent Peterson still ranting about jurisdiction, they drove away, leaving him in a cloud of reddish dust.

"Agent Peterson seems to be a thoroughly unpleasant person," she said.

"To say the least."

She could see that Lucas was angry again. He aimed the Jeep directly at a sagebrush and plowed over it as if running down Agent Peterson himself.

She asked, "So, what next?"

"For the rest of the day, I'll meet with my men and go

over the evidence we've gathered to this point. Hopefully, we'll have the coroner's report to give us more answers. You're staying with Mo, at the ranch house, right?"

"She wouldn't have it any other way."

"Good. I won't worry about you there with my deputy on guard and the family looking out for you. Tomorrow, if you're up to it, we'll meet again and talk about possible motives for your abduction. Maybe I can have that conversation with your father."

Lexie was almost sure of that. "In the meantime, I have a bit of information that just might turn this case around."

"Oh?"

"Ian Solé?"

"Gesundheit."

Despite the situation, she smiled. "It's a name. Ever heard it before?"

"No. Should I have?"

"He's a mercenary. A killer for hire."

"And where did this gem of information come from?"

"St. Novia," she told him and then went on to explain how she'd used her time on the mountain to make the calls to her father's office.

"Sounds as if we need to move Mr. Solé to the top of the suspect list," Lucas said. "I must admit, I'm impressed by your investigative skills, Lexie."

She wished she could find a way to smile under his compliment, but the strange and disturbing news from St. Novia left her feeling less than cheery.

"All right," he said, "I guess turnabout is fair play. I've got a bit of information for you."

"Yes?"

"Deputy Ferguson tracked down Seth Rockwell's next of kin. As it turns out, he didn't have to look very far."

"Why was that, Lucas?"

"The murdered BLM employee was a distant cousin of the St. Novian ambassador."

"Lady Margaret's husband?" Lexie almost couldn't believe her ears.

"Lord Edward Roche, himself."

That connection bothered Lexie deeply. She'd experienced the pain of betrayal and hoped to heaven she wouldn't have to go through that again. Deep down, she couldn't believe the jolly ambassador had had anything to do with the abduction attempt. And yet, she couldn't deny the news of his connection to a murder was just another disturbing brush stroke in a big picture that was becoming darker and more foreboding by the moment.

Chapter Nine

The sniper crept silently through the cover of night. The high meadow grasses veiled him from sight, and the crisp breeze whispering through tree branches masked the sound of his footsteps as he approached the Garrett ranch house. A rustic log fence bordered the yard, and he glided, like a shadow, along the perimeter.

The lights in the house had blinked out, one by one. Only the lamps in the great room and kitchen were still shining.

The sniper went down on one knee. The barrel of his rifle balanced on the fence rail, as he peered through the night-scope.

Only one man stood guard on the porch. With clear night vision, the sniper aimed at the center button on Deputy Eli Ferguson's shirt. An easy target.

If the man on the porch had been Sheriff Lucas Garrett instead of his deputy, the sniper would have pulled the trigger without hesitation. The small-town sheriff was much too clever and tenacious for his own good. He was a threat. And with the princess constantly at his side, the man posed an even greater obstacle.

As the sniper watched through the scope, rifle at the ready, the princess came onto the porch with a steaming mug of coffee for the man on guard. *She was serving him.*

Again, her behavior was completely out of character. If

she had known enough to behave like royalty, his original plan would have succeeded. He would have successfully kidnapped her on the trail and the ransom might already be his.

But she hadn't acted as he'd expected. She'd ridden back to help Hugh Miller and put too much distance between herself and the truck. *Why, little princess? Why should you care about a virtual stranger hired to follow you at a silent distance?*

His aim shifted. Through the scope, he saw her shimmering blond hair. She'd ruined his carefully laid plans. He did not abide failure. She deserved to die.

His finger twitched against the sensitive trigger.

But what use was she to him dead? He needed a live princess for his ransom demand.

Another man meandered onto the porch, one of the ranch hands. The sniper lowered the rifle and sank down into the grasses behind the fence. He couldn't afford a bloodbath.

Stealing her from the house would be far too risky. He would have to wait, bide his time. But that time would come. His plan would go forward. He had waited far too long for the right moment, the precise opportunity.

This abduction would be his finest hour, the grand finale of a long and remarkable career.

After he received the payoff, he would take his revenge against Princess Alexandra. He could wait. A professional knew that time was always on his side.

LUCAS LEANED BACK in the wing chair in the great room. With Mo gone to bed, there were no restrictions about resting his heels on the edge of the pinewood coffee table, and he stretched out his legs and sighed. It was past eleven, and he was wiped out. His scribbled notes on the canary legal pad blurred into an unintelligible mess of question marks.

Either he needed a second wind or he might as well pack it in and head for bed.

Unfortunately, that meant driving back to his own house. All three guest bedrooms in the ranch house were occupied. Lexie had one. Eli and another deputy shared another as they alternated guard duty. And Virgil Blackburn, the ranch foreman, had moved in from the bunkhouse to add his support to the ring of protection around Lexie.

Two of Mo's guest cabins—those rented by Lexie and Hugh Miller—had been designated crime scenes. The other two were occupied by Fulton Bobek and Lady Margaret.

Lucas doodled a star beside Lady Margaret's name on the legal pad. Her semihysterical behavior when he'd informed her of the murder of her husband's cousin caused Lucas to realize that Lexie had been amazingly reasonable under interrogation. Though Lexie, the princess, had been evasive, Lady Margaret had shrieked and moaned and swooned.

Lucas was too much of a gentleman to accuse Lady Margaret of faking, but he noticed that her fainting spell had landed her neatly on the sofa in the living room. When she regained consciousness, without a hair out of place, she threatened lawsuits and international incidents. Talk about a royal pain in the butt!

When the front door opened, Lucas looked up to see Lexie closing the door behind her. "I took your deputy some coffee," she said. There was a brightness in her eyes as she moved deeper into the room and sat down opposite him. Just the sight of her gave Lucas a much-needed surge of energy. Though she had to be as tired as he was, her violet eyes sparkled.

"It's a beautiful night," she said as she kicked off her shoes and curled up on the sofa. "There's only a sliver of moon, but we're so close to the stars and the sky is so clear, I feel like I could reach up and grab one."

"You'd like that, wouldn't you?"

"To have that kind of freedom, yes. Not to mention a star of my very own."

"Well, maybe I'll get one for you," he said.

Her lovely mouth curved in a smile. "Would you?" Her eyes danced like a child's at storytime.

"Absolutely."

"Tell me, Lucas. Tell me how you'd fetch me a star."

"Well, I'd saddle up G-Bar and ride him to the summit of Mount Destiny. When the going got too rough for my horse, I'd hike the rest of the way on foot. I'd climb and climb, until I was right out there, face-to-face with the satellites. Then I'd take out my lariat, and I'd swing it over my head until I lassoed the brightest star in the heavens. When I got back down the mountain, I'd put it in a pendant you could wear forever, so you'd have starlight, even on the darkest nights."

Unconsciously, her hand went to her throat. Her fingertips outlined the delicate hollow in her collarbone. "I'd treasure that gift forever, Lucas."

He hadn't intended to wax on with such poetic enthusiasm, but the dreamy light in her delighted eyes as he'd spun his cowboy yarn had made him want to go to any lengths to please her.

Spinning tall tales was not his style, but this lady was having a profound effect on him, and Lucas was finding it more and more difficult to think about what life would be like when she left Destiny Canyon Ranch.

He couldn't kid himself into believing she'd ever consider staying. Lexie was a princess, like it or not, and that meant she had responsibilities. Preparing himself for that inevitable disappointment, he said gruffly, "I don't suppose a cowboy's pendant could compare with the crown jewels of St. Novia."

She gazed into his eyes and said, "It would mean more to me than the most perfect diamond."

It was only the thought of her ultimate departure that stopped him from gathering her into his arms and carrying her upstairs to the nearest vacant bedroom. His mouth remembered the taste of her lips. His arms would never forget the sensation of holding her slender body. But that was before, before he'd known her real identity.

Lucas had always had an image of the woman he'd marry, a woman who'd share his dreams for building the kind of life he'd watched his father and mother build here on Destiny Canyon Ranch. Lexie had no idea what that life was like. She had come from another world, a world as far from Destiny Canyon Ranch as his lasso was from that illusive star he wished he could capture and hang around her creamy neck.

Instead of acting on the impulse to kiss her, he gazed down at the legal pad in his lap. "Can you think of anything else I should ask Lady Margaret?"

Lexie thought a minute. "I think your phone conversation with her husband covered all the bases."

"Her husband, the ambassador," Lucas said with a wry smile. Lady Margaret never said one without the other. The phrase was almost one word: my-husband-the-ambassador. "He wasn't nearly as upset about his cousin's death as she was."

"Edward Roche is a reasonable man," Lexie said. "He's not melodramatic. Didn't he tell you that he'd never even met Seth Rockwell?"

Lucas flipped back a few pages in the legal pad to review his talk with the ambassador. "He said they'd never done more than exchange Christmas greetings. Rockwell wasn't even a citizen of your country. He was born in the United States. The only reason they stayed in touch was some kind of St. Novian trust fund which netted Rockwell less than two hundred American dollars per annum."

"That's not unusual," she said. "Business managers handle most of the commerce in St. Novia, and they pay stipends to the landowners.''

''Is there any reason to be suspicious of the ambassador?''

''Not that I know of.''

Briefly, Lexie recapped, ''I contacted him, looking for a place to stay where I could have total privacy. He suggested Colorado. Actually, his first idea was Aspen, which I vetoed immediately. Then, the ambassador said he would do some checking around and get back to me. Later, he told me he'd talked to his cousin and that he'd recommended Destiny Canyon Ranch. I had no idea that cousin was Seth Rockwell.''

Lucas tapped his pencil against the legal pad. ''Seth knew you were coming here. So did the ambassador. Who else?''

''I requested my plans be kept secret. But there are always information leaks at any embassy and the St. Novian embassy is no exception.''

Again, Lucas was distracted by her royal heritage. *The St. Novian embassy?* It sounded like a fancy place with ballrooms and servants in uniforms and lots of people wearing white gloves. Even though Lexie had explained that it was only a suite of offices with fewer than ten full-time employees, Lucas figured he'd feel out of place in any kind of embassy.

He dragged his brain back to the investigation. ''I think we have to assume Seth Rockwell was somehow involved in the kidnapping plot.''

''Why?''

''Because I don't believe in coincidence. The kidnapper used Rockwell's BLM truck, and Rockwell was one of the few people who knew you were coming here. Not only that, it seems he went out of his way to get you here.''

''But the killer could have stolen the truck and killed Seth not knowing his connection to St. Novia,'' she said.

''The odds against that kind of random circumstance are astronomical.''

The way Lucas figured it, Seth and the killer had been cohorts. ''Do you remember your theory about more than one kidnapper?''

''Sure,'' she said as she reclined against a sofa pillow. Her eyelids seemed heavy.

''Maybe you were right. And maybe that second man was Seth Rockwell,'' Lucas said. ''But someone got to him first. He wasn't there on the trail to make the grab because he'd already been killed.''

''I know this may sound self-serving,'' she said with a sigh, ''but I hope your theory is correct. If Mr. Rockwell were involved in a plot, I wouldn't feel so guilty about his death.''

In Lucas's opinion, Lexie had proven herself anything but selfish. Few people were as concerned about the welfare of others.

She reached for her coffee mug on the table, then seemed to think better of it. Her voice sounded sleepy when she said, ''Do you think Seth Rockwell was behind this whole thing?''

''Nope,'' Lucas said. ''I'm going to stick with our mercenary, Ian Solé. It's my guess that Solé contacted Rockwell. Solé, if he's involved, was the mastermind.''

Unfortunately, that line of thinking circled back around to the FBI. They had records on Solé and knew he was considered a dangerous man in any country. They had communication and voice prints. They did not, however, have a recognizable photograph.

In a fairly civil conversation with Agent Paul Browning, Lucas learned that Solé was a master of disguise and had never been accurately captured on film. He also had a reputation for marksmanship and familiarity with high-tech weaponry.

But we don't know what he looks like, Browning had said. That fact alone convinced Lucas that he should stay on the case instead of turning over all his evidence to the FBI. In spite of their fancy electronics and high-powered networking, they were as much in the dark as Lucas when it came to identifying Ian Solé.

The killer might have left Destiny and Bluff County after the murder and failed abduction, but Lucas didn't think so. His gut told him that danger still stalked Lexie, and by extension his own family. The ransacking of Lexie's rental cabin showed a violent, ruthless personality, someone prone to senseless destruction, someone who wouldn't accept failure or defeat. There had been nothing in Lexie's cabin or in her possession that the intruder could have wanted. The act of vandalism had been meant to simply terrorize her.

Besides, if the FBI really believed Solé had fled, Lucas doubted they would have shown so much interest in this case.

When he looked up from his notes, ready to share that thought with Lexie, he saw that her eyelids had closed. Her soft lashes formed golden crescents on her smooth cheeks. Her pink lips parted slightly, and her breathing was steady and even.

Lucas took the opportunity to study the sleeping princess, to memorize her perfect features, to study the graceful curve of her throat and delicate proportions of her slender body. He'd never seen a more beautiful woman. Truly, she was a perfection—the result of guarded bloodlines.

Yet, she was flesh and bone, he knew, capable of every human emotion from fear to fierce determination. And passion. A passion he'd only glimpsed but couldn't forget.

Lucas rose from the wing chair and moved toward her. As he approached, she didn't stir. He smiled down at her. She was already in deep sleep.

Gently, he slipped one arm under her shoulders and another under her knees. When he lifted her from the sofa, she shifted, snuggling against him. Her sweet, feminine warmth felt good in his arms as he carried her up the stairs and down the hall to the guest bedroom.

The covers on the bed had already been turned down, and Lucas placed her on the freshly laundered sheets. Still not waking, she stretched out on the bed. He might have undressed her, but Lucas didn't trust himself to withstand the temptation.

Leaning over her, he placed a kiss on her smooth forehead. "Good night, Princess Honey," he whispered. "Sweet dreams."

AT DAWN the next morning, Lexie awoke on the guest room bed, fully dressed. She wasn't quite sure how she'd gotten there, but a pleasant sense of contentment flowed through her veins. Despite a few stubborn aches from the minor injuries she sustained in her battle with the kidnapper, her muscles were relaxed. She couldn't remember the last time she'd felt so well-rested and at peace.

Despite all the turmoil, staying here at Destiny Canyon Ranch had been the right decision. It was time to stop running. Princess Alexandra had taken charge of her own life, and she was anxious for the new day to begin.

She left the bed and went to the window. Outside, a glorious sunrise colored the vast Colorado skies a pinkish hue. The long meadows and rocky mesas stretched to the edge of blue-tinted mountain peaks. Confronting this incredible natural beauty, it was difficult to remember that somewhere out there was a murderer, a kidnapper. Perhaps an internationally known mercenary waiting to pounce.

Was it the oddly named Ian Solé? A faceless specter of evil incarnate? She shuddered at the thought—infinitely thankful she'd escaped the attempted abduction. *There were some things worse than death.*

She showered and dressed quickly. Mo had the foresight to retrieve enough of her belongings from the ransacked cabin to allow Lexie a fresh change of clothing and a minimum of makeup. She didn't need much. A pair of softly faded blue jeans, a cotton T-shirt and soft leather boots suited her just fine. The royal pageantry of a lifetime caused Lexie to prefer the casual minimum in her personal grooming. With a dash of mascara and a whisper of lipstick, she was ready for the day.

Downstairs at the kitchen table, Lucas was already sipping his first cup of coffee.

"Did you spend the night here?" she asked.

"There wasn't a free bed. My sister seems to think she's running a boarding house instead of a ranch house."

Lexie went to the coffeepot. "Did you give Rocky a pat on the head for me?"

"Ever since he met you, that silly mongrel has been acting weird. If I didn't know better, I'd say he's lovesick."

"The feeling is mutual. I can't wait to see that handsome canine again."

"Don't pour any coffee," Lucas said as he pushed away from the table. "We're going to have breakfast at The Timbers."

"Why? Mo says the food is horrible."

"It's not as good as Mo's cooking," he said, "but that's a sacrifice we have to make for the sake of our investigation. I want to talk to the owners of The Timbers about the waitress who was dating Seth Rockwell and I figured you'd want to be there."

"An interrogation," she said delightedly. "This time, I get to be the one asking the questions!"

"Back off, honey," he feigned gruffness. "It's not like we're going to grill Inez and George Estes."

"But I think we should." She liked the idea of playing a role, being a detective. "Do you guys really do that good cop-bad cop thing, like in the movies? Is that how you break down a suspect?''

''They aren't suspects,'' Lucas said.

''Nevertheless, if it comes to that, I'll be the good cop, okay?'' She slipped into a light jacket to ward off the morning chill and followed him outside to the Ford Explorer. The crisp clean mountain air was almost invigorating enough to eliminate the need for a morning dose of caffeine.

She sensed that Lucas felt the same way. They'd made good progress on their investigation last night. Their goals were clear: Find Solé and discover what connection, if any, Seth Rockwell had to the murder of Hugh Miller and the thwarted abduction attempt.

As they drove into town, Lexie was surprised to see how many people were out and about so early. The wide two-lane road through the center of town had several cars parked on either side, most of them gathered outside The Timbers which was situated on a corner beside the one stoplight.

''Everyone is up so early,'' she said.

''Farmers and ranchers,'' Lucas explained, ''their day starts at dawn.''

''I've always loved morning,'' she said. ''It's the most peaceful time of day.'' The farmers and ranchers of Destiny, Colorado would have been surprised to know Princess Alexandra envied them their lifestyle. ''It must be wonderful to wake up every morning feeling good about who and where you are,'' she said wistfully.

Lucas pulled up to the curb in front of the restaurant. ''Some people might find that certainty boring.''

''Not me.'' She emerged from the car and stepped up on the curb where she noted on the meter that parking was free until eight o'clock. ''I can't think of anything more appealing.''

''Lexie,'' he said, ''I don't have to pay for parking. I'm the sheriff.''

"Well, that doesn't seem fair."

He chuckled. "It's not like I'm royalty or anything."

He'd never know how relieved she was to hear him making jokes about her title. All she'd ever wanted in life was to be treated like everyone else and Lucas seemed to have no problem doing just that.

The moment they stepped inside the café, the hum of conversation went silent. The men at the counter swiveled around on their stools. A group of four older men, dressed in jeans and cowboy boots and a woman seated at a small table by the window stared openly at her. A couple dressed for office work set down their coffee cups simultaneously with a loud clink.

A plump blond woman in a gingham waitress uniform with a white apron bustled toward them. She bent her knee in a curtsy. "Your Highness," she said, "to what do we owe this honor?"

"We were hoping for sausage and eggs," Lucas said dryly.

"And coffee," Lexie said reaching out to help the woman up out of her awkward curtsy.

"Did I do it right?" she asked. "I mean, is that the proper way to greet a princess?"

"That was a perfectly lovely welcome," Lexie said, not wanting to embarrass the woman. Lowering her voice, she confided, "But from now on, it won't be necessary to curtsy. And as for the Highness, bit, I'd much prefer you just call me Lexie."

The woman smiled broadly. "I'm Inez Estes," she said.

Lexie accepted the offered hand and gave it a firm shake. "I'm pleased to meet you, Inez. Is it all right if we take that booth?"

"You betcha."

After they were seated and Lexie had picked up the one-page menu, the hum of conversation slowly resumed. Many of the café patrons stole surreptitious glances, but no one had the nerve to approach the booth.

Lucas leaned toward her. In a low voice, he asked, "Is it always like this?"

"Only when I'm recognized." She'd never understood the fascination with royalty, but unfortunately, she'd never lived any other way. "Now you understand why I prefer to remain anonymous."

After they'd placed matching orders for sausage and eggs and were served, Inez hovered by their table. "Is everything all right? Can I get you anything else?"

"Just a minute of your time, if you can spare it," Lucas said. "Pull up a chair, Inez. I want to ask you a couple of questions."

Eagerly, Inez grabbed a vacant chair from one of the tables and sat at the end of their booth. "Shoot."

"I want to talk about Seth Rockwell."

Her full lips pursed. "I was sorry to hear what happened to him, but I have to admit I didn't have much use for the man when he was alive."

"Why's that, Inez?" Lucas asked.

"He was rude." She leaned forward. "And a lousy tipper, too."

"I seem to remember he was dating one of your waitresses."

"That's right," she said. "Her name was Dottie Butterworth. She dated Seth until about a month ago, then she up and quit her job and moved back to Arizona. If you ask me, Seth was one of the reasons she wanted to get out of town."

"Why?" Lexie questioned.

"Oh, a woman knows when a man has no intention of ever settling down and getting hitched. And everyone knew Seth was too cheap to ever share anything he had with a wife. That man squeezed every single penny. And he was always looking for an angle, a way to make a buck the easy way. I remember when he and Dottie bought a winning lottery ticket. It wasn't a big winner, just fifty bucks. Now, we all knew how hard Dottie worked for every dollar, but what does Seth do but try to cheat her out of her half by claiming he was the one who'd picked the numbers. Never mind that it was Dottie who'd paid for the ticket! And then there was the time he came in here too late for the special and tried to con me into giving him the cheaper price anyway because his wristwatch was wrong. Mind you, we're only talking an extra buck fifty, which may not seem like much to some, but George and I have to look out for ourselves, you know. I mean, it's not like we make a killing in this business…'' Her round face instantly flushed red. "Oh my! I guess that was the wrong thing to say.''

"That's all right,'' Lexie assured her.

"Tell me what else you remember about Seth,'' Lucas urged.

While Inez listed more examples of Seth's cheating ways, Lexie drew the obvious conclusion. If Seth Rockwell saw a way to profit from her presence in Destiny, he'd have jumped at the chance. But would he have dared to become involved in a murder plot and a kidnapping?

"When was the last time you saw Seth?'' Lucas asked.

"I believe it was last week.'' She frowned, concentrating hard. "Or maybe it wasn't that long. Let me see…I guess it was Wednesday.''

The day before Hugh Miller had been murdered, Lexie thought.

"Are you sure?'' Lucas asked.

"Positive. Our special on Wednesdays is fried chicken, and Seth fussed about wanting an extra helping of white meat. The guy with him got so tired of hearing him complain that he gave him part of his own dinner just to shut Seth up.''

"Seth was with someone?'' Lucas asked.

"Yes. But I didn't know the man." Inez shook her head. "Kind of an odd looking guy with long hair and a beard. And he had a baseball cap pulled down low on his forehead. I'd never seen him before."

The beard and cap sounded like a possible disguise. Half-excited and half-afraid, Lexie couldn't help wondering if the infamous Ian Solé had been here in the company of Seth Rockwell.

"Can you remember anything else about the man?"

"Well, I couldn't really see much of his face. But he had real strange eyes. Nothing else unusual, though."

"What about his eyes?" Lexie asked.

"Gee, now that you ask, I can't remember. All I recall is that they seemed...well, strange. Maybe it was all that hair that made him seem different. Sorry, Lucas," Inez said. "I guess I wasn't paying all that much attention."

"Did he speak with an accent?" Lexie wanted to know.

"No," she said. "I would've remembered that."

"How was he dressed?" Lucas asked.

"Let's see..." Inez thought a minute. "I just remember him as dark. I think he might have been wearing black. All black."

Inez's description of the man's clothing struck Lexie as a certain indictment. Though she hadn't been able to clearly take note of the clothing worn by her attacker, it *seemed* like he was an image in black. A black ski mask covering his face. "Black jeans," she said. "And a black turtleneck?"

"I think so," Inez said.

"Would you recognize him again?" Lucas questioned. "If you saw this man, could you pick him out of a line-up?"

"It's possible. We don't get all that many strangers in here and he did look different, with the beard, and all. Who was he, Lucas? Somebody dangerous?"

"If it's who I think it is, he's someone you don't want to

mess with, Inez,'' Lucas warned. "If he comes in again, call my office immediately and tell them to contact me wherever I am."

Inez's face went pale. "Will do, Sheriff," she said soberly.

They finished their coffee and departed after Lexie insisted that Lucas pay the tab and leave an outrageously generous tip.

Lexie tagged along with Lucas through several other interviews, including one with the BLM office manager, the coroner, Deputy Eli Ferguson and Sylvia. As far as Lexie was concerned, the most important information of the day had been gathered during breakfast at The Timbers Café. On Wednesday night, Seth Rockwell had shared a chicken dinner with a stranger. A stranger in black, who in Lexie's mind loomed as a dangerous international mercenary.

It was evening, nearly seven by the time they returned to the ranch house, and as Lucas pulled up in front, Lexie realized she didn't want her time with him to end.

When he parked in front of the house, she asked, "Should we tell Agent Browning about Inez seeing Solé?"

"We don't know who she saw, Lexie," Lucas said. "At this point, it's only conjecture."

"But who else could it have been? Are you suggesting there might be someone else besides Solé and Rockwell involved?"

"I'm not suggesting anything, Lexie. At this point, anything's possible. There could have been a complicated network of operatives or it could have been one man working alone. It's just too soon to tell."

"But regardless of the number involved, only one was ruthless enough to kill both Seth Rockwell and Hugh Miller," Lexie pointed out.

The sun had dropped behind the mountain peaks in the distance when Lexie reached for the car door and opened it.

She glanced over at Lucas's profile to see it bathed in shadows. "Are you coming in?"

"I don't think I'm up to another scene with Lady Margaret." Without looking at her, he took her hand. "You were a great help today. Thanks."

"Really?" Her heart beat a little faster.

He turned toward her. "Not that it matters, but yes, you were."

"What do you mean it doesn't matter?"

"It doesn't matter because I like being with you, whether it helps the investigation, or not. That isn't a very professional thing to say, is it?"

"No," she admitted, "but it's nice to hear."

"The fact that you're turning into a great little investigator is only icing on the cake as far as I'm concerned."

Take me home with you, Lucas, she longed to say. *I don't want this day to end.*

The day was behind them, but there was still the night. And she wanted more than anything to spend that night in his arms.

"Good night," he said with an air of finality. "Sweet dreams, Princess Honey."

THREE HOURS LATER, Lexie had once again made an important life decision and acted upon it. She decided she had to find a way to meet with Lucas privately, had to talk to him and warn him before he fell under the full force of her father's pressure.

Although she already knew the proud lawman well enough to guess it wouldn't make a difference, she still felt obligated to warn him that his future was on the line. No one knew better than Lexie how miserable King Frederick Dubois could make things for anyone who defied him.

True, Lucas was a man of experience, a man of the world, but when it came to bucking the kind of power Lexie knew her father could wield, Lucas needed to be prepared. She felt responsible for the trouble she'd caused everyone at the Garrett ranch, but especially the trouble she felt Lucas was riding toward with a vengeance.

After donning a dark sweater and jeans, she slipped silently from the house. After years of evading bodyguards whose sole purpose was to observe her every move, it was child's play sneaking past the unsuspecting deputy who stood guard on the front porch of the ranch house.

Gliding through the shadows, she made her way to the barn and quickly saddled the mare she'd been riding the day of the attack. She was leading the animal through the darkened barn when she felt the presence of someone behind her. With her heart racing, she spun around to face the menace stalking her.

Chapter Ten

From the shadows in the barn, Lucas watched her. Lexie's gaze darted left, then right, frantically searching. In a trembling voice, she demanded, "Who's there?"

At least, he thought, she had the good sense to be nervous. Before he could step forward and identify himself, she whipped around and ran toward the rear of the barn.

"It's okay." He took off after her. "Relax, Lexie. It's just me."

When he came around the edge of the stall, she was waiting for him with a pitchfork braced in both hands. Her face, in the moonlight, was a study in determination. Her soft lips drew back from tightly gritted teeth. Her eyes squinted, seeking a target for the pointed tines.

If he'd ever had doubts about her courage or her innate survival instincts, the sight of her wielding that pitchfork banished them. The woman was prepared to defend herself, even if it meant impaling her attacker.

"Lexie, honey," he said calmly. "It's all right."

"Damn you, Lucas! What kind of joke was that?"

"Hold on." He wasn't about to let this situation reverse itself. "You're the one who's out of line, here."

"How can you say that?" She stormed away from him, circling the wooden floor of the barn, the pitchfork still in her hand. "I might have killed you."

"I appreciate knowing exactly how lethal you are, but I have just one question—what the hell are you doing out here?"

She came to a halt in front of him and jabbed a finger at his chest. "I was coming to see you, Sheriff Garrett! I wanted to tell you—"

"What?" he encouraged as he cautiously removed the pitchfork from her hand.

With a groan, she sat down hard on a wooden bench. "To be careful."

"Oh, that's a good. You're the one drugged and almost abducted, there's a killer still on the loose and you were on your way to warn *me* to be careful. Sorry, honey, but you're going to have to do better than that."

"Just forget it!" she snapped.

But there was no way Lucas could easily dismiss the fact that Lexie had been willing to go to such lengths to see him. And there was no way he could deny that the attraction that had been pulling them together from their first meeting was growing stronger by the hour.

At the moment, however, that undeniable force had to be put on hold. A more pressing concern had to be addressed.

"I know I frightened you," he said as he sat down beside her on the narrow bench. "But I can't really say I'm sorry. As you may have noticed, there's a deputy posted twenty-four hours at the front door of my family's ranch house. You might also have noticed that the ranch hands are taking turns watching the back entrance and the side doors. My nephew, Cal, hasn't slept in days. Even his foreman has taken up residence in the ranch house. For all I know, Pop is sleeping with a gun under his pillow! Do you understand why my family's house has been turned into an armed garrison?"

"Of course I know," she grumbled. "And I hate it!"

"I can't help how you feel. The fact is, this is all about you, Lexie. All for your protection."

"But I don't need—"

"The hell you don't!" Although she glared at him, he sensed his outburst had hurt her feelings and, although he'd wanted to make an impression, he hadn't meant to wound.

"Lexie, honey," he began again in a gentler tone, "you're a target for a killer. It's my responsibility to see that nothing happens to you."

She sighed as though the weight of the world had been dropped on her pretty shoulders. "I know all of that. And I'm sorry to have caused everyone so much trouble. Don't you see, that's why I had to talk to you. I don't think you know just how much more turmoil is headed your way."

"You could have called," he reminded her.

She nodded. "I know. But...I was feeling so—so claustrophobic with all those eyes watching me."

"I understand."

"Do you?" she challenged him. "I don't see how."

"You're right. I don't know what it feels like to have my wings clipped or to feel hemmed in and overprotected. But I don't think *you* understand what we're dealing with here. This isn't a game, Lexie."

Lucas had spent the evening gathering information by phone and on the computer. Through his official contacts, he'd located a federal marshal based in Los Angeles who had been involved in investigating a professional hit made by Ian Solé.

Over the telephone, the plain-talking marshal described the brutal methods used by Solé. The man defined the term mercenary. With no loyalty to any country or cause, motivated only by his own gain, Solé recruited cohorts who would sell out their own mother for a price, the lowest form of humanity.

Upon hearing the details of the murders in Bluff County

and the abduction attempt, the marshal had agreed that it sounded like Solé's M.O., right down to the murder of Seth Rockwell. Although Solé preferred to work alone, he had been known to recruit assistants. But he had never been known to leave a witness. The man was a ruthless killer who would stop at nothing to achieve his goals.

When Solé started something, he finished it. It was part of his profile, clearly a point of twisted honor with him. If Ian Solé was after Lexie, everything in his past indicated he wouldn't quit until he had her in his grasp.

After the conversation with the California marshal, Lucas hadn't been able to sleep. He hadn't been able to stop thinking about Lexie and how important she had become to him. The thought of her in the hands of a man like Solé made his blood run cold. Though he'd arranged for round-the-clock protection, he still couldn't rest until he was there to protect her himself.

"All right. I know it was a foolhardy thing to do," Lexie finally admitted, "but I really am quite adept at moving around undetected."

"Obviously," Lucas said with a humorless smile.

"And believe it or not, I usually have sense enough to watch my back. I sensed your presence, didn't I?"

He allowed her that much. "Before I call my deputy to task for falling down on the job, do you mind telling me how you got past him?"

A look of deep concern creased her pretty brow. "You're not going to fire him, are you, Lucas? It wasn't his fault. You don't understand. I'm really good at this! Please, Lucas. Don't punish your deputy for what I've done."

Despite the situation, he had to smile. "Lexie, honey, will you stop worrying about everyone else long enough to help me save your own sweet little tail? Now, tell me. How did you get out of the house unseen?"

Briefly, Lexie explained how she'd made her escape.

"Deputy Ferguson presented the biggest challenge, so I waited until the shift change. I slipped out a window onto the porch while the other deputy's back was turned." When she told him how she'd dropped down into the bushes from the porch roof, he shook his head. "I guess I should be glad you never decided to take up a life of crime. You're a born cat burglar."

She didn't find any humor in his back-handed compliment. "Unfortunately, I've had a lot of experience with this sort of thing. All my life, I've had to find creative ways to steal some privacy."

"I've got to ask why, Lexie? There are a lot of people who would give anything to be in your position."

"And I'd give anything to have a normal life. Do you know what it means to a fifteen-year-old to be able to meet with friends for a pizza? To go to a movie without being shadowed by an armed guard? All I've ever wanted was my freedom, the kind of simple freedom normal people take for granted."

"But, Lexie, this situation is different. It isn't about privacy or freedom, it's about saving your life."

"I know." Her voice brimmed with emotion.

"No one here is trying to box you in. We're just worried about your safety. All of us. Did you stop to think what would happen if Mo had awakened and found you gone?"

"Actually, I did. I put a note under her door letting her know I'd be at your place tonight."

That stopped him cold. Lexie Dale, aka Princess Alexandra Dubois, was a walking contradiction. Sneaking out was completely irresponsible, but she had been considerate enough to leave a note so his sister wouldn't worry. She was half-princess and half-street urchin.

And all woman. A woman who had boldly planned to spend the night with him.

"Sounds as if you were pretty sure I'd let you stay."

She did smile finally. "I guess I was. But then, we do have quite a lot to discuss…don't we?" She ran a hand through her hair. "I mean, about the investigation and my father and Solé…"

"All of which could have waited until morning."

"Maybe," she allowed.

"But maybe you just wanted to see me?"

"Maybe," she said again, a spirited light shining in wide, violet eyes.

"Well, now that's quite a coincidence," he said with an exaggerated drawl as he stood and reached his hand out to her, "because I wanted to see you, too."

With her gaze fastened on his, she took his hand and moved willingly when he pulled her into his arms. Pressed tightly against him, her warmth mingling with his, she felt like the fulfillment of all his wants and expectations.

He kissed her, long and hard, feeling nearly overwhelmed by the need to release the passion that had been building inside him all day, all night—hell, he had to admit it—from the moment he'd laid eyes on her. If he didn't know better, didn't know who and what she was, he'd have sworn this was the woman he'd been waiting for all his life.

He ended the kiss and stood looking down at her. It was impossible not to stare; she was just so beautiful. Her features could not have been more perfect.

His voice was husky when he said, "Is this what you thought might happen when you got to my house?"

"Pretty much," she said, but her eyes weren't laughing. Instead, they were shining with desire. Slightly breathless, she gazed into his face. "Take me home, Lucas."

He'd never heard more beautiful words.

Though he wanted to fly back to his house, Lucas was cautious. He helped her onto the saddle in front of him and they took the long way around the ranch yard to avoid being seen. Until Mo discovered Lexie's note in the morning, this would be the perfect diversion. With his deputies standing guard at the ranch house, no one would suspect Lexie was with him.

As they rode slowly, her body pressed intimately against him. He breathed in the fresh clean scent of her hair and tried to remember if anything had ever smelled a sweet or looked as good as Lexie in the mountain moonlight.

Silently, she pointed at the sight of a doe and fawn at the edge of the forest. The starlit darkness was alive with the chirp of cicadas and the soft murmuring of nocturnal life in the forest. The cougars came out at night. Raccoons marauded. But there were no signs of other men, no sign of ambush or some unnamed foe lying in wait to attack.

Lucas sensed they were safe. For tonight, it seemed, the investigation could wait.

INSIDE LUCAS'S HOUSE, Lexie and Rocky greeted each other like long lost friends. She knelt on the hardwood floor in front of him. "Did you miss me, boy?"

As before, she waited for the tawny German shepherd mix to make the first move. He inched closer and closer, wrinkled his snout and lapped at her cheek.

She patted him gently at first, but it wasn't long before he'd stretched out on his back with his three paws in the air, allowing her to scratch the soft fur on his tummy. Lexie stretched out beside him on the floor. "I love this dog!"

"Apparently," Lucas said. He'd done a quick check of the house, as if he were expecting an intruder, and headed for the back door again.

"Is something wrong?" she asked. "What's going on?"

"If I seem overly cautious it's because I spent some time this evening checking out Solé. He's bad news, Lexie. About as bad as they come and we can't afford to take any chances." He headed toward the door. "I need to check on

Miss Molly once more tonight. Do you want to come with me?''

The night air was turning cooler. "It's cozy in here. I think I'll wait.'' When he hesitated at the door, she said, "I'll be fine. Rocky's here to protect me.''

Lucas laughed. "Right now, he looks fairly well disarmed, like he couldn't do battle with a butterfly.''

Rocky gave a growl that turned into a moan of pleasure.

"Pathetic,'' Lucas said as he left to do his chores.

Lexie stood up and looked around, once more taking in the comforting sights and smells of Lucas's home. Though Lucas was right about the foolishness of sneaking away from her protectors, she couldn't help feeling delighted to be here, in his domain, with his masculine presence all around her. Although she wasn't sure exactly how this night would end, she had the deep sense that for once in her life, she was exactly where she belonged.

If tonight went the way she expected it might, Lexie was about to take a giant step forward in her emotional development. Since she was fifteen, she'd dreamed about this moment. About the moment she'd give herself for the first time to that one special man.

Making love for the first time represented a milestone in the lives of all women, but Lexie had been taught that it was especially momentous for a princess. Even more than most women, Lexie had more to consider than just momentary gratification. Not only were the emotional ties more complex, but there was always the issue of pregnancy. Any child Lexie bore would immediately become an heir to the throne of St. Novia. Although her offspring would be nowhere near the front of the line of succession, they would still be royalty.

The weight of that responsibility, coupled with the complications inherent in trying to explain her identity and the special considerations that went along with dating her, had caused Lexie to avoid potentially intimate situations. Until Lucas, there had only been one other man with whom Lexie had even considered sexual intimacy.

Jeffery Vance was the first man to break Lexie's heart, and the last. Three years ago, she'd discovered he'd taken money from a tabloid to plant cameras in her apartment and sell the pictures along with the story of his involvement with the young woman the press had dubbed the reluctant princess. Luckily, Lexie had stumbled over one of the hidden cameras before Jeffery's plan for betrayal could be enacted. Her father had stepped in and paid for Lexie's unscrupulous fiancé's silence.

The incident devastated Lexie. It had taken time for her to recover the confidence in her judgment that Jeffery's betrayal had shaken. But with time, Lexie had also gained maturity and perspective, and now she understood that what she'd felt for Jeffrey had been nothing more than infatuation—an infatuation he had calculatingly encouraged.

Countless times since her break-up with Jeffery, Lexie had thanked her lucky stars that she'd been spared the added humiliation of having shared a sexual liaison with a man who had courted her with such devious intent.

Since that unhappy incident, Lexie had learned to control her passions. Until now. Until Lucas.

"Well, what do you think, Rocky? Is this the right time? Is Lucas the right man?"

As if in answer, the dog rolled over and stood. When Lexie moved to the sofa in the living room, the dog followed her and hopped up onto the cushion beside her.

When Lucas returned to the house and saw them sitting so cozily, he looked the dog in the eye. "Sorry, old man, but you're cramping my style."

Rocky made a low rumble in the back of his throat as he reluctantly climbed down off the couch.

"I know you like her," Lucas said, "but tonight, she's all mine."

Lexie warmed to the sound of that claim.

When he sat down and draped his arm around her shoulders, she leaned against him. It seemed the most natural thing in the world, for the two of them to be together this way.

When he tilted her chin and brushed her lips with a light kiss, a rush of longing surged through her. She shivered with anticipation as his hand trailed along the length of her arm.

All those years of abstinence culminated in this moment, and she realized that she hadn't been avoiding passion because of St. Novia or her royal duties. She'd been waiting for a man like Lucas.

He kissed her again and she felt lost to his touch. His arms pulled her closer and she felt her self-control slipping away. When his hand moved over her breast, she realized that very soon, there would be no turning back.

"Lucas," she whispered huskily, "I—I need to explain something before we…I mean —" How to tell him she was a virgin? Would he be put off by her lack of experience? "It's just that—"

"What is it, honey?" he asked gently.

She shook her head. "Well, you see, a woman in my…situation, with my background, my position and title—"

He lifted her chin and grinned slyly. "What are you trying to tell me, honey? That we need some sort of royal dispensation?" His laugh was a low, sexy chuckle. "Or are you asking to see my pedigree papers?"

She averted her gaze so as not to have to see his face when she told him. "I'm a virgin, Lucas."

He didn't say anything for a moment, or move a muscle. Lexie held her breath, waiting.

"I'm glad you told me," he said finally, and then kissed

her with such exquisite tenderness she thought her heart might burst. ''I want everything to be right for you, Lexie. And not because of your position or your title.''

''No?''

''No,'' he said, firmly. ''Because you're a special woman, honey. Because you deserve nothing but the best.''

''I want you, Lucas,'' she said, leaning forward to kiss him in a way that let him know that as far as she was concerned there could never be anything better than the two of them, here and now.

When he pulled slowly away from her, her eyelids opened slowly, and she drank in his features. From his rugged brow to his firm jaw, he was utterly masculine. His blue eyes were the only contrast, hinting at sensitivity and gentleness.

I need you, Lucas Garrett, she longed to tell him, but instead she replied with her movements, slowly and deliberately reaching for him. Tentatively, she unfastened the top two buttons on his shirt. Her hand glided inside and she caressed his warm flesh. The light sprinkle of chest hair felt springy and crisp.

His chest was magnificently broad and muscular. She leaned forward and kissed him.

''It's my turn,'' he murmured as he rained kisses along her cheek and down her neck.

With practiced skill, he opened her blouse, revealing the fine lace of her bra. Her breasts felt heavy. Her hard nipples pressed against the white lace. When he touched her, a searing fire raced across the surface of her skin. When he pushed away the lace, she moaned with pleasure.

Rocky growled.

Slowly, Lucas turned toward the dog who sat directly in front of the sofa, staring at them with unblinking eyes. ''Relax, old man.''

''He thinks he needs to protect me,'' she said.

''And he'd be right.'' He tasted her lips and then stood

slowly. "I want you, Lexie. But only when the time is right. For your sake, for both our sakes, you need to be sure."

She stood slowly and linked her hand with his, and led him down the hall to the bedroom. If she'd wanted to object, she had every opportunity. He certainly wasn't rushing her, wasn't forcing her.

She had had enough time to question her motives and review all the ramifications of her behavior. The answer from her yearning body to her brain to her heart was a resounding yes. She wanted this man with every ounce of her body and soul. She wanted him to make love to her. Lucas Garrett was fated to be her lover. He was her destiny.

Chapter Eleven

Hours later, they lay together, entwined in the sheets. She had trusted him with her body and he had welcomed her gift with infinite gentleness and loving respect.

She had no regrets. She was glad that Lucas had been her first lover. Somehow, she felt she'd been waiting all her life for him. Never before had she felt so vulnerable and yet so completely protected.

He lazily stroked her hair and murmured, "You're a hard woman to understand, princess."

"Please call me honey."

"Okay, honey." He kissed her forehead. "Sometimes, you've got this imperial majesty thing going on. Other times, you're the scrappy little girl next door. Kind of a tomboy."

"I could say the same about you." She snuggled against him. His chest hair tickled her nose. "You're a tough, no-nonsense lawman who talks in two-word sentences. The next minute, you're a cowboy poet, telling beautiful stories about roping the stars and stringing them around my neck."

"I'm a Garrett," he said. "Just like my dad. We're not hard to understand. We love our land. We take our responsibilities seriously. And when we give our heart or our word, it's forever."

A shiver went through her. Would he give her his heart? Had he fallen in love with her? Could he?

"Tell me about your mother. From what you've said, I'm guessing she and your dad had a very special relationship."

"My mother's name was Rose. Not only was she a great mom, but she was the perfect partner for my dad. They built Destiny Canyon Ranch to what it is today out of dreams, a cowhand's meager wages and years of hard work and dedication."

"Were they childhood sweethearts?"

He shook his head. "She came out here from the East to marry him after they'd exchanged letters for a year. But to meet her, you'd never know that she hadn't been born and raised in the West. She loved the animals, the land and the lifestyle."

"Rose Garrett," Lexie mused. "I bet I would have liked her."

"You would have. Like you, she was a fine lady, soft-spoken and gentle. Hardly ever raised her voice. But she could handle the old man with a single look." He smiled. "He would have given his life for her, and she would have done the same for him."

Lexie heard a wistful longing in his voice, but Lucas wasn't sad when he spoke of his family. There was a sweetness and a pride that was as much a part of him as an arm or a leg.

"I like your dad," she said. "He's—how do you cowboys say it—a straight shooter. I like that. Honest, straightforward. No pretenses."

"He likes you, too. My whole family does."

"I'm glad." Being involved with Lucas meant taking on his whole family, and the prospect pleased her immensely. Though Lexie had no shortage of blood relatives, they had never been a family, not in the true sense of the word. Not the kind of family she saw in the Garretts.

"So, Will and Rose didn't inherit their land?"

"No. They built the ranch from the ground up," he said.

"And it wasn't easy. There was always lots of worry about financing and refinancing. The bank was always breathing down their necks. In the beginning, they worked the whole place themselves because they couldn't afford to pay for help. In all that time, I never heard them say a cruel word to each other. They liked being together. Just sitting on the porch or taking a walk at sunset. There was a kind of glow around them. Will and Rose had a perfect, ideal love."

"And yet, you've never married," she said. "Didn't you ever want a family of your own?"

"Of course! But it's something that doesn't just happen. A life like that has to be built, tended, nurtured."

Lexie felt moved by the reverence in his voice.

"You know, Lexie, it seems like I've been building all my life. Building my skills in the military, building experience as a cop and then a few years ago, building support to be elected county sheriff. I built my house and, now, I'm building a reputation as a breeder of one of the finest bloodlines of quarter horses in the West."

"And after you've built all of that, then what, Lucas?"

He shifted and put his arms behind his head and stared up at the ceiling with a hopeful expression on his face that Lexie found endearing and irresistible. "Well, I guess I'll settle down and start building a family, enjoying the fruits of my labor." Softly he added, "With a woman I love."

Could he ever love her? Was it possible that he might think of her as the kind of woman who could help him build that family, that future?

Cuddled against his muscular body, she closed her eyes and allowed herself to dream of just such a future. This beautiful home he'd built with his own hands would be her palace. They would work together by day, training and tending the animals that would be the pride of their own Destiny ranch. In the evening, the well-deserved peace of a satisfying day would strengthen the bonds of their love.

Could a princess become a ranch wife? The prospect of cooking and cleaning and nurturing children seemed at first daunting. But the idea warmed her, touched her deeply and filled her with unexpected yearning and joy.

"But enough about my future," he said, propping up on one elbow and staring into her eyes. "Tell me what you see in yours."

"I'm a princess," she said. To Lexie, that inescapable fact sealed her identity; her past, present and future were all the same.

"That's just a title, honey. If I wanted to know about the title, I could buy a copy of *The Exposé* and read all about it. I want to know *you*, want to see the real you, the woman behind the facade."

She had never been encouraged to share any part of her private life. In the world of pretense, frank disclosures were discouraged. "You've seen as much of her as anyone, cowboy," she said with a teasing smile. "What do you think of what you've seen so far?"

When he didn't respond to her playful overture, Lexie realized what she'd sensed from the beginning. When Lucas wanted answers, he couldn't be manipulated or distracted.

"I think I've seen a woman who's much stronger than anyone knows," he said finally. "Someone who's willing to take chances in order to carve out her own place in the world."

She felt slightly taken aback by his expansive description of her.

"You're obviously made of strong stuff, Lexie. Tell me, how'd you get so brave?"

She rolled away from him on the bed, separated but still holding his hand. "What makes you think I'm brave?"

He touched her shoulder. "I know you are. That day on the trail, you rode back to help Hugh Miller. In spite of the sniper and the danger to yourself. You didn't think twice, but acted on pure instinct. I'm a cop and I know what it's like to witness a violent death for the first time. I can't imagine how terrified you must have been, but helping Miller was your first thought. That's bravery.''

''Except that it wasn't the first time,'' she said quietly, still not looking at him.

After a short silence, he said, ''Tell me about it, honey.''

She shook her head. ''It was so long ago.''

''But it still hurts.'' It wasn't a question, but a simple statement of fact. ''It helps to talk about these things. Trust me, I've been a cop long enough to know.''

The memory was buried deep inside her brain, locked away in a dark and frightening place where she seldom dared to venture. ''I was just a child,'' she began. ''Only five years old…'' Her voice trailed off.

''Go on, honey.''

She shuddered. The years of enforced silence weren't ignored easily. ''I'm sorry, Lucas. I've never talked about this with anyone…It's just too…unspeakable.''

He sat up in the bed and gently placed his hands on her shoulders and turned her around to face him. ''Do you mean to tell me that you witnessed a murder as a child, but that you've never talked about it to anyone? Not even your father?''

''The royal family of St. Novia does not discuss unpleasant subjects,'' she said.

He muttered a curse under his breath.

''It's just the way it is, Lucas. We're a different breed. I tried to tell you….''

''But what about a teacher or a counselor? In all these years, hasn't there been anyone you could talk to?''

''A princess seeing a shrink would make headlines.'' The bitterness in her tone could not be concealed.

''To hell with headlines!'' he said angrily. His voice was calmer when he said, ''Listen, honey, it's the twenty-first century. Talking about the terrible or frightening things that have happened in our past doesn't make us crazy, but repressing them sure can.''

The well-trained defenses of Princess Alexandra rose to the fore. ''Oh, so now the cowboy cop is a psychologist?''

''No,'' he said solemnly, ''I'm just a man who cares about you.'' His simple statement smashed through those defenses with the force of a hammer blow. ''You can tell me anything, honey.'' He prompted, ''So, it happened when you were five years old....''

She swallowed hard and nodded and gave him a nervous smile. ''Going on six.''

He gave her hand a reassuring squeeze.

''I'd had the same bodyguard from the time of my birth. He was a kind man with a round, shiny, bald head. His name was Danton. As a child, I remember thinking he was a giant. Danton used to push me on the swings when my nanny was otherwise engaged. And even when Nanny was around, he'd make shadow puppets with his hands on the wall and tell me bedtime stories.''

Danton's tales had leaned a bit toward the Brothers Grimm school of brutal consequences, but Lexie adored having the big man's full attention. Her father and mother, always occupied with important affairs of state, seemed to have little time and less talent for parenting.

By the time she was five, Lexie's brothers and sister had been shipped off to boarding schools and she was the one and only child in the palace.

''There was no one to play with but Nanny and Danton. I loved them both and spent far more time with them than either of my parents. When I lost Danton, it was like losing a member of my family.''

''How did it happen, Lexie?'' Lucas asked.

''I remember it was a very warm day,'' she began, ''Danton and my nanny took me for an outing at a private beach just beyond the city limits. We'd made the same trip many times before. I loved the beach and I'd paddle around in the water and pretend that I was a champion swimmer. I remember the day we left, everyone else in the household was very busy. My brothers and sisters were home from school, but they didn't want to come with us to the private inlet. The Jubilee Ceremony was upcoming and they were all old enough to be included in the celebrations.'' She smiled at him. ''It was a huge blowout, very formal, lots of dignitaries and black-tie affairs.''

As her thoughts shifted to the glittering events held in the palace ballroom, she described for him the string of elaborate events that took place during that week. ''I was too young to take part, of course, but I always managed to find a way to get out onto a balcony to watch the beautiful ladies and elegant gentlemen dancing to the music of a full orchestra.''

''Early training for your cat burglar routine,'' he noted dryly. ''Let's get back to what happened that day at the beach with Danton and your nanny.''

She hesitated. ''I'm not sure I can talk about this.''

He leaned over her. The buttery light from the bedside lamp shone on his handsome features. The look in his eyes was warm and reassuring. ''I know the princess isn't supposed to talk about anything unpleasant, but those rules don't apply here. Tell me, honey. Believe me, once you let it out, it won't have the power to hurt you so much.''

She *did* believe him. With him at her side, Lexie felt protected and strong, and for the first time safe enough to push open the door to her darkest memories and expose them to the light of day.

''The water sparkled like a sea of crystals. Danton and Nanny waited on the shore, watching me as I splashed and dove. I was using my snorkel.''

''When you were five?''

"St. Novia is a coastal country and I was a princess who had been trained by the best swimming instructors money could buy. I learned to swim before I could walk. And I loved it! Danton used to tell me that if I didn't stop spending so much time in the water, one day I'd grow a tail and turn into a mermaid. I delighted in his teasing. He made me feel so special, as if he really cared for me." She sighed. "You know, even after all these years I still miss him." A feeling of sadness washed over her like the rippling waves of the crystal sea.

"I'd been swimming for I don't know how long, when two men appeared at the water's edge. I don't remember what they looked like. They might as well have been faceless."

"Like Solé," he murmured almost to himself.

"Yes," she said. "Anyway, I saw them arguing with Danton. Then, one of them grabbed Nanny and hit her. She fell back, limp and unconscious. Danton's gun, the one he wore in a holster around his shoulder, was drawn. But something must have gone wrong, because they shot him in the chest while I stood there watching, chest-deep in the water, terrified."

In her mind, she heard the tearing blast of gunfire, ripping her idyllic life to shreds. She saw the burst of crimson blood on her bodyguard's shirtfront. And she felt the pain again, as deep and fresh as if she were experiencing the horror all over again. She could hear the child's screams—her own agonizing cries—echoing through her memory.

"I heard Danton calling my name. He shouted at me to swim." She shuddered. "I started to wade out of the water, toward him, but he yelled at me to stop. He had never used that tone of voice with me before and it frightened me. He ordered me to swim away, to kick my legs and swim hard. He sounded so angry, so desperate. I knew, instinctively, that this was the most important thing he'd ever asked me to do. And I knew I had to obey.''

"After one last look at the shore, I ducked under the water. I swam as hard and as fast as I could. My heart and lungs burned. I used my snorkel and tried not to come up for air.''

She was unaware of the tears that had slipped from the corners of her eyes to slide silently down her cheeks. "I wanted to be a mermaid, to live at the bottom of the ocean where there were no men with guns and no pain. When at last I had to come up for air, I saw the two men moving clumsily in the water, trying to catch me. And I saw Danton on the shore. His shirt was covered in blood, but he rose up on his knees and fired once and then once more. His aim was true, but one of the men turned and fired at Danton again before he fell facedown into the water for the last time.''

Lucas held her hand tighter.

"I waded through water stained red with their blood to get to Danton, but it was too late. He was dead.''

She shuddered; the flood of memories left her weak. "I can't really remember what happened next, except that I soon had a new nanny and a new bodyguard. Much later, I learned that my nanny had been arrested for her part in the kidnapping attempt. I also learned that Danton had had three children of his own, three daughters, the youngest one only a few months older than I.''

"Oh, Lexie. I'm so sorry.''

"I don't remember exactly how I came to realize Danton had died trying to save me, that his children would grow up without their father because I was a princess. But I do remember wishing from that day forward that I could be someone—anyone—else. I didn't want to be different, didn't want to be a princess. I couldn't bear knowing that other people had to lay down their life for me." She choked back a sob. "And now another man has died...."

Lucas gathered her in his arms. His strength reassured her and helped fill the chasm of sorrow her memories had carved in her heart. She accepted his solace, leaned into his caresses and, finally, hours later, fell asleep, exhausted, in his arms.

THE PERSISTENT RINGING of the telephone beside his bed called Lucas away from his dreams and back to reality. He groped for the cordless phone and dropped it beside his mouth. "What?"

The ringing continued, and he realized that he hadn't pressed the "on" button. This took way too much concentration. Through squinted eyes, he saw the light of day slicing through the blinds in his bedroom. How could it be morning already?

A slender, feminine hand plucked the telephone from his fist. He opened his eyes to see her clutching the sheets over her bare breasts.

"Hello?"

Lord, she was beautiful. First thing in the morning with mussed hair and sleep-clouded eyes, Lexie was still the loveliest woman he'd ever seen.

"Hi, Sylvia," she said. A small smile touched the corner of her lips. "Yes, he's here. I'll put him on the line right away."

She held the phone out to him. Her troubled expression warned him there was another disaster brewing, and he definitely didn't want to deal with it. His preference would be to pull beautiful Lexie into his arms and carry her off into the sunset, to a place where he could fill her days and nights with lovemaking and laughter, where nothing would ever hurt her again. But the phone she held out to him said that fantasy would have to wait.

Gruffly, he spoke into the phone. "What is it, Sylvia?"

The dispatcher's normally tranquil voice was uncharacteristically shrill. "You better get down here, pronto. Those FBI agents are all over the place. They're going through files and confiscating all your records on the Hugh Miller case."

He sat up abruptly. "What?"

"You heard me, Sheriff. They have some kind of paper, saying they're in charge."

"Put Agent Peterson on the phone, Sylvia."

While Sylvia summoned the agent to the phone, Lucas looked at Lexie who had left the bed and slipped into the white shirt he'd been wearing yesterday. The shirttail skimmed her pretty knees. "Damn, you look cute," he said. "If that's what you do for an old cowboy shirt, I can't wait to see you in a tiara, Princess Honey."

This was not the way he'd planned their morning to begin. His plan had been to serve her breakfast in bed, from a tray decorated with wildflowers gathered from the front yard.

"I'll put on the coffee and let Rocky out," she said as she headed for the door, with the devoted dog hot on her heels.

Lucas crawled out of bed and pulled on his jeans. Somehow, he felt like he ought to at least have his pants on when he dealt with Agent Simon Peterson.

"Sheriff," Peterson snapped into the phone.

"I understand you're looting my office," Lucas said.

"Appropriating records," Peterson corrected. "As duly authorized by the powers that be at the State Department."

"We'll see about that," Lucas grumbled. He wasn't prepared to take on the entire justice department before he had the facts. "In the meantime, as a professional courtesy, would you mind waiting until I can get to my office before you confiscate any more of my records?"

"Is that what you call them? Your notes seem pretty sketchy, to me, Garrett. Haven't you ever heard of proper documentation?"

Lucas was in no mood to argue procedure with the pompous bureaucrat, but he was secretly glad he hadn't had time to input all his notes. Specifically, he was relieved he hadn't had time to file a report on his conversation with Inez at The Timbers. After learning more about Ian Solé and his penchant for not leaving witnesses, Lucas was glad he held the advantage of knowing Seth Rockwell had been seen meeting with a stranger. Information like that could be dangerous and the last thing Lucas wanted was to put another witness in harm's way.

Swallowing his irritation at the FBI, Lucas offered, "Obviously, you're going to need my assistance in deciphering my notes. I'll be there in less than an hour."

"You sound suddenly cooperative, Sheriff," Peterson said. "Why the change of heart?"

"Last night I garnered some information about an individual, one Ian Solé."

Peterson was silent.

"I know you boys are familiar with the man. If what I've learned is correct, I need all the help I can get to rid my county of this vermin." He hated to admit to the arrogant agent that he needed his help, but Lucas was too smart to let pride get in the way of solving a murder case. "You boys are the experts when it comes to profiling guys like Solé."

"We're the FBI," Peterson reminded him. "Our data banks and our investigative techniques are second to none."

"Yeah, well, I just hope all those resources can help us catch this guy. That is the whole point, isn't it, Agent Peterson?"

Lucas sensed the other man's hesitation. "Yes, well, of course. Half an hour, then. I'll be waiting."

His officious tone rankled Lucas's pride, but he said nothing. For Lexie's sake, he needed to catch a murderer. And if that meant putting up with Peterson's attitude to get the job done, then so be it.

"One more thing, Agent Peterson. I wonder if you've checked into the background of Ramon Acardi."

"The photographer?"

"That's the one. He works for a rag called *The Exposé.* Seems strange he'd turn up here even before you guys."

He heard the sharp intake of breath on the other end of the line and knew he'd hit the intended nerve.

"It might not be a bad idea to check out Mr. Acardi's alibi for the time of the murder and abduction attempt. As I understand it, no one knows what this Solé character looks like."

"You're saying you think Ian Solé could be posing as a photographer?"

"Could be," Lucas said. "And while you're checking backgrounds, what about Fulton Bobek?"

"The little guy with Lady Margaret? Isn't he an emissary to the St. Novian ambassador based in Washington D.C.?"

"An emissary with access to a private jet," Lucas supplied. Lucas found it ironic reminding this supposed FBI hotshot that even Destiny, Colorado was part of a global community. "I think we ought to at least check out his story."

With the phone still in his hand, Lucas shuffled down the hall to the kitchen where he leaned against the doorway and watched Lexie grinding fresh coffee beans. She hummed to herself as she set out two mugs and checked the sugar bowl. Having her here, part of his daily routine, helped remind him why he had to play politics with Agent Simon Peterson.

"See you in thirty minutes," Lucas said into the phone.

"See that you're on time," Peterson grumbled.

The doorbell rang once, then immediately again.

Over the noise, Lucas reminded Peterson, "Look, we both want the same thing, don't we? To apprehend the killer and if that ends up being an international mercenary, then we've both done the world a big favor.'' He wanted to add that if Solé was apprehended, there would be plenty of glory to go around, but further irritating the nerves of the already prickly agent wouldn't help the investigation. ''Our goal is to get this guy in custody,'' Lucas said. ''No matter what it takes.''

Lexie slid past him to open the front door. ''It's probably Rocky,'' she mouthed.

''Okay,'' Peterson agreed. ''You've made your point, Sheriff.''

Lucas set the phone down and turned to see Lexie open the door to reveal a tall, barrel-chested man silhouetted by morning sunlight. His navy blue uniform was trimmed in scarlet, with gleaming gold buttons. A glittering array of medals and ribbons decorated his chest. Thinning gray hair had been combed back neatly from his forehead. His complexion was ruddy. His scowl, ferocious.

Calmly, Lexie said, ''Good morning, Daddy.''

Lucas wasn't quite sure how things could get much worse. Lexie was standing in the doorway, wearing his white shirt and nothing else. Lucas himself was bare-chested. It was fairly obvious that King Frederick of St. Novia knew he hadn't interrupted a game of chess.

Without saying a word, Lexie's father strode through the door. In his wake were two other men dressed in dark suits.

Though Lexie had her hands full, trying to control Rocky—who had slipped past the king—she managed to affect a royal decorum. ''Daddy, I'd like you to meet Sheriff Lucas Garrett. Lucas, this is my father, King Frederick of St. Novia.''

Lucas stuck out his hand and met the King's steely gaze without blinking. ''Sir.''

Frederick's lip twitched in a snarl. The red of his face darkened to a dangerous magenta, and Lucas thought for a second the man might either spontaneously combust or be stricken by a sudden coronary. Instead, he gripped Lucas's hand and squeezed hard.

Big mistake, Your Highness. Lucas was younger and more muscular. Even if he hadn't been able to match the king's strength, he wouldn't have flinched. For a few tense seconds, neither of them relented, but continued to tighten their respective grips by degrees.

"Well, then." Lexie patted their hands, giving them a reason to break apart. "I need to get dressed," she said without apology. "Lucas was just about to have some coffee. Would you care to join him, Father? Gentlemen?"

"You're coming with me," her father decreed.

"Father, please," Lexie said firmly. "Obviously, this is a difficult and awkward situation, but there's no reason we can't all act civilly."

Once again, she'd slipped on the royal facade, but watching her father's furious expression, Lucas worried that Lexie at her most imperious best was no match for the king.

"There will be no more discussion," King Frederick decreed. "I've come to take you home, where you belong. Ulster, escort Alexandra to the car. Harris, gather her things." The taller of the two men stepped forward and reached for Lexie's arm.

"Father, please…I'm not even dressed!"

Ulster's hand moved toward Lexie's elbow, but Lucas's reaction was immediate. "Touch her and you'll be carrying that hand in a sling 'til Christmas."

The second man took a step forward and Lucas tensed, ready to take them both on. Rocky growled a warning.

"Stop!" Lexie came up behind him. "Please, Lucas." She turned to her father. "Just give me a minute to get dressed and then we'll go."

The tension in the room crackled as the two men glanced uncertainly between the king and his daughter. Finally, King Frederick gave a curt nod and both men stepped back.

Lucas didn't move a muscle until he felt Lexie's hand on his arm. "Let's go finish dressing," she said softly.

In his bedroom, Lucas dressed in minutes, anger propelling his every action.

"Was that Agent Peterson on the phone?" Lexie asked him as she slipped into her own clothes.

Lucas nodded. "He's waiting for me, now, at my office. Sylvia said he and his men were confiscating my files, but I convinced him to hold off until I could meet with him."

"Then you'd better get going," she said as she quickly pulled her long hair into a ponytail and smoothed the loose strands behind her ears.

"I'm not leaving you here to deal with your father alone," he said.

"But you have to go, Lucas. Don't worry about me, I can handle Daddy."

Torn between the desire to protect Lexie and his need to keep the FBI from running roughshod over the case, he searched her face. "But I don't want to leave you."

"You have to go, Lucas. If Peterson is willing to meet you halfway, you have to grab this opportunity."

The war of nerves with King Frederick of St. Novia and his entourage seemed like a mere warm-up for dealing with Agent Peterson and Agent Browning.

"You handle the FBI and I'll deal with my father," she said, giving him a quick hug.

"If I go, you won't feel like I'm running out on you?"

"Of course not."

But Lucas couldn't help wondering if that was the response of the always appropriate princess or a flesh-and-blood woman who realized that as much as he wanted to be with her, he had to tend to his professional duty.

"Promise me…" he said, gripping her shoulders. "Promise me you won't let him push you into doing anything you don't want to do."

"Don't worry. I'm not going anywhere." But he could see the worry in her violet eyes, along with a sadness that made his heart ache. "Don't worry," she said again. "You're not going to get rid of me that easily, Sheriff."

He kissed her quickly. The petal softness of her lips reminded him of last night's passion. Investigation or not, how could he leave her? Now or ever? She was everything he wanted. The perfect woman for him, the only woman he'd ever longed to call his own. "Everything's going to be all right, honey. I promise."

But at the moment, he had no idea how the hell he was going to go about fulfilling that promise.

The man in his living room was no doubt ready to order his execution. The man waiting at his office was poised to undermine his professional standing. In the meantime, a murderer was still at large, a ruthless cold-blooded killer who had tried to abduct the woman—the *princess*—Lucas had decided to make his wife.

Chapter Twelve

Twenty minutes after breaking every speed limit, Lucas squealed up in front of the police department, parked the SUV and marched into his office.

Agent Paul Browning, in his usual dark blue suit and white shirt, sat in the waiting area. His laptop computer rested on his knees and he was typing efficiently. Agent Simon Peterson, looking smug in his FBI windbreaker, had taken the chair behind Eli's desk. "It's about time," he said.

"With minutes to spare," Lucas said. "All right. Let's get down to business, shall we, gentlemen?"

"The only thing that's in order around here are the coroner's reports," Peterson said. "But I don't think they'll be of any use except as evidence in a later court proceeding."

"Oh, I wouldn't say that." Browning looked up from the computer screen. "The coroner's report confirmed my suspicion that the same weapon was used to kill both Miller and Rockwell."

"But he wasn't able to pinpoint the time of Rockwell's death," Peterson reminded him, "other than to say it was within a couple of hours of Miller's. Unfortunately, we don't know if that was before or after."

Lucas was fairly certain of the timing. Without mentioning that Inez had seen Rockwell having dinner with a stranger the night before Miller's murder, he said, "I think we can assume Rockwell died before Miller. We found tire tracks at the Miller crime scene that match that of the stolen BLM truck.''

"Yes, what about that truck?" Peterson asked. "Why haven't your men found it, yet?"

Lucas shook his head. It was as if the truck had vanished. "We've had an APB on the vehicle from day one. My men have combed the area where the vehicle was last seen, but there's been no sight of it, yet."

Agent Peterson sneered. "I thought you were supposed to be the expert on this territory, Sheriff. Seems to me a vehicle with such a distinctive description would be fairly easy to spot."

Lucas didn't bother to explain that they were dealing with a huge area of rugged terrain, dotted with canyons and caves, and acres of timber. Even something as large as a truck could easily be concealed, especially a truck painted BLM green.

"We might have better luck searching from the air," he said. "The department has access to a plane and a pilot we hire for extraditions."

"A single plane and a citizen pilot," Peterson scoffed. "Sounds like a monumental waste of time and money, Garrett." He addressed Agent Browning, "Get on the horn to the Bureau and make the proper request." To Lucas, he said, "We'll have a thorough air search organized in less than twenty-four hours, Sheriff."

"There's an Air Force training facility twenty miles north of town," Lucas told Browning. "The FBI's air team can use that strip to prevent interrupting local air operations." The airport that served Destiny consisted of only one gate. The entire operation was small and ill-equipped to handle even a minor increase in air traffic.

"All right, now we're getting somewhere," Peterson said. "The FBI will head up the search for the truck." He wheeled on Browning. "Well? What are you waiting for, man? Get on it!"

"I was just wondering if the Bureau will approve this kind of effort for something as minor as a stolen truck," Browning said.

"It's not *just* a stolen truck, you imbecile," Peterson rebuked. "If Garrett is right—and this time I think he just might be—that truck could be the key to finding our killer."

For the first time, Lucas found himself in full agreement with Agent Peterson.

"You know, that's always been your problem, Browning. You move too slow and think too small. Sometimes I think you spend too much time on that computer. There's more to police work than reports. Maybe it's time you took that retirement you've been yapping about, get on that old tub of yours and sail off into the sunset."

Though Browning's face didn't reflect any change in expression, Lucas could well imagine the resentment simmering beneath the surface of Agent Browning's cool demeanor.

"I'll contact the Bureau," he replied stiffly.

As a man accustomed to leading men, Lucas would have advised Agent Peterson to change his insulting tactics, but he doubted the arrogant agent would have listened.

"You see, Garrett, that's why I'm lead investigator," Peterson said while Browning made his call on his own cell phone. "Even though Browning has seniority. He's a detail man, so focused on dotting all his *i's* and crossing all his *t's* he can't see the big picture."

"I like to be thorough," Browning said simply, with a hand over his phone.

Within a few minutes, Browning let them know that the air search for the missing BLM truck had been approved.

When Peterson left to refill his coffee mug, Browning turned to Lucas. "Sheriff, I'd like to go over the list of evidence you've gathered so far on the crime scenes."

Lucas was glad to oblige. Another set of eyes, especially ones fine-tuned to detail, might be able to spot a clue his own men had missed.

For the next hour, using information gathered by his deputies, Lucas covered the probable events at the scene of Hugh Miller's murder for the two FBI agents. Next, he moved on to the Rockwell case.

"Once again," he concluded, "we found tire tracks that would be typical of the tires on the BLM truck. Also, the tarp used to cover the body bore the BLM stamp."

Thoughtfully, Browning said, "That doesn't sound like standard procedure for Solé. He never leaves anything to chance, follows a meticulous plan and uses a minimum of equipment. The Rockwell murder sounds amateurish and spur of the moment."

"Yet the weapon used in both murders was the same," Lucas reminded him. "But you could have a point, Browning. At this point, maybe we're wrong to focus all our efforts on this Solé character." He leaned back in his chair and looked from one agent to the other. "But then, you boys would be more informed about that subject than I. Do you really think Ian Solé is our primary suspect?"

"We have reports that indicate his latest movements put him in the West," Browning said without hesitation. "But it could be premature to conclude he's our man. And then there's the fact that Solé usually operates on his own."

"He's involved," Peterson said with a finality that did not invite contradiction. "The weapon had his signature all over it. She's a princess, for goodness sake. Who else would try to pull off such a caper?" He stood and paced impatiently across the room. "Now, let's stop wasting time and go over the rest of the evidence. Fill us in on the incident at the cabin, Garrett. What was going on there? You've had almost constant access to Miss Dubois. What has she told you? Has she given any indication what the intruder might have been after?''

Lucas shook his head. Lexie had said she hadn't been carrying anything of value. ''The few pieces of jewelry she had with her weren't taken. Obviously, robbery wasn't a motive.''

''Then what was?'' Peterson demanded.

''I don't —'' Browning began.

Peterson sank down into his chair. ''I'll tell you what I think. I think it was pure unbridled rage. I've done a fair amount of profiling, and it looked to me like someone mad as hell tore that place apart. A real head-case.''

''Another reason to eliminate Solé,'' Browning said. ''He's always been known as cool and controlled. I fed all the information into my computer and the profile just doesn't fit.''

''I don't give a damn what your computer thinks. Solé kills people for a living,'' Peterson pointed out. ''And if that's not a head-case, I don't know what is. Call him cool, but to me the man's a psycho. It's pretty basic, Paul. People who murder aren't normal. They can't keep their personality from disintegrating forever. At some point, they lose it!''

Peterson was so adamant Lucas could only assume that this was not the first time the two had discussed the varying aspects of a murderous personality. Obviously, there was a power struggle going on between them. Peterson wanted to be the boss, but to Lucas it seemed Browning, although less aggressive, was the more intelligent and experienced of the two.

Peterson continued, ''I think it's a waste of time to focus any more effort on the ransacked cabin.''

''A detailed analysis of the scene might help,'' Browning insisted. ''Garrett's men lifted a dozen prints.''

''Which we've forwarded to the Colorado Bureau of Investigation,'' Lucas said. This was another area where the

Feds might prove extremely useful. "But if you guys can get the Bureau to run those prints, we'd have the results a lot faster."

"It's already been done," Peterson informed him.

Lucas could only stare when Peterson laughed. "You didn't really think I'd sit around waiting for your backwoods procedures, did you? I contacted the CBI my first day on the case and this morning I received a positive identification for Hugh Miller."

As much as Lucas would have liked to personally cram Peterson's laughter down his neck, he was glad the jerk had taken the situation with the CBI in hand.

"So, who was the mysterious bodyguard?" Lucas asked.

"Well, to begin with, he was no bodyguard." Peterson rose from the chair and strutted across the office. The fabric of his black windbreaker rustled as he moved. "Hugh Miller was an ex-con with a rap sheet longer than my arm. His real name was Hubert Miller Jones. Apparently, he shortened his first name and dropped the last."

Lucas couldn't believe it. A felon had been hired to protect Lexie? "Who the hell was responsible for hiring Miller as a bodyguard?"

"Here's where it gets interesting," Peterson said. Lucas sensed Agent Peterson would have stopped short of revealing this much information, but he didn't seem able to resist letting everyone know he had the upper hand. "Miller was hired at the recommendation of Seth Rockwell, who was in communication with the St. Novian ambassador, Lord Roche. Seems Rockwell and Roche are relatives."

"Distant cousins," Lucas said distractedly. His mind was quickly assessing this newest piece of the puzzle. "Then, it's possible Miller might have been part of the abduction plot. But why was he killed? A double cross?"

"If it was Solé," Browning said, "he would have used Rockwell until the end, until he had his hands on the ransom.

He wouldn't have risked fouling his original plan by cluttering the scene with a dead body.''

If it was Solé?

"It was Solé," Peterson said disgustedly. "And it should be obvious he had the so-called bodyguard in his pocket. We found out Miller had been bragging to his cronies about a big score, a cool million he was getting for a job in the West. He'd bragged that this one would set him up for the rest of his life.''

As it had turned out, the rest of that life had been short-circuited by his accomplice, Lucas thought.

"As far as Ian Solé, our intelligence shows he's opened a line of communication that reaches all the way to King Frederick himself."

Lucas could hardly wait to hear who and what that connection might be.

"Unfortunately, we don't have any names, at this point. Suffice to say, someone in the king's circle has sold out to Solé.''

"Which reminds me," Lucas said. "The king, himself, has made an appearance. In fact, I just met him.''

"He's here?" Peterson asked. "The king came here? Oh brother! That's all I need. All right, Garrett, I don't want you mucking this up. We're to handle His Majesty with kid gloves, understand?''

Lucas didn't respond.

"My orders are clear. We're not to ruffle any royal feathers. Damn it! How am I supposed to crack this case with royalty breathing down my neck?''

Lucas couldn't resist. "Oh, come now, Peterson. Don't tell me a little political heat can keep you from getting your man?''

Peterson glared at Lucas, but Lucas only laughed.

As if they needed any further distraction, Tucker Oates

burst into the office—Sylvia hot on his heels, apologizing for the intrusion.

"Lucas!" Tucker shouted. "I got a big problem. You have to talk with that photographer guy. He's way out of line. All right, I admit it," the words gushed out of the excited old man like water, "I was wrong to call him. But how was I supposed to know the man was a liar and a cheat?"

"Calm down, Tucker," Lucas ordered. "And tell me what's going on?"

"Well, for one thing, he's trying to back out of giving me the money he promised when I called him. A hundred bucks ain't much to some folks, but I can use that cash! And if that wasn't bad enough, he's making a play for a married woman."

"What woman?" Lucas asked.

"Inez Estes, over at The Timbers. For the past two days, he's done everything he can to get her alone."

Warning bells went off in Lucas's head. He had to warn Inez. If Acardi was Solé, he would be worried that she could identify him as the stranger who had met with Seth Rockwell the day before his death. And if Acardi was Solé, the man had to be desperate. From the botched abduction to the death of Seth Rockwell, nothing in his scheme seemed to be going smoothly.

"But that ain't the half of it, Lucas," Tucker continued breathlessly. "He's out there at the ranch again, with all sorts of long-range lenses. Hell, everybody's there and the fat is in the fire, I can tell you that much! Be darned if the King of St. Novia himself didn't show up at Mo's front door," Tucker said, his eyes growing wide. "And believe you me he is raising a royal ruckus."

Lucas glanced around his office. Given a choice of protecting his files and protecting his family, he knew what he had to do.

"I need to get out there," he told Peterson. "Help yourself to my files. Sylvia can answer your questions on procedures."

"Gee, thanks," Peterson replied, his voice dripping sarcasm. "But we'd better go, too, Browning. Obviously, I'm going to need to get control of the situation."

"With all due respect," Browning said, "we have a great deal of investigative work to do right here."

Agent Peterson drew himself up to his full height. "Right now, you and I are the only representatives of the United States government on the scene, Paul. And my orders are clear. I need to assure King Frederick that everything's under control. Hell, you should know what to do. Now, get out there and do it! You're supposed to be the expert on foreign affairs. You're the only one I've ever known who's actually made a study of St. Novia."

"I *am* the expert," Browning said coldly. "And by the way, if you plan to meet the king, I suggest you change out of that windbreaker into a coat and tie." No one could miss the glint of satisfaction in Browning's eye at having for once the upper hand on his arrogant boss.

"Good point." Peterson headed for the door. "I'll go to the motel and be back with the car."

As soon as he left, Browning turned to Lucas and confided, "If Ian Solé was, in fact, involved, you can bet he's long gone, Sheriff."

Lucas had to ask the question that had been nagging him for days. "Peterson says you're the international expert and you seem to have the inside track on this character Solé, so, why is it you're not in charge of this investigation?"

Browning bent down to gather up his laptop computer. "Peterson is up-and-coming. He needs the field experience. I'm on my way out. Actually, I was hoping this would be my last major case before retirement."

"I'm ready for a change in career myself," Lucas said as

Browning walked with him to the door. On days like this, he'd be happy to turn over the sheriff's job to Eli Ferguson.

"I understand you raise horses."

Lucas nodded. "Eventually, I'd like to concentrate on that full-time."

"Time to settle down, Sheriff?"

"Maybe," Lucas said as they walked out into the sunshine together.

"With the princess?"

Lucas raised an eyebrow. "You don't miss much, do you, Agent Browning?"

"You'd be surprised, Sheriff. But it didn't take long to figure out that if I wanted to locate Alexandra Dubois, all I had to do was find you. And vice versa."

He realized Lexie did figure into his plans for settling down. After last night, it was hard to imagine a future that didn't include her.

"That true, Lucas?" Tucker asked. "You making time with that little princess gal?"

"Never mind," Lucas growled at the older man. "Let's get going."

He was anxious to return to the ranch and put the brakes on whatever havoc Lexie's father was wreaking. Maybe he should have felt more respect for the man. He was her father, after all, and a king, to boot. But how could Lucas respect a man who hadn't had time to parent his own daughter, who'd shipped his kids off to boarding schools and left them to be raised by nannys and bodyguards? Obviously, King Frederick was more concerned with the royal image than Lexie's happiness.

Browning followed Lucas to his vehicle. "Well, good luck with your future plans, Sheriff."

"Same to you, Agent Browning. Will you go back to D.C. to retire?"

"I'm not sure. For a while I thought I might move to this

area. When I was at the Air Force academy, I always thought I'd come back to Colorado. But now, I'm thinking more of sandy beaches and cool trade winds.''

"Peterson mentioned a boat…''

Browning smiled. "The *Sea Lion*. Like your horses to you, my boat is my pride and joy. Someday I hope to set sail for a long vacation.''

"Well, best of luck, Browning.''

"Same to you, Garrett. No matter what Peterson says, you've done a fine job on this investigation.''

Lucas wasn't so sure he was right. There were too many loose ends, too many unanswered questions and half-truths that didn't add up. A part of him hoped Browning was right, that Solé had left the area. At least for the moment, Lexie would be safe.

ESCAPING THE FUROR inside the Garrett ranch house, Lexie slipped out the front door onto the porch where Deputy Eli Ferguson stood gazing at the meadow in the distance.

"Is it safe out here?'' she asked.

The sun glinted off his dark glasses and he grinned at her. "Well, there could be a sniper hiding out in the sagebrush, but I haven't seen him.''

Lexie sighed. "Even at that, I think I'd be safer out here than in there.''

"You must have felt like a referee at a tag-team wrestling match,'' Eli noted.

Lexie sighed. "That's a pretty accurate description, Deputy.'' On one side were the colorful St. Novians—Lady Margaret, Fulton Bobek, the entourage and her father. On the other side was Mo Garrett, Lexie and Cal. The St. Novians were furiously debating all the reasons why Lexie should pack up her belongings and go home like a good little princess. Mo Garrett was arguing Lexie's right to choose, reiterating Lexie's own assertion that it was better for her to face the danger than to spend her life running and hiding.

"Frankly," Eli said, "I don't understand the problem. It's your decision."

"Except that I've never had much freedom in making my own decisions," Lexie confided. "Sometimes it seems I need royal approval to cross the street."

Lazily, Eli lifted the gleaming rifle to his shoulder and took aim.

"What are you doing?" she asked.

"Just warning a hyena to keep his distance," he said.

She followed his line of sight. Beyond the fence in the field, she saw a head poking out from behind a rock. "Who is it?"

"That damn photographer."

"Acardi?"

"That's the one," Eli said. "He's been hanging around here for a couple of days and Lucas told me to keep him away from you."

Even from that distance, Acardi's high-tech telephoto lens would be able to capture her image. "He must be going crazy with me and my father so close and yet so far."

A loud wail from Lady Margaret drew her attention back to the house. "I'd better get back in there," Lexie said, "before they kill each other."

"I'm betting on Mo," Eli informed her with a knowing smile.

"You don't know my father."

Inside the house, Lady Margaret was explaining the life of a princess, how Lexie could never be happy without the opulent luxury to which she'd become accustomed.

"You can't be talking about the same gal I know," Mo said. "Lexie's as down-to-earth as anyone raised in the West."

"You're all missing the point," Cal said. "Lexie wants

to stay here until the killer is apprehended and she has the right to do that.''

King Frederick boomed, ''What my daughter wants and what she needs are two distinctly different things. You Americans have no respect for parental authority or protocol. It's up to me to decide what's best for her.''

When Lexie moved into the room, her father turned to glare at her. His face was so red that she feared for his blood pressure. ''For the last time, pack your things, Alexandra,'' he said. ''Despite whatever romantic notions you've spun around your fling with that cowboy last night, you cannot be seriously considering staying here.''

All eyes turned to Lexie. Now, it was her turn to blush. In a small voice, she said, ''It was not a fling.''

''Have you forgotten?'' he demanded. ''I caught you at his home, half-naked this morning.''

''Well, I'll be damned,'' Cal said.

''Well, all right! Lexie and Lucas,'' Mo exclaimed with satisfaction. ''I just knew you two were right for each other.''

''Right for each other?'' The King gave a very unregal snort. ''Absurd! Alexandra has made a mistake, but it's behind her now. She will return to St. Novia where she will find a suitable match.''

Cal stepped forward. ''Are you saying my uncle Lucas isn't good enough for your daughter?''

''I cast no aspersion on the good sheriff.'' Her father's tone was so overtly condescending Lexie felt embarrassed for him. ''But anyone can see this is not an appropriate match for a princess.''

''Of course it isn't,'' Lady Margaret chimed in. ''There's a perfectly charming duke who's just been waiting for her to give him the smallest word of encouragement. Why, even Fulton would be a more appropriate match than that long-legged cowboy!''

Fulton Bobek took a step toward Lexie. Before she could object, he snatched her hand and went down on one knee. "Princess Alexandra, I would be honored."

"Get up, Fulton!" she said and pulled away from him so suddenly that he fell backward.

"Ow!" he shouted. "My tailbone!"

"Oh, Fulton! Oh, dear," Lady Margaret wailed. "Dear Lord, she's assaulted him."

"Good grief." Mo laughed. "She did nothing of the kind, although why she didn't is beyond me. You've got some gall, Mister."

Fulton bounded to his feet. Furious, he confronted Mo. "You know nothing about me."

Lexie had never seen Fulton so angry. For a moment, his foppish manner faded, and she saw him as a potentially dangerous man.

Apparently, Cal recognized the same possibility. He stepped forward. In a firm voice, he said, "Back off, little man."

"You'll be sorry you said that, you barbarian. You have no idea who you're dealing with."

Cal took another step toward Fulton when Lady Margaret put her wrist to her forehead. "I feel faint," she exclaimed.

One of the entourage rushed forward to catch her as the front door swung open and Lucas strode into the room. Behind him, his face bright with expectation, was Tucker Oates.

Lucas surveyed the room calmly. "Good morning, everyone. What seems to be the problem in here?"

Chapter Thirteen

When Lucas walked through the door into the house he'd called home for most of his life, he'd immediately encountered a seething hostile atmosphere that had never been there before. The temperature inside must have been a good twenty degrees hotter than on the porch.

It was a shame, he thought. The Garrett ranch had always been known for western hospitality. Neighbors knew there would always be a cup of hot coffee and a homemade cookie or a slice of pie for anyone who dropped by. If his mother were still alive, she would never have allowed such turmoil in her home.

The sight before him was disturbing, but at the same time almost comical. The group of cranky St. Novians faced down Cal and Mo, who seemed to be holding their own. In the middle of it all was Lexie. She'd told him, again and again, that he couldn't possibly understand what it meant to be a princess. But the ugly scene unfolding in the living room gave him a pretty good idea.

Lexie looked as upset as she had the day she'd been attacked. Her complexion was pink and flushed. Her violet eyes flickered with panicky desperation. He wanted to take her in his arms and comfort her. This morning, he'd promised everything would be all right, and he'd meant it. Now, he had to make good on his promise.

"What's the problem, here?" he demanded again.

Several people started talking at once, and Lucas held up his hand for silence. "Lexie?"

"My father has ordered me back to St. Novia, but I wish to remain here."

Agent Simon Peterson darted around Lucas and greeted King Frederick. After his official spiel, "on behalf of the United States government," he concluded with, "Of course, Your Highness, the FBI stands ready to assist you in any way we can."

"Finally, a reasonable man," King Frederick said. He straightened his broad shoulders within his crisp blue uniform. "I want my daughter out of here," he said simply.

"But I'm afraid that's not the way it works in this country," Lucas interrupted. "Lexie's a grown woman. She's free to make her own decisions."

"Do not presume to lecture me on the ways of government, Sheriff. As a father, I'm acting in the best interests of my daughter. An abduction attempt has been made on Princess Alexandra, proving this is an unsafe situation."

"That attempt might never have happened had she been adequately protected."

Lexie gasped at Lucas's assertion.

"I have always provided my children with protection. Lexie has had a bodyguard from the time of her birth," the king said.

"But her bodyguard, in this case, just happened to be an ex-convict." Lucas kept his gaze trained on Lexie as he continued, "Hugh Miller was a convicted felon. What's more, it's possible he was involved in the abduction plot."

In a voice so quiet that only Lucas could hear, she whispered, "Then, he didn't...die for me."

"Probably not. It's looking more and more like he was one of the bad guys," Lucas said.

She closed her eyes and lowered her head as if she were

briefly offering a prayer of thanksgiving. When she looked back at Lucas, he saw fresh clarity and renewed strength of resolve in her gaze. The burden of guilt had been lifted.

"Lady Margaret!" the king thundered. "What is the meaning of this? Hugh Miller was hired through the auspices of the ambassador's office."

"My husband, the ambassador..." Words failed her. This time, when her eyes rolled back in her head, she fainted for real and fell gracelessly into the unsuspecting arms of one of the St. Novia delegation who had to peer around her towering gray hair in order to lift her into a wing chair.

The king turned on Fulton Bobek. "What can you tell me about this, Bobek?"

Bobek eyes shifted, as though he were looking for some means of escape. Fulton Bobek might not have been an admirable human being, but Lucas didn't seriously believe he was the dangerous mercenary, Ian Solé.

"Bobek!" the king thundered.

"Yes, Your Highness. All I know is that the arrangements to hire Miller were made through the Ambassador's cousin, Seth Rockwell."

"A man who was subsequently killed," Lucas said. "It's likely Seth Rockwell was conspiring with Solé."

The king turned to Agent Peterson. "Ian Solé? That murdering madman is involved? Is this true?"

"It's a theory," Peterson said. "There's nothing to worry about, Your Majesty. The FBI has jurisdiction of this case, and we will find the killer, whoever it is."

"Surely you don't require the assistance of my daughter in your investigation. She has told me she's been questioned and has given her statement."

"Absolutely not," Peterson said. "In fact, I'd feel much better knowing she was safely away from the area."

"And if you fail?" Lexie said. "If you are unable to apprehend Solé, what then? Am I to spend the rest of my life hiding from him? Looking over my shoulder and wondering when the next abduction attempt will occur?''

''The FBI won't fail,'' Peterson assured her.

She went to her father. ''Father, I have never asked you for anything, but I'm asking you now to listen to me. Regardless of the outcome of this case, I refuse to live under constant surveillance. We've tried it your way and look what's happened. Miller is dead. Danton—''

''That was a long time ago,'' King Frederick interrupted.

''Face it, Father. If someone wants to do me harm, nothing you or anyone else can do will stop them.''

''You'll have better bodyguards. I, personally, will hire them.'' His bluster had faded, and he almost sounded like the concerned father instead of the embarrassed monarch. ''Alexandra, if you come back with me and let me protect you, I will do everything in my power to make sure no danger ever comes close to you again.''

''And that's what frightens me most,'' she said softly.

Lucas stepped up. ''If she stays, I'll guarantee her safety.''

''You?'' The king regarded him with deep hostility. ''Your services are not acceptable.''

''I'm not offering a service. I'm giving you my word.'' He would never let anything bad happen to her. She was more precious to him than anything, more precious than this land, his house, his horses and even his own life. This woman who had been a stranger such a short time ago had somehow become the center of his life. ''I'll take care of her, Sir.''

King Frederick brushed past his daughter. He confronted Lucas eye to eye. ''And help yourself to her inheritance and enjoy her fame, as well, I'm sure.''

''I don't need her money and who the hell would want to pay the price for that kind of fame?''

As King Frederick stood glaring at him, Lucas sensed Lexie's presence beside him.

Poor little princess. With a father like this man, how had she turned out so honorable, so normal?

"I'm finished talking," King Frederick declared. "Alexandra, we're leaving in one hour. This is not a request, it's an order."

"No one gives orders in my house, but me." At the sound of the voice behind them, all eyes turned to see Will Garrett standing on the stairway. The shotgun in his right hand was aimed at the floor.

His clothes hung on his emaciated body like a scarecrow's rags. He was obviously painfully frail and tired. But at that moment, Lucas had never been more proud of his father.

In a quiet but firm voice, Will Garrett said, "I won't have any more arguing under my roof. Now, everyone who isn't family or a paying guest, get the hell out. Now!"

Agent Peterson started toward him. "Sir, if you'll allow me. I'm sure I can explain all of this. Let me introduce myself. I'm Agent Simon Peterson, from the FBI and—"

"I don't give a damn if you're Buffalo Bill Cody." Will lifted his gun and waved it in Peterson's direction. "I'm a sick old man, with one foot halfway through the pearly gates and the other one on the proverbial banana peel. In short, I don't have much to lose. And I don't intend to give up my last few days of peace and quiet. Now, if you don't want your backside filled with lead, clear out. All of you! You've got exactly one minute to vacate the premises."

There was a gleam in his father's eyes that Lucas and everyone else seemed to know indicated that the old man wasn't bluffing. As he stood watching from the stairway, the assembled group quietly prepared to comply with the old man's orders. Fulton Bobek was the first one out the door.

LEXIE, OF COURSE, stayed behind with the Garrett family. Even as she watched her father and her countrymen leave, she felt no guilt about staying behind. With Lucas and his family, she felt more cared for than she ever had in St. Novia. The warmth and genuine caring the Garretts had shown her was something she'd never experienced from her own relatives. Her father knew how to give orders and issue edicts, but she couldn't remember him ever telling her he loved her.

After the others had filed out, Lexie and Mo helped Will onto the sofa, while Cal relieved him of his shotgun.

"For goodness sake," Mo fussed at him. "What were you thinking, Pop? You could have killed someone!"

"It isn't loaded," he told her and smiled. "And if anyone was going to get hurt it wouldn't have been my fault. If I hadn't come down when I did, Lucas and Lexie's father might have gone at it and we couldn't have that, could we?" He winked at Lexie and patted Lucas's hand.

"Thanks for backing me up, Pop. Mom would have been proud."

A smile of pure joy lit his ravaged face. "Rose always did like it when I took a stand, as long as I did it her way, of course."

"Too bad your gun was empty. A little lead in the britches might have loosened up those stuffed shirts," Cal said. "No offense, Lexie, but I don't know how you put up with those high-handed people."

"When I walked in, it looked like you'd had enough of Mr. Bobek," Lucas said.

Cal rubbed his fist into the palm of his other hand. "The man did try my patience."

"I'm glad you didn't hit him, Cal," Lexie said. Had the situation come to fisticuffs her father's bodyguards would have stepped in and possibly hurt someone seriously.

"Yeah, I'm glad you managed to control yourself," Lucas

said with mock seriousness. "Because if you'd punched Fulton, I'd have had to arrest your sorry butt."

"Oh, yeah?" Cal laughed. "I'd like to see you try."

"But you couldn't arrest Cal if you wanted to," Tucker Oates put in from the doorway. "Not now anyway."

Mo grumbled at him, "Why are you still here, old man? And what on earth are you babbling about?"

Tucker shuffled across the room and sank into the wing chair where, only moments ago, Lady Margaret had collapsed. His expression was troubled. "I heard them talking outside, Lucas. Peterson and that Bobek fella. You've been temporarily relieved of duty by order of the state's attorney general. Eli is the acting sheriff for the interim and the FBI has official jurisdiction of the Miller and Rockwell murder cases."

Lexie watched the shock register on Lucas's face and felt helpless to comfort him.

"But this is ridiculous. They can't do that!" Mo cast a harsh look at Tucker as if it were his fault. "You're still the sheriff, Lucas. It's just this one investigation."

"Just this one. The most important case of my life." His sky-blue eyes focused on Lexie. "I'm sorry, honey. I've managed to botch this whole thing."

When he strode across the hardwood floor toward the kitchen, she followed and stood watching as he paused beside the telephone, flipped open the local Yellow Pages, found a number and dialed.

Lexie couldn't for the life of her think of what she ought to say. Because of her interference, Lucas had been relieved of his duties. His authority as sheriff of Bluff County had been usurped.

This never should have happened. The decision to remove Lucas had been purely political, because of her father's power and Agent Peterson's complaints. Lucas Garrett had handled this investigation with tireless brilliance. He'd methodically tracked down clues and made intelligent deductions. But the fact remained: The attempted abduction and double murders had not been solved.

On the telephone, Lucas said, "This is Sheriff Garrett. Let me talk to Inez."

Lexie inched closer to him and placed the palm of her hand on his shoulder. Immediately, he turned and offered her a forced smile. Lexie put her arms around him and snuggled against his broad chest. Though they had only been apart for a few hours, she'd missed his touch.

"Inez," he said into the phone. "Do you remember that conversation we had the other morning? About the stranger?"

Lucas nodded while he listened. Then he said, "If you see him again, don't let him know you recognize him. This is real important, Inez. Are you paying attention?"

He nodded again. "Good. And if he comes in, get out of there as fast as you can and contact Sylvia. She'll patch you through to me wherever I am. Understand?" He smiled. "Thanks, Inez. Take care of yourself."

He hung up the telephone and looked down at Lexie. "I guess we have to trust the FBI to locate and apprehend Solé."

"And I thought we were doing so well on our own."

"We're a regular Sherlock Holmes and Dr. Watson," he said wearily. "Damn it, Lexie. I want this guy caught. I know how important this is to you."

"But not like before," she said. Now that she knew Hugh Miller had been in league against her, the deep feelings of guilt had been greatly alleviated. She regretted his death, as she would the death of any human being, but if Miller had sold out to a killer, then he'd put himself in danger.

"Lucas, I don't understand. If my supposed bodyguard was in on a plot to kidnap me, why was he killed?"

"More than likely, he was double-crossed," Lucas said.

"According to Peterson, Miller was planning on a million-dollar payoff for his part in your kidnapping. From what we know of Seth Rockwell, I'm guessing he demanded an even bigger share and probably convinced Miller to do the same. If they demanded more money, Solé might have decided it would be easier to eliminate them both. Of course, I believe he would have killed them anyway."

"Because he doesn't leave witnesses," she said with a shudder. "Did you tell the FBI about Inez? So they could question her?"

He shook his head. "I don't want to take chances with Inez's safety. She saw a guy wearing a beard, and it was just for a minute. What if they drag her in for questioning and she can't make a positive identification? No one knows what Solé looks like. He could be watching her, even now. If Solé sees the FBI questioning Inez, he won't hesitate to kill her."

She rested her head against his broad chest. Below his rib cage, she could hear his heart beating strong and steady. He seemed solid as a rock, confident in his abilities, in his proud identity as a Garrett. Even with his badge temporarily taken from him, Lucas still knew who he was, where he'd come from and where he belonged.

In contrast, Lexie had felt cut adrift her whole life, with no real home, no real family. Her roots, her heritage, her title all came from St. Novia, but there was no place there for her. No chance for real happiness as a princess.

"So, what now, Lucas? What are you going to do?"

"I'll do what I can to protect Inez, of course. And I'll see what I can find out from Eli about the investigation. I can't be a real part of it, now, Lexie. There's no way I can defy an order from the attorney general's office."

She understood that even a man as independent as Lucas had to heed certain boundaries.

"What about you?" he asked. "There's no real reason

for you to stay here, now. Agent Peterson is so intent on pleasing your father, he won't involve you in any way in the investigation. You won't be questioned or even asked to identify a suspect if one is apprehended.''

''I know,'' she said unhappily.

''But if you're still interested, I'd like you to stay.''

Her heart skipped a beat. Had she heard him correctly? ''What?''

''I think we need the chance to get to know each other better.''

''What are you saying, Lucas?''

''I care about you, Lexie. Last night—'' He exhaled a long sigh. ''I don't want you to leave. I want to explore the possibilities. Together. Our possibilities, honey.''

Together. ''Lucas, I don't know what to—''

He pressed a finger gently to her lips. ''Don't say anything. Don't tell me about the trials of loving a princess or becoming part of your very special life, because none of that matters. All that matters is that I think I'm falling in love with you.'' He gazed into her eyes and let that amazing declaration register before he added. ''And if I had to guess, I'd say you were falling in love with me, too.''

''Oh, Lucas. I want to believe....''

''Then do,'' he said and kissed her. ''Believe it, Princess Honey, and remember that nothing else matters. Not your father, not St. Novia. None of that matters. Just the two of us, Lexie. We can make this work. I know we can.''

''Show me,'' she begged him. ''Convince me, Lucas. I want to believe we can make it happen.''

He ducked his head and kissed her again. The insistent pressure of his lips against hers tantalized her senses, and she opened her mouth to receive him more fully.

Sparks of desire ignited her memory of last night—the most wonderful night of her life. How could anything come between her and something that felt so right?

He drew away from her. "Convinced?"

"Yes," she whispered.

He smiled. "Then you'll stay?"

"My father is going to keep pushing me to leave. And if I stay, he's going to insist I need protection."

"I'll be your bodyguard, round-the-clock protection, guaranteed." His smile was sexy and filled with promise.

"I'm sorry my father was so rude to you, Lucas," she said sadly.

"I'm willing to cut him some slack. It had to be a shock, even for a king, to walk in on his daughter the way he did this morning." He took her hand to lead her out of the kitchen and into the hallway. "In his way, I think he cares for you more than you know, Lexie."

They joined the others in the living room where the conversation was lively. The ranch foreman, Virgil Blackburn, had come in from the barn and was hearing a recap of Will's heroics.

Later, when Eli Ferguson came in from the porch to hear the story repeated, Lexie had the feeling that a brand-new Garrett legend was about to be born: The day Will Garrett chased King Frederick of St. Novia and the FBI off Destiny Canyon Ranch.

Sitting between Lucas and Will on the sofa, Lexie felt like part of the family, especially when Cal started teasing her about being a princess. But this easy time could only last for so long on a working ranch. Virgil and Cal soon headed back outside. Mo returned to the kitchen to prepare lunch and Tucker followed her.

When Lexie and Lucas were alone with Will, he sighed and leaned his head back against the sofa cushion. "I knew the good Lord was letting me hang around a few more days for a reason."

"To threaten the FBI and the king of St. Novia with a gun?" Lucas asked teasingly.

"No, son. I'm talking about the two of you," Will said. "For years I've wanted to see you settle down, Lucas. And now I see you've finally found the right woman."

Lucas beamed, but Lexie only wished she felt as sure.

"Do you really think we have a chance, Mr. Garrett? My background makes things difficult."

"It's Pop," he corrected her. "And of course you have a chance. You've got every chance in the world. When Rose and I started out...well, if there were ever two people with more going against them, I don't know who it would have been." He sighed, seeming suddenly even older than his years. "But that's old history," he said. "The point is, you two have the power to determine your future. It's up to you. If you love each other, nothing can stop you from building a wonderful life together."

"Nothing will," Lucas promised. "Not if we decide it's what we want."

Will slapped his knee. "So, you've already talked about it. Good."

"I'm glad you're happy...Pop," Lexie said.

Beside her, Lucas couldn't stop smiling.

"But there's one thing bothering me," Will said. "I just ran your father out of my house with a shotgun. That's no way for Lucas to start a relationship with his in-laws."

Lexie couldn't imagine King Frederick joining this warm, easy-going family. Among other things, her father was much too easily affronted for all the Garrett family teasing. "He'll get over it," she said.

"It's not right," Will said firmly. "Remember, Lexie, when we talked before. You can't run away from your problems. You've got to stand up to them and face them head-on."

All her life, she'd tried to avoid confrontation with her father. Either she acquiesced to his demands or she'd worked around him by moving to Boston or signing up for more college courses. She couldn't recall a single instance when they'd discussed a situation and found a way to compromise.

Perhaps she'd been unfair to him. Maybe if she took the time to really explain how she felt, her father might understand. "I'll talk to him," she promised.

"Lexie, honey." Lucas squeezed her hand. "You don't have to put up with his dictatorial ways."

"I know. And I won't. But your dad is right. I need to make peace with my father if I intend to really get on with the independent life I keep saying I want."

"If that's how you feel, I'll support you." Lucas rose to his feet. "Let's get it over with."

She stood beside him. "I appreciate the offer, but this is something I need to do by myself. He's staying in town."

"I'll have Eli drive you when my other deputy comes to relieve him. I need to go see Inez and then I'll drive out to my place and wait for you." He kissed her and then walked with her to the door.

As she watched him walk away, Lexie could only hope just knowing Lucas would be waiting for her would be enough to sustain her through the confrontation with her father.

ONCE IN TOWN, it wasn't difficult to figure out where King Frederick of St. Novia was staying. Two stretch limousines were parked outside a charming two-story bed-and-breakfast house. As Eli pulled his SUV to the curb, Lexie inhaled a deep breath, attempting to fill herself with fresh air for courage. "Thanks for the ride."

"I'll be right here when you're ready to go back." He pulled his sunglasses down on the end of his nose and peered over the rim.

"I'm sure my father can arrange to take me back to the ranch."

"No way. Lucas would have my hide if I left you in

anyone else's care'' Eli said. ''Let's don't forget there's still a murderer at large.''

With that ominous warning still in mind, Lexie walked across the threshold of the B & B. Immediately upon entering the beautifully decorated home, she was greeted by the two men who had accompanied her father this morning. The one she remembered as Harris ushered her into a private sitting room, lovingly decorated with ornate Victorian furnishings. Her father sat in a perfectly restored Chippendale chair beside a claw-foot table where he sipped tea from a delicate china cup.

He had removed his ornate blue uniform jacket, and was dressed in khakis and a knit shirt that made him seem much more human, more approachable.

Unfortunately, when he spoke, he exuded the formal air that kept everyone—even his daughter—at arm's length. ''Ah, I see you have come to your senses, Alexandra. I had a feeling you might.''

''Indeed, I have come to my senses, Father.''

She approached the table but did not sit until he offered, ''And just in time for tea. Won't you join me?''

''Thank you.''

Now that she was actually here, she didn't know if she could go through with her good intentions. What had made her think she could really talk to this man? She busied herself pouring from the matching china teapot and adding sugar, cream and lemon. Where to start? Years of emotional distance stretched between them and left her tongue-tied.

Without knowing what she intended to say, Lexie opened her mouth and said, ''Did you love my mother?''

His eyes widened in surprise. ''Your mother was a perfect lady, a perfect queen. Gracious, knowledgeable, sophisticated. She handled her position with style, grace and perfect aplomb.''

''But did you love her?''

"I respected her more than any other person I'd known before. Or met since, for that matter."

"But did you—"

"Yes, Alexandra," he interrupted. "I loved her."

Though his statement sounded a lot like an official press release, it was a start. "Then, you understand what it is to be in love."

He held up one hand. "I can see where this is heading and I don't want to hear it, Alexandra. One night of passion does not equal love."

She persisted. "I don't want to leave him, Father."

"Alexandra, please—"

"At first, I thought I needed to stay because I had a responsibility to do what I could to help the authorities apprehend my bodyguard's killer. To an extent, that was a valid reason. But now I realize that there was something even more important holding me here."

"Say no more." He made a slashing motion with his hand, cutting off her words. "That's quite enough. I'm sorry, Alexandra," he said, his tone softening perceptibly, "but I don't want to hear this."

He didn't touch her, didn't take her hand. In fact, other than polite kisses on her cheek her father had never expressed any real affection toward his youngest daughter.

Okay, it's up to me. She rose from her chair and circled the table, stood before him and reached for his hand and held it between both of hers. "You're my father," she said. "And I love you."

She stared at him a moment, then bent at the waist and hugged him. It felt awkward and unnatural, but Lexie persisted. He didn't respond, didn't return her embrace, but he didn't pull away, either.

After a moment, Lexie stood and stepped back. His eyes—the same unique violet color as her own—seemed filled with uncertainty. "I...love you, too, Alexandra."

A burst of laughter tickled the back of her throat. "Now, that wasn't so painful, was it?"

"Alexandra, I must say, I don't understand."

"There's nothing very complicated about it, Father. I'm your daughter and you're my dad and once in a while it's good to remember what we mean to each other."

"Of course," he said. "And the hugging, too. Maybe we should do that more often, as well."

Lexie laughed again and resumed her seat. "Probably." It was a beginning, she told herself, feeling more light-hearted and hopeful than she had in years.

She lifted her cup and took a sip of tea.

"Alexandra, we must talk."

"Of course. That's part of it, too."

"No," he said, his expression growing serious and fore-boding. "I mean, I have something unpleasant to discuss with you. Please try to understand, this is not something I want to do. It is not my wish to hurt you. But because you are my daughter and I am your father, there are things I must tell you, things you won't want to hear."

On an impulse, Lexie reached for his hand across the table and squeezed it. "All right, Father. What is it?"

King Frederick returned the slight pressure of her touch and then withdrew his hand. "This man...this Lucas Garrett, he is not what he seems."

Lexie couldn't have agreed more. At first impression, Lucas appeared to be merely the most handsome man to walk the face of the planet. It was only after she'd gotten to know him that she'd come to appreciate his depth of character and his intelligence.

"Two days ago," her father said, "Fulton Bobek informed me that there seemed to be a relationship building between you and the sheriff. I immediately enlisted the aid of St. Novian intelligence to research the background of the

Garrett family. As you know, this is standard procedure whenever any of you children becomes...emotionally involved.''

Of course, she knew. Her father's ''research'' had put an end to several ill-advised and potentially embarrassing relationships for her older brothers and sisters. ''I'm not worried,'' she said. ''The Garretts are salt-of-the-earth people. Hardworking and completely honest. Lucas would've told me of any dark, horrible secrets in his past.''

''If he knew.''

A tightness constricted her lungs. ''What are you trying to say, Father?''

''In choosing a mate, bloodlines are all-important. Though you may never sit upon the throne, one of your heirs might.'' He scowled darkly. ''At the rate your brothers and sister are going, I doubt that any of them will find an acceptable spouse. It is entirely possible that you will be the only one of my children to produce a suitable heir to my throne.''

''Father, what is it? What are you trying to say? That the Garrett bloodline is unworthy?'' She came to her feet, emotion burning her cheeks. ''I won't listen to this. I don't know why I came here. I should have known—''

''Sit down, Lexie.''

Hearing him address her by her shortened name caught her by surprise and she sank into the chair without argument.

''In all likelihood, Lucas Garrett does not know the secrets of his family's past. It is my understanding that his father and mother, Will Garrett and his wife, Rose, kept the episode to themselves. Their shame was buried deeply, beneath years of cover-ups and forged records. But the truth was finally uncovered in the records of a custody case brought before the Bluff County court some thirty years ago. And it was within those records that the dark truth was revealed.'' He sighed and an expression of dread moved like a cloud across his ruddy features.

"Alexandra, I'm sorry to have to tell you. Will Garrett is not Lucas's father. Rose Garrett was raped. Her son, Lucas, is the product of that rape. Lucas Garrett is a bastard."

Lexie momentarily stopped breathing. *This could not be true.* The core of Lucas's identity rested on the bedrock of the Garrett name. He felt justifiably proud of his roots, of his father's name. Family ties meant the world to him. This strange twist seemed too unbelievably cruel to be true and she told her father as much when at last she could find the strength to speak.

"But I'm afraid it is all too true." The king shook his head. "I wish it were otherwise, for your sake. But I assure you, I've demanded the story be checked and double-checked. I went so far as to contact the family doctor—a Doctor Rogers—myself. He was the physician who tended Rose Garrett the night of the...attack. He was there when Will and Rose made the decision not to report the crime. And he was there, nine months later, when he delivered the child. That child, Lucas, is not a Garrett by blood."

Lexie drew in a ragged breath. "Are you sure he doesn't know?"

King Frederick nodded. "I must say, Will Garrett is quite a man. To have raised the bastard child as if he were his own son takes an unusual character. But the fact remains, Alexandra. Lucas Garrett would not be an appropriate mate for you, nor a fit addition to our royal bloodline. Not to mention the heyday the press would have with this kind of scandal."

Her hands knotted at her throat, and she pressed hard, trying to force herself to breathe, to think. "What if...what if I said I didn't care?"

"But we both know what's at stake. It isn't just you, Alexandra. Think of the family. His family, as well as your own. You have no choice but to end this relationship. If not for yourself, for your family, do it for the Garretts." He paused to allow his words to sink in. "Just thinking of the tabloid frenzy makes me shudder."

In her mind, she could already see the headline: The Princess And The Bastard. Lucas would be devastated. "I could never put him through that."

"Then you understand what you must do," he said.

She nodded, numbly, feeling shell-shocked and stunned by the information her father had imparted to her. To pursue a relationship with Lucas would mean his ultimate destruction. She had no choice but to leave Destiny, Colorado, to leave Lucas Garrett and never return.

With her mind still reeling, she stiffened her spine and walked out of the bed-and-breakfast. Her royal facade was firmly in place, the iron mask she would be forced to wear for the rest of her life.

Chapter Fourteen

Fully engaged in his alter-ego identity, Ian Solé entered The Timbers Café. Watching him go about his day-to-day life, no one would suspect he was the internationally known killer. The mastermind criminal who had evaded capture and identification for the past ten years. No one had come close to unmasking him. No one ever would.

He enjoyed immeasurable satisfaction knowing he was the best that had ever been. But, at times, he experienced a loneliness that might have undone a lesser man. A less motivated man.

If his life had gone in another direction, if he'd just once received the respect and accolades he deserved, he might not have resorted to his mercenary activities. He would have been proclaimed a hero instead of an infamous killer for hire. But now was hardly the time for second thoughts.

This was the time to measure every step, watch every word and prepare himself for the grand finalé.

As he sat in the booth, across the table from his companion, he marveled at how inconspicuous he had become. To all the world, he was a harmless nobody, placing his order for a cheeseburger without onions and a glass of iced tea. For an ordinary man in a similar circumstance, it might have been enough to have evaded capture, once again. But Ian Solé was not an ordinary man. And the need to complete the plan that had been so ridiculously interrupted by the unpredictable Princess Alexandra burned within him. Never had he experienced such chaos in the midst of a caper. Never, once it had begun, had he aborted a mission.

And the planned abduction of Alexandra Dubois would not be the first.

Thinking back, he wondered if perhaps it had been a mistake to kill both Rockwell and Miller before he had the princess in his grasp. There would have been time enough after the physical abduction to eliminate them both. But Rockwell's greed had enraged him, insulted him. Petty criminals disgusted Solé. They were irrelevant, unnecessary. They gave experts like him a bad name.

The notorious killer affected a placid demeanor, while inside he grew restless to collect the five million dollars he would demand for the princess's return. It wasn't the money—he had already amassed a respectable fortune from his many other exploits. But this final score would put him in a league all his own. In the annals of law enforcement, no one had ever dealt with the likes of Ian Solé.

He'd decided this would be his last venture. The premature killing of his cohorts and the overwhelming moment of rage when he'd felt driven to destroy all of Alexandra's belongings had convinced him it was time to retire. Although he was still head and shoulders above any of his peers, he knew deep down he was losing his edge, becoming too emotional. Emotional men made mistakes. No one knew that better than he. Without even realizing it, the small-town sheriff had almost entrapped him.

"Here we are." The waitress returned to the table. She placed the orders in front of him and his companion.

"That's fried chicken for you. And a cheeseburger with no onions for you, right?"

Solé glanced at the waitress and nodded and instantly spotted the flicker of recognition in the woman's eyes. Had she made the connection with Rockwell? Impossible! He'd been well disguised that night. It was only his nerves playing tricks on him.

He glanced down at the name badge pinned to her uniform. "Thank you, Inez."

Her smile was bright and friendly. Yes, it had simply been a case of nerves. He'd only imagined that she'd recognized him and made the connection to the dinner he'd shared with his sleazy cohort the night before Hugh Miller's death.

But even as he carried on mundane conversation with his companion and smiled as the waitress refilled his glass, that look haunted him. What was she thinking?

The moment of decision was upon him. He could easily eliminate the waitress or proceed and take his chances. If he chose to kill Inez, that meant another loose end in a plan that seemed to have been unraveling before his eyes almost from the beginning.

How many more ragged ends could he afford to leave before the FBI and the persistent Sheriff Garrett uncovered his identity?

The waitress smiled when she brought the check, and Solé felt an imaginary noose tightening around his throat. He couldn't afford any more mistakes, couldn't afford wasting another day in this backwater town, teaming with potential witnesses and lawmen. He had to act and act fast, grab the reluctant princess and complete the crime of the century.

He pushed aside his half-eaten sandwich, dabbed his mouth with the paper napkin and said to his companion, "Catch the check, will you? I have to get going." Feeling an unaccustomed and unwelcome surge of desperation, Ian Solé fled the diner before his companion could respond.

When he stepped outside into the sunlight, he steeled himself against the tide of emotion that threatened to destroy him. By the time he was on the road again, he felt better; the old confidence had returned. He was the infamous Solé, master criminal, ever strong and triumphant. He would finish this job and he would not fail. Not now. Not ever. If he had to take out a simple waitress, so be it. And that went for the pesky sheriff and the Garrett family, as well. He would get to Princess Alexandra, this time, and nothing and no one would stop him.

LUCAS FINISHED the chores around the house and tended his horses while he waited for Lexie's return. Miss Molly still hadn't foaled and the vet had said she could go as long as another week. No point in worrying. Nature would take her own sweet time. Some things in life just couldn't be forced. Couldn't be planned or predicted. They just happened. Like Lexie.

Though he hadn't been expecting it or seen it coming, the woman had hit his life with the impact of an emotional tidal wave. He smiled, realizing that in some ways, Lexie was a force of nature unto herself—impossible to control, unstoppable, but yet as lovely as the delicate petal of the native Columbine.

He tilted back in the chair on the porch and stared across the meadow. For the rest of his life, he knew thoughts of Lexie would never be far from his consciousness. But this evening, the beautiful blond wasn't the only thing on his mind.

There was something about the investigation that bothered him. Something that nagged at the back of his mind and his lawman's instincts told him that he was on the brink of a solution.

The vanishing BLM truck bothered him. They'd put out the APB right away, and his deputies had searched half the county. If the vehicle had been on any road in the area, his deputies would have spotted it by now.

As Agent Browning had suggested, the killer might have left the area, but Lucas didn't think so. The ransacked cabin the day after Hugh Miller's killing confirmed it in Lucas's mind. Had Solé used a second vehicle? A rental? Maybe the green pickup, driven by Ramon Acardi. Was it possible that the tabloid photographer could be an internationally feared killer?

Lucas reviewed the information. Ian Solé was a faceless phantom. He never left a witnesses. He'd never come close to being caught. And he never gave up. Somewhere in that narrow profile there had to be an answer to the man's identity, some clue as to what he would do next. In the past few hours, Lucas had become convinced the international mercenary was the killer. Agent Peterson's unshakable conviction, along with the forensic evidence seemed to leave little doubt.

And now all the FBI had to do was find the man and stop him. But how? Although he'd officially been removed from the case, Lucas knew he wouldn't rest until he had the answer to that question. Solé had to be apprehended. Lexie's life depended on it.

Rocky's low growl drew Lucas's attention to a vehicle at his gate. It was Mo in her Jeep with Tucker Oates sitting beside her.

"Quiet, Rocky." Lucas scratched the tuft of fur between the tawny dog's ears. "I know you're not too fond of Tucker, but try to put up with him. For Mo's sake."

Although Lucas couldn't guess why, somewhere deep in his sister's bountiful heart, she cared for the old reprobate. He was the only man she'd ever loved. Good old big-mouth Tucker with his red suspenders and scraggly beard. Who knew, someday, Mo might actually take pity on the old guy, and agree to marry him and spend the rest of her life trying to fatten him up.

But not today. When they parked and came toward the porch, Lucas could see that Mo was obviously annoyed at something and he figured it was a good bet that something was Tucker.

Her lips were puckered up tight and she actually shoved Tucker's shoulder when they got to the porch. "Go ahead, you old billy goat. Apologize."

"Well, hell," Tucker drawled. "A man makes mistakes. But I swear, Lucas, I didn't mean no harm."

"Okay." Slowly, Lucas nodded. "But do you mind telling me what this is all about?"

Mo poked him again. "Show him."

Reluctantly, Tucker unfolded the tabloid newspaper he had tucked under his arm and placed it Lucas's lap. "It's today's edition of *The Exposé*."

A grainy photograph of Lucas himself stared back at him from the front page of the paper. The headline said: Reluctant Princess In Love Tryst With Cowboy Cop.

Unsure whether he should be amused or outraged, Lucas scanned the accompanying article which gave a sketchy description of the murder of Lexie's so-called bodyguard and the abduction attempt. He was referred to as "the strong, silent type" and the "dashing small-town cowboy sheriff."

"Dashing?" he mumbled. "That's a new one."

"I wouldn't blame Lucas if he locked you up and threw away the key," Mo declared. "Having his picture plastered all over the country. Blabbing his private business."

"Aw, now, Mo...it ain't all that bad," Tucker insisted. "I wouldn't care if it happened to me. In fact, it might be kind of fun."

"Well, it isn't any fun for Lucas. Or Lexie either!" Mo glared at him. "Tell him, Lucas. Set the old fool straight."

"I can't say that I like it," Lucas replied honestly. Having his face staring out from every grocery checkout stand was an uncomfortable feeling. He was naturally inclined to keep his business to himself. "But it's not all that big a deal, Mo. Not really. It'll pass. By next week, it'll be someone else people are gossiping about. Nobody'll even remember the *dashing* Lucas Garrett.''

But it wouldn't be so easy for Lexie. She'd had to fight this invasion of privacy every day of her life.

She'd tried to explain it to him, what it was like living in a fishbowl. This small splash of notoriety gave him an inkling of what she had been trying to explain.

''All in all, I don't think I care for being famous,'' he said. ''And I know it's difficult for Lexie.''

From inside his house, the telephone rang, and he left Tucker and Mo on the porch while he went to answer. It was the reporter from the local newspaper, asking if he wanted to share his reaction to the article in *The Exposé*. As soon as he said, ''No comment,'' and hung up, the phone rang again.

This time, it was a woman he'd dated four years ago. She wanted to know if it was true that he was involved with a princess.

After the third call, Lucas turned off the ringer and turned on the answering machine. He wasn't about to waste anymore time dodging questions about his personal life.

When he returned to the porch, he glared at Tucker. ''Maybe I should think again about locking you up, for everyone's sake.''

''Sorry, Lucas. I didn't mean to cause you or Lexie any trouble.''

''You weren't thinking,'' Mo said. ''Just like always, you went off half-cocked.''

''How many times do I have to apologize? There's nothing I can do about it now.''

Still scowling, Mo turned to Lucas. ''While I'm here, how about I rustle up some dinner for you?''

It was only four o'clock in the afternoon, but Lucas didn't object. His sister needed to work off some of her anger, and the way she generally accomplished that was by cooking something delectable. "Thanks, Mo. You know where to find everything."

"Grab an apron, you old coot," Mo ordered Tucker. "You might as well put yourself to good use."

Once again, Lucas found himself alone, waiting on the porch, staring nervously toward the road. Though he hadn't consciously decided to be a sentinel, he knew he'd be useless at anything until she came back and he found out how her conversation with her father had gone.

If King Frederick had convinced Lexie to return to St. Novia, Lucas wasn't sure what he'd do. Would he follow her? Well, why not? If she couldn't adjust to life in the West, maybe he could adjust to another country? The very thought of leaving his place startled him. Nothing and no one had ever tempted him to forsake the Garrett way of life. Until now.

But if he was to have a chance with Lexie, he had to be willing to make a few sacrifices. And he wanted that chance, believed with everything in him that all they needed was time to build a once-in-a-lifetime relationship, the kind of relationship that his mother and father had shared. The kind of relationship Lucas had been waiting for all his life.

When, at last, he spotted Eli's SUV, Lucas rose from his chair and started walking toward the gate. Rocky was right beside him, wagging his tail. "She's back, old man. I guess it takes more than a king to keep her away."

The mutt gave an enthusiastic yip.

Quietly, Lucas said, "Now, all we have to do is convince her there's a way she can stay."

As soon as the car stopped, Lexie jumped out and started toward him. The mere sight of her filled Lucas with more happiness than he'd ever dreamed possible.

Lucas waved to his deputy as Eli turned his SUV around and pulled back out onto the road.

Then Lucas turned, scooped Lexie up into his arms and

off the ground and spun her around in a wide circle. In that moment, they were the center of a bright, shining universe. Nothing outside them existed. It was just the two of them. Life was good. The future held nothing but promise.

They walked together to the porch and he held her pretty face in his hands and kissed her. "So, tell me," he said finally. "How did he take it, when you told him you were determined to stay?"

The next thing he knew, she'd started to cry. The tears slid unchecked down her ivory cheeks.

"Lexie, honey! What happened? What did he say to you? What did he do?" He was ready to fight.

She shook her head and swallowed hard. "He—he didn't do anything."

"Wait a minute," Lucas said, "it's not that stupid tabloid, is it? Because if it is, you're wasting your tears. It doesn't matter. It's a picture and a ridiculous story. It's not important. Really."

She brushed away her tears and blinked up at him. "What tabloid? What are you talking about?"

He reached down and picked up the copy of *The Exposé*. Lexie cringed. "Oh, Lucas. I'm so sorry. How could this have happened?"

"The day when Ramon Acardi showed up here, he snapped those pictures of me, remember? If I'd known it would upset you this much, I would've taken his camera and smashed the damn thing."

"It wouldn't have done any good," she said bleakly. "He'd just come back with another one. They always come back."

He shrugged. "But you see it doesn't matter. Let them come. I don't care if we have to deal with the likes of Acardi for the rest of our lives. It's worth it, isn't it? Just being together. We'll figure this out, Lexie. Trust me. They can't hurt us."

"You don't understand. And it's all my fault," she said. "I've disrupted your entire family. Because of me, you've been damaged professionally. And now this!" She threw the paper on the ground.

Sensing something far more than the tabloid article had upset her, Lucas caught hold of Lexie's hand and said, "Come on. Let's take a walk."

In silence, they strolled around the house to the barn and finally to the corral where they stopped to stand side-by-side watching the horses graze contentedly.

He looked down at her. "All right, honey. Tell me. What is it that has you so upset?"

She sighed and looked up at him with eyes so full of sadness Lucas felt his own heart ache in sympathy.

"This is so difficult. The hardest thing I've ever had to do. But I must tell you. I want you to hear it from me." She paced a few steps away from him. Her shoulders were trembling. "I swear, if this ever hits the tabloids…I couldn't bear what it would do to you."

"It's okay, honey. Whatever it is, I'll survive. It can't be that bad."

"But it is!" she declared. "And it's all my fault. I bring pain to everyone who cares about me."

He didn't want her to feel guilty about him. She'd carried needless remorse for too many years. "The tabloids are a joke. Forget about it. You haven't hurt me, Lexie."

"But I have." She sighed and swiped the tears from her eyes. "Do you remember how you once said there were worse things than dying?"

"I remember."

"This is one of those things, Lucas."

He leaned back against a fence post and folded his arms across his chest. No matter what she had to say, he could take it. "Tell me, Lexie."

"When my father heard there might be something between us, he had the St. Novian Intelligence Minister look into your background. We may be a small country, but our intelligence is connected with Interpol and the CIA. We have operatives all over the world. They've been trained by your own FBI and they're quite efficient.''

He smiled. ''Your father had all those international agencies shaking my family tree?''

''I'm afraid so.''

''Pop won't believe this,'' he said and shook his head.

''Unfortunately, he found something.'' She wrapped her arms around herself to still the shudder that shook her.

''What? What could he possibly find? To my knowledge, there aren't many skeletons rattling around in the Garrett closet.'' He would have smiled if not for her grave demeanor.

''It's about your parents.''

He couldn't imagine what she was talking about. ''Go on.''

''Your mother…you see, a long time ago, your mother was involved with a man who was obsessed with her. Even after she married your father, this man wouldn't leave her alone. He stalked her. He followed her to Colorado. He attacked her.''

Lucas felt a cold chill race down his spine.

''She was raped, Lucas.''

He felt like she'd driven a nail into his heart. His mother, Rose Garrett, had been raped. Lucas gritted his teeth. As bad as it was, he sensed there was even more. ''What else?''

''After the rape, she discovered she was pregnant.''

Lucas felt as if he'd been gut-shot. ''Go on,'' he managed.

''With you, Lucas. She was pregnant with you.''

His mouth went dry and he felt strangely light-headed. Without realizing what he was doing, he took a step toward her. His hands were clenched at his side. ''Are you telling me my biological father, my real father, is a rapist? Are you telling me Will Garrett is not my father?''

"They kept the secret between them, told no one but Doc Rogers. They put Will's name on your birth certificate. But later, when you were just a toddler, to spite them, your biological father filed a custody suit. After all those years, he was still trying to make trouble for your folks. The whole story is in a deposition taken from Rose in a Kansas City lawyer's office.''

Lucas was struck dumb. His world tilted on its axis. If what Lexie said was true, his entire identity, his whole life had been based on a lie.

Slowly, he turned away from her and gazed with unseeing eyes at the animals. Their breeding was pure, carefully documented from generation to generation. And Lucas respected that lineage.

Everything was a product of what came before. Lucas Garrett, the sheriff of Bluff County, was the son of a rapist, the lowest form of criminal.

"It can't be,'' he said his voice hoarse with emotion. "Pop—he never treated me like anything but his son.''

"He's an incredible man.''

Lucas's emotions reeled, his pride lay shattered at his feet. His life was a sham. "He's a damned liar! Damn it! Why didn't he tell me?''

"I don't know, Lucas,'' Lexie said quietly.

"Well, I'm going to find out.'' With that, he stormed past her toward the house.

Inside, the answering machine blinked wildly, signaling half a dozen messages. But anger and shock blinded Lucas to everything but his burning need to confront Will Garrett.

"Keep an eye on her,'' he ordered Mo and Tucker. "Don't let her out of your sight until I get back.''

"Where you headed, Lucas?'' Tucker asked.

But Lucas didn't answer. He couldn't. A lump the size of

Mount Destiny had formed in his throat. An angry mix of confused emotions propelled him out of the house, past the silent and staring Lexie.

Minutes later, with a single question searing his brain, he steered the SUV onto the highway and headed for Destiny Canyon Ranch and the answer that would change his life forever.

Will was sitting on the porch in an easy chair when Lucas pulled up in front of the ranch house. A plaid blanket had been draped over his lap and smiled at Lucas when he saw him coming up the walk. Lucas did not smile back.

"Son," Will greeted him, but Lucas merely stood staring down at the old man who was either the self-same man his children had always thought him to be or a bald-faced liar. The time had come to find out, but for a few seconds Lucas seemed unable to find the words. All he could do was stare at the old man who matched his gaze with a questioning expression. In the corner of Lucas's mind, hope urged him to go on looking. To keep searching for some glimmer of himself in Will Garrett's care-worn face that would dispel all the doubt, return Lucas's life as he'd always known it, and breath the life back into his numbed senses.

"What is it, son?" Will asked, his voice betraying his deep concern over Lucas's strange behavior. "What's happened? Is Lexie all right?" He half rose out of his chair, so great was his concern.

When he finally spoke, Lucas addressed Will through clenched teeth, "I'm only going to ask you once. And I want the truth." He paused, everything in him hoping and praying Will could and would deny the story Lexie had told him. "Are you my biological father?"

Will's mouth opened slightly and an expression of sadness Lucas would never forget crept over his face. As several seconds of silence ticked by Lucas knew he already had his answer.

"Rose was your mother," Will said, finally. "The day you were born, I gave you my name and have been proud to call you my son ever since." He swallowed hard, but kept his gaze locked on Lucas's face. "I've loved you from the minute you were born, Lucas. I love you now."

Lucas steeled himself against the emotions Will's uncharacteristic declaration evoked. "Why didn't you tell me I wasn't yours?"

"Your mother…" He did look away, then, to gaze off at the peaks in the distance. "At first, I thought we should call the police. But Rose—she just couldn't relive it all again. Try to understand, son."

Lucas winced at the word.

"Lucas, please. She couldn't go through it all again with the authorities, but she couldn't give up her child, either. It wasn't her fault, Lucas. It wasn't anything she brought on herself. But she was ashamed. I kept quiet for her sake. She made me promise we would keep that one secret between us always, that we would take it to the grave." He sighed and slumped down lower in his chair. Had Lucas not been so distracted by his own grief, he might have grieved the poor health that had never been more evident on Will's face than it was at the moment.

"She was one in million, Lucas. She didn't deserve the horrible thing that was done to her that night. No woman does."

And what does that make me? The product of my mother's worst nightmare. His father was a rapist.

"I had a right to know." The sound of his own voice rang cold and thin in Lucas's own ears. I had a right to know, he repeated himself. A right to know about his tainted heritage, his shameful pedigree. The blood flowing through his veins held the stain of a vile criminal. "How could you let me live a lie?"

"Lucas, listen to me. son, please—"

"I'm not your son."

"Please, Lucas. Think about what you're saying. Has it been so bad?" Will leaned toward him, pleading. "Being Lucas Garrett? Carrying my name." His veined and knotted hands gripped the sides of his chair.

"It's not my name," Lucas said flatly. "And you're not my father." With that, he turned and walked away.

LEXIE WAS WAITING outside by the corral when Lucas drove in. Her heart felt shattered in a million pieces. In a few minutes, she would be forced to say goodbye to only man she'd ever really loved. What choice did she have but to leave? To stay would mean exposing Lucas to the kind of pride-shattering ridicule that would destroy a man like him. Eventually, he'd grow to hate her as the source of all that humiliation.

She watched him climb out of the SUV and cross the distance between them. She drank in the sight of him, memorizing the expanse of his broad shoulders, the curves of his muscular arms and tight, narrow hips. She cherished every feature, his blue eyes and black hair, his courageous heart. Later, when she was alone, she would recall every part of him. Every moment they'd shared.

He walked past her without meeting her gaze. He put a foot on the bottom corral rail and draped his arms over the top. "It's true."

"No one else need ever have access to this information, Lucas," she assured him. "My father promised the file would be sealed. He gave me his word."

"But I know, don't I, Lexie? And so do you. We both know I'm not the man you thought I was. In fact, we don't know who the hell I am, do we?" The anger radiated off him in waves.

"You're right. I do know you, Lucas," she said gently. "I know that what you told me last night was true, that a person is more than a name or a title. You're Lucas Garrett, the man who told me that together we could work anything out. You're the same man today that you were yesterday. Responsible. Brave. Intelligent. The biological makeup of your DNA changes nothing. You're a fine person, Lucas, the same fine person who made love to me last night.''

He still didn't look at her, but stood staring at his horses. ''Last night was a mistake.''

She choked back the crushing disappointment that felt like a hand at her throat. ''Yes,'' she managed. ''I guess it was.''

They stood for a moment in taut silence. Finally, Lexie took a step toward him, reached out and touched his arm. When she felt his muscle tense beneath her touch, her heart broke anew.

''You don't have to say anything, Lexie. Just go. I understand if you've changed your mind about staying.''

''No. I don't think you understand anything, at all,'' she informed him bitterly as she withdrew her hand.

''You'd better get going if you're going to make that flight with your father.''

He'd hurt her deeply, shattered her hopes and dreams with a single blow. She'd been a fool to hope he'd beg her to stay, to believe him when he'd said they could find a way to build a future together.

She turned to leave, but her heart stopped her. If she walked away without giving their love one last chance she knew she'd regret it the rest of her life. ''You said nothing mattered but the two of us,'' she reminded him, ''that together we could work through anything. Nothing's changed, Lucas. Don't you see? We're still the same people. You were right. Nothing else matters as long as we're together.''

She watched a muscle work in his jaw, but still he didn't look at her. ''I was wrong,'' he said firmly. ''I didn't know then who I was—what I was.'' He released a tired sigh and finally turned to face her. "Go on, Alexandra. Go home with your father. Everyone knows this is no place for a princess."

His words hit her with the force of a physical blow. She took a step backward and stumbled. Her legs felt numb. Her heart leaden.

Somehow, she managed to make her way to the house. In the kitchen she asked Mo if she could borrow the Jeep.

"What's the matter?" Mo asked. "Has Lucas been snapping at you? If he's upset about that tabloid, it should be Tucker he's growling at."

"I have to go," Lexie managed. If Lucas chose to share his true parentage with Mo, that would be his decision.

Mo handed her the keys. "Of course, Lexie. Lucas can take us back to the ranch house." Mo frowned. "You look upset, sweetie. Do you want me to drive you?"

Lexie shook her head and clutched the keys tighter. She would leave Mo's Jeep in town and have one of her father's minions return it. "No. I just...n-need to go."

She couldn't bear to look at Mo or even Tucker, knowing she would never see them again. The genuine concern in their eyes bruised her aching heart. This special moment in her life was over. The warm, loving home and family that she'd dreamed of joining would now hate her.

Her life would consist of strangers and bodyguards. Choking back a sob, she ran from the house toward Mo's ragtop Jeep.

Before she drove away, she took one last look at the handsome log home Lucas had built with his own hands. For a brief moment, she'd thought this place could be her home. That the man who'd built it with pride and love could be her destiny. What a cruel joke fate had played on them both.

Rocky trotted toward her, and she knelt to hug the tawny mongrel. She wrapped her arms around the dog, saying goodbye for the very last time. "Take care of him, Rocky."

Lexie climbed behind the wheel of the Jeep and started

the engine. She should have been sobbing, but her sorrow went too deep even for tears.

Navigating the ruts in the dirt road, she tried to create a memory of every twig and shrub. Each view of the landscape was precious because it belonged to Lucas. It was a part of him. A part of the life she would never share.

TEN MINUTES LATER, on the deserted two-lane road leading back to town, Lexie drove without thinking. She hadn't realized how slow she'd been driving until she saw the truck looming in her rearview mirror. The truck was going too fast. There was no way he could stop. The adrenaline shot through her when she realized a collision was inevitable.

Even as she stomped on the accelerator, she knew it was too late. She cried out, but the sound was lost in the sickening crash of metal against metal.

Chapter Fifteen

Lucas had heard the door slam. He'd watched Lexie run from the house and watched as she'd stopped to say goodbye to Rocky. At any moment, he could have called out to her and stopped her from leaving. He could have done whatever it took to convince her to stay.

Instead, he'd stood motionless where he was, immobilized by the revelation that had turned him inside out and stripped him of his identity and ravaged his pride.

He was a bastard, the product of a brutal rape. His mother's shame. The object of Will Garrett's pity. Lexie was a blueblood, a princess. What dirty trick of nature had caused their fates to collide?

The hollow ache inside him caused his heart to thud painfully in his chest. Who the hell was he? When he looked in the mirror, whose eyes would be staring back?

The blood that ran through his veins was the blood of a stranger. A criminal. A man without honor or pride. A man he'd never know but would despise for the rest of his life.

His dark thoughts were interrupted by the sound of Mo calling him to supper. Hearing her voice, the voice of the woman he'd thought was his sister, brought the reality of his changed life crashing down on him in a dozen different ways. From now on, everything would be different.

First and foremost, he had to pay Will Garrett for this

land, the land that had been deeded to him under false pretenses. That would be a first priority. There was no way he could continue as the sheriff of Bluff County. He'd resign his position immediately. How could he demand the respect of others when he no longer respected himself? He could never again be a lawman. But maybe it was just as well. He'd throw himself into raising his horses, take that early retirement he'd been working toward.

Retirement, he thought. *Retirement.* The word seemed stuck in his brain and it repeated itself over and over for seemingly no reason. As he turned it over in his mind, he had the nagging sense that he'd missed or forgotten something.

Someone else had used that word recently, hadn't they? It had been Agent Paul Browning. Lucas replayed the conversation in his mind and recalled the agent saying something about retiring to someplace with sandy beaches and trade winds. He'd mentioned retirement after he'd tried to convince Lucas that Solé was not involved in the murders. Well, hell. The agent was supposedly the expert, the individual who knew the most about the infamous criminal. If Browning thought Solé had left the county, then he probably had.

Then why did the conversation bother him, Lucas wondered. Especially now, when he had his own devastating personal crisis to deal with.

But thoughts of that conversation wouldn't go away. Something just didn't add up. Although information about Solé was scanty, what was known seemed carved in stone: The man was a brutal, cold-blooded mercenary. Until now, he had remained faceless to those who sought to bring him to justice. He was a marksman of uncanny ability. He had been involved in another kidnapping. He planned his crimes with meticulous attention to detail. He left no witnesses.

And he never gave up, never walked away from a plan once he'd committed to it.

"He never gives up," Lucas said to himself, staring out across the vast expanse of his ranch with unseeing eyes. But if that were true, if Solé considered it a point of pride to finish a job once he'd started, then why would Browning—the FBI agent with detailed profiling information on a known mercenary—believe that Solé had walked away from his one?

It was a simple question, but one for which Lucas could not conjure a logical answer.

Now, completely distracted from thoughts of his own problems, Lucas found himself suddenly refocused more keenly than ever before on the case that had brought Alexandra Dubois into his life.

He could at least give Browning a call, he decided, and ask him to explain why he thought Solé would walk away this time. Lucas told himself he had no illusions about trying to restore his career or even to assist in this investigation.

In essence, his career had been pulled out from under him, anyway. At this point, his resignation was almost unnecessary. The FBI and Eli would solve this case, he told himself. But a phone call to Browning was harmless enough. It would be nothing more than an attempt to satisfy his own curiosity.

He returned to the house, but mumbled an excuse when Mo asked him to sit down to supper.

Grabbing the phone, he dialed his office. When Sylvia answered, he asked, "Are the FBI agents still there?"

"That obnoxious Peterson is," she said in a low voice. "But Agent Browning hasn't come back from lunch."

Lucas glanced at his watch. "But it's nearly five."

"Maybe the Feds have better hours than the rest of us," Sylvia joked. "So, where are you, Lucas? I've been trying to reach you for an hour."

Only then did Lucas remember having turned off his phone's ringer. "I'm sorry, Sylvia. What's up?"

"Inez called from The Timbers looking for you. She said it was urgent. Here's the number."

Lucas disconnected the call to his dispatcher and punched in the number to The Timbers so fast his fingers slid from one number to the next. If his unprofessional conduct—first turning off the ringer and then wasting precious time wallowing in his own self-pity—had resulted in anything happening to Inez, he would never forgive himself.

When he recognized Inez's voice on the other end of the line, Lucas felt almost weak with relief.

"Geez, Sheriff, what took you so long?"

"I'm sorry, Inez. I just got your message. I take it you've seen him?"

"Sure did," Inez exclaimed in an excited voice. "He's shaved the beard and upgraded his wardrobe, but I'm sure it was the same guy. And you know what? I think he knows I recognized him. He had this kind of weird look in his eye. It was his eyes I recognized. Pale green, you know? With a kind of hungry look, like some wild animal."

"When was he there, Sylvia? How long ago?"

"Just a couple of hours."

"Do you have any idea who he is? Did he identify himself?"

"I don't know his name," Sylvia said. "But I can describe him right down to the black suit and white shirt," she said. "I think he's one of those FBI guys."

"Good Lord, Inez! Are you sure? Which one?"

"I'm sure, Sheriff. He's the older one, the one with the hair going gray."

Browning! The logic of his guilt came together quickly in Lucas's mind. Who better than an FBI agent to outsmart the agency? He had all the access to intelligence information, the inside track to every effort to track the infamous Solé.

Armed with that intelligence, Browning had outmaneuvered law enforcement's every strategy. In fact, he, himself, had probably designed some of them!

Who knew how long Ian Solé had been involved in his double identity? Planting false clues and misdirecting all efforts to put an end to his deadly crime spree. Just as he had today when he'd made a point of convincing Lucas that the killer had probably left the area.

Lucas's lawman's instinct told him he had the truth of Solé's identity, at last. And with Inez to back him up, he had an eye witness that put Agent Browning in Destiny a full day before the FBI. Agent Paul Browning was Ian Solé. Lucas would bank his career on it—that is, if he could reclaim that career. And suddenly, he knew he could and that he would.

"Inez, this man is extremely dangerous," Lucas warned. "Stay right where you are. I'm sending a deputy over to get you."

Lucas's next call was to his dispatcher. In moments, Lucas had Eli Ferguson on the phone and had ordered him to The Timbers to take Inez Estes into protective custody.

"She's ID'ed Solé," Lucas explained.

"Damn!" Eli said.

"It's none other than Agent Paul Browning."

"Double damn!"

"Don't take any chances, Eli. Solé is a cold-blooded killer. If you see him, shoot first and ask questions later."

After he finished talking to Eli, Lucas disconnected the call and headed for the door. He would call Sylvia on his radio and give the order to mobilize the rest of the Bluff County deputies.

He glanced over at Mo who was staring at him, wide-eyed. Even Tucker Oates had been shocked into silence by the events of this tumultuous evening.

For no real reason, Lucas gave Mo a brief hug on the way

out the door. "I don't have time to explain, but you've got to do as I say. Stay here. Lock the doors. If you see Agent Paul Browning, shoot the son of a bitch."

His hand was on the door when the telephone rang again. Lucas crossed the room and grabbed it.

"Garrett, here."

"Is Mo all right?" It was Sylvia again.

"Why wouldn't Mo be all right?"

"I just had a call reporting an accident. Burt found Mo's Jeep off the side of the highway near mile marker 320. It had obviously been in a collision, but no one was in the vehicle."

Lucas's heart stopped. Lexie!

WHERE AM I? Lexie's eyes opened slowly, but still she couldn't see. She couldn't move. She'd been blindfolded and hog-tied, her wrists bound and secured to the cords that held her ankles.

She was lying on her side, curled up in a ball, being jolted painfully. She was being transported in some sort of vehicle; she could feel the movement and hear the whine of an engine.

She tried to cry out, but the gag over her mouth muffled the sound.

"You're awake," a voice from somewhere out of the darkness said. "Good. I wondered if maybe the ether had worked too well this time. I hope you know you've been more trouble than you're worth, Princess Alexandra. I'll have to adjust my demands on your father to compensate for my trouble."

Her head bumped painfully against the cold metal floor. Desperately, she struggled to move her arms. It was impossible. She was helpless. Sheer terror raced through her. She couldn't see, couldn't breathe. The more she fought, the closer she edged to full hysteria.

Stop! She commanded herself. *Calm down. Breathe through your nose.*

Gradually, her mind cleared and she remembered the crash, the truck ramming her from behind. *The stolen BLM truck!* She remembered seeing the logo seconds before the crash.

And now she was a captive, the helpless prisoner of Ian Solé. The worst had happened.

"You should be honored," the voice said. "Your kidnapping is my final act as the infamous Solé, my swan song. Your name will forever be part of the annals of international intrigue."

Despair mingled with her fear. She would not survive this ordeal. Even after he'd collected the ransom, there was no way Solé could let her live. The precious moments of her life were numbered. She could expect no pity from the mercenary who had killed two men in cold blood.

She felt the truck grinding to a stop, but the motor was still running. She heard the door open. He had climbed out of the cab. His actions reminded her of the last time she'd gone through the gate to Lucas's house.

Oh, Lucas, why couldn't things have been different? Now, there really was no hope of ever seeing him again, of ever reconciling or building the kind of wonderful future she had so foolishly allowed herself to believe they might share.

Hot tears of despair sprang to her eyes and she felt the moisture seep into the blindfold that obliterated her vision. She choked back her sorrow and told herself she would not give this kidnapper the satisfaction of knowing how devastated and hopeless she felt. If death was her fate, she would die honorably, without hysterics and tears.

Seeking a place of inner calm to still her reeling emotions, she retreated into her mind and relived each moment of her short time with Lucas. Last night, she had experienced the kind of love some people searched a lifetime to find. She could almost feel his touch on her body, his hands so skillful and strong. In her ears, she imagined his voice whispering her name, as gentle as a caress. Through his sky-blue eyes, she'd seen a glimpse of a beautiful world, filled with possibilities, freedom and independence.

If this really was the end—if Solé was preparing to take her life—at least she had the memories of what it had been like to live. To really live. At least for awhile. And to love and be loved.

BEHIND THE WHEEL of his SUV, Lucas raced against time, pushing past speeds of one hundred all the way to town. Over the police radio, he yelled at Agent Peterson.

"The air search, when was it supposed to begin?"

"I don't know," he admitted. "Browning was supposed to have made all the arrangements, remember?"

Lucas felt like he'd been punched.

"And what's all this talk about Agent Browning? I heard your put out an APB on him. What's going on, Garrett? What kind of game are you playing?"

"It's not game, Peterson. Your man, Browning, is Ian Solé."

"What? Have you gone crazy?" Peterson shouted. "Browning has been an agent for twenty years. He's done some decent work, but he's not smart enough to pull off the kind of crimes you're talking about. Why, in twenty years, the man has only had three promotions."

Browning's motivation presented itself to Lucas in a flash of insight. In addition to his darker, more psychotic motives, Browning must have taken pleasure in deceiving the law enforcement agency that in his opinion had failed to acknowledge his true brilliance.

"I have a witness," Lucas said into the police radio. "Browning was seen in Destiny the day before the first killing and the abduction attempt. He met with Seth Rockwell.''

''Impossible. Browning wasn't even in this area.''

''Where was he?''

''He was in Denver.''

''Are you sure about that?''

''I talked to him.'' But there was a hesitation in Peterson's voice. ''On the phone, I mean. I left a message, and he called me back.''

''So, you don't know for sure that he was calling you from Denver.''

''No, but I had no reason to doubt his word. We met at the airport in Destiny because Browning said he wanted to fly his own plane in. He's a pilot, you know. With an old single-engine Cessna.''

Lucas careened to a halt at the side of the road. Browning was a pilot.

Suddenly, another piece of the puzzle came clear. The military training facility, twenty miles north of town, the deserted airstrip—it was the logical place for Browning to have taken Lexie. Browning could have flown in and out of there undetected, without filing a flight plan or leaving any incriminating records behind.

That's where he'd hidden the BLM truck! There were several outbuildings on the facility, and Lucas's deputies wouldn't have searched there. The area was secured by a chain-link fence, posted with No Trespassing signs.

Lucas gunned his engine and aimed in that direction. He was taking a chance, betting everything on his hunch that Solé was headed for the airstrip.

Lucas took note of his surroundings and realized he was only fifteen miles away. For a moment, he considered informing Agent Peterson of his conclusions, then he decided against it. Peterson would go after Browning with guns blazing and Lucas was unwilling to take even a small chance that Lexie could be caught in the cross fire.

The thought of any harm coming to Lexie curdled his blood. Panic and rage shimmered at the edge of his peripheral vision, but he told himself he had to keep his mind clear. He had to maintain control, keep his senses sharp if he was going to outsmart Solé and save Lexie. And he had to save her. A strange twist of fate had given him a second chance and he would not risk losing the woman he knew, with every fiber of his being, was his destiny.

His foot pressed the accelerator to the floor, but he didn't turn on the siren. The last thing he wanted to do was give Solé any warning.

Gripping the police radio in his free hand, he contacted Eli to arrange for backup.

THE TRUCK had stopped again. This time, Lexie sensed that they'd driven into some kind of building. A garage maybe. When her abductor slammed the car door, the sound echoed as though against metal.

The door on the passenger side was sprung open. Rough hands yanked at her body.

"I am going to untie your feet, Princess. You're going to walk to the airplane."

Her legs were pulled from the floorboard of the truck at a painful angle. Behind the gag, she made a muffled sound of protest.

"I'd planned to carry you, Your Highness," he said with mocking deference, "but I seem to have twisted my ankle when I ran your Jeep off the road."

A single thought formed in Lexie's mind and took full possession. She could not allow him to force her onto that plane. Once airborne, there would be no hope of rescue.

He finished untying her feet and dragged her body from the truck and propped her upright against the side of the truck. Blinded by the dark cloth over her eyes, Lexie felt dizzy and disoriented. She was only half-pretending when she allowed her legs to go limp and slid to the floor. She landed on concrete, hard. The surface was cold and unforgiving.

"Don't even try it, Princess." His tone was sharp. "I won't tolerate any games. At this point, it would be easier to kill you."

With his hands pulling at her arms, she staggered to her feet. He shoved her forward. "Get going," he ordered. Blindly, she stumbled, tripped and fell again.

"I can't see," she mumbled behind the gag.

"All right, all right," he said and ripped the blindfold from her eyes.

Though the light inside the airplane hangar was dim, it hurt her eyes. She squinted and focused on the face of FBI Agent, Paul Browning.

"Surprised?" he asked with a sneering smile. "Most people are. The few people who have had the privilege of learning Solé's real identity can't believe Agent Browning could be capable of anything more than detail work behind a computer screen. But they're wrong. All of them are wrong. Those details have allowed me free rein, carte blanche. Oh, and, by the way, Princess, none of them lived to set the record straight."

In Lexie's mind, he was making it clear he had no intention of letting her be the first.

Frantically, she scanned the building, searching for an exit. He'd said his ankle was hurt. If the opportunity presented itself, maybe she could outrun him.

"Get moving, Princess. Over there. Into that plane."

The small aircraft was only a few feet away. She had to act now. She had to escape. She wanted to live. More than anything, she wanted to live to have another chance at a future with Lucas Garrett, the man who would always be her only love.

PARKED AT THE TOP of a small rise, Lucas had the military training facility in sight. Four buildings, including a hangar, lay at the bottom of the hill some three hundred yards in the distance. The National Guard had used this place for winter maneuvers for as far back as Lucas could remember. The troops were flown here in snow gear and full backpacks for a twenty-five-mile survival exercise.

Solé must have gone through that training when he was stationed at the Air Force Academy in Colorado Springs. When he was planning his escape route, he must have remembered the facility. Lucas guessed the airstrip had been part of Solé's plan from the start and that meant Seth Rockwell had been in on the scheme from the beginning, arranging through Lord Roche to entice Lexie to the area.

And now, Solé was preparing the final phase of his scheme. He jogged down the hill to see the padlock on the chain-link fence had been broken, confirming his suspicion that Solé was somewhere on the facility.

With his sidearm in the holster and the rifle in his hand, Lucas made his way toward the hangar at the far end of the field.

His deputies would be arriving momentarily, but Lucas couldn't afford to wait. Every moment brought danger closer to Lexie. It took an act of sheer will not to be distracted by his thoughts of her. Later, he would let her know how deeply he regretted chasing her away. And right after that, he'd apologize to his father and beg Will to forgive him.

But now was not the time for self-recrimination. The last thing Lucas needed was a flood of emotion clouding his judgment.

Right now, he had but a single thought: Stop Ian Solé.

Quickly, silently, he moved around the outside of the old hangar. He was willing to bet everything he owned that Solé's plane was inside.

Behind the structure, Lucas decided that rather than risk charging inside and putting Lexie in even greater danger, he should wait to make his move until Solé pushed the wide metal doors of the hangar open in order to taxi the plane out onto the runway.

With every nerve in his body tensed, Lucas settled down to wait a few yards away, at the edge of one of the nearby shacks. He wanted the best possible view of the hangar. Crouched low, his eyes riveted on the hangar doors, he waited and prayed that the mercenary inside was feeling confident. Hopefully, Solé was just arrogant enough to think no one had yet figured out his identity and his plan. If his defenses were down, Lucas would at least have the advantage of surprise.

Within a few minutes, even as Lucas watched, the doors at the front of the hangar started to crack open in the middle. Paul Browning alias Solé limped as he dragged one heavy metal door to the side and returned for the other.

Inside the hangar, Lucas could see the plane. A white, single-engine Cessna. Parked just behind it was the missing BLM truck.

Carefully, Lucas took aim. His rifle wasn't a state-of-the-art weapon like the one Solé had used to eliminate his targets, but Lucas was a crack shot. This time, his aim would have to be perfect. There wouldn't be a second chance.

Suddenly, there was another figure outside the hangar. Lexie, with her wrists tied behind her back and a gag in her mouth, ran through the opened door.

Solé saw her dash past him and drew the automatic pistol from his shoulder holster and took aim.

Lucas squeezed his trigger. The sound of the rifle shot

split the quiet evening air at the same time Solés gun discharged.

With a scream of pain, Solé went down. Lucas saw blood spurting from the mercenary's thigh. His eyes scanned the tarmac and his heart froze when he didn't see Lexie. Dear God, if she had been shot, he would never forgive himself.

When he finally saw her, relief flooded him. She was alive and well and running as fast as she could, crouched like a trained soldier, moving through the thick underbrush beside the runway toward him.

Keeping his rifle trained on his prey, Lucas stepped out from his hiding place. "Throw your gun over here, Browning."

"Sheriff?" Unbelievably, Solé began to laugh. "Is that you?"

"I don't want to kill you, Browning, but I will. Throw the gun over here. Now."

The sound of laughter died. "Where's your sense of humor, Garrett? Don't you think this is ironic? With all the international law enforcement agencies searching for me, I'm caught by a backwoods county sheriff. A nobody!"

But that was where he was wrong. Lucas knew exactly who he was. He was a man who had been raised by a loving family who had taught him right from wrong and instilled in him a deep sense of duty and honor. In short, he'd been raised a Garrett. And that's who he was. Who he'd always be.

Lucas took his eyes off Solé as Lexie stumbled toward him. Blood matted on her forehead where Solés bullet had grazed her skin. She looked half-dazed, and the sight of her in pain tore at his heart. "Oh, Lexie!" He gathered her into his arms and held her, pressing her precious body against his heart.

What an incredible woman she was. Even in the face of mortal danger, she'd done what she had to do to survive. Without a doubt, she was the bravest woman he'd ever known. But if he had his way, she would never have to outsmart or outrun another pursuer. Never again would he allow her out of his sight. No matter what the consequences, he would love and protect her forever.

The sound of movement drew his gaze back to the killer. Solé had another gun. He pulled it. "Ian Solé never gives up." He aimed, but Lucas was quicker and when he fired again his bullet found Solés chest.

From the gate at the end of the field, Lucas heard the shouts of his deputies. They ran across the tarmac, headed toward Solé. Lucas barely registered the commotion. His full attention was focused on Lexie.

He threw down his rifle and tore the gag from her mouth.

Gulping for air, she collapsed against his chest. "I thought I was going to die."

He took out a pocketknife and cut the ropes binding her wrists. With her arms free, she embraced him.

"Lexie, I'm so sorry," he whispered into her silky hair. "I acted like a fool. My damn pride could have gotten you killed. Forgive me, honey."

"It was all my fault," she said. "I should never have left. I should have stayed and pounded some sense into your stubborn head."

"Promise you won't ever leave me, Lexie," he said. She felt so good in his arms, like the fulfillment of his destiny. "I love you, honey. And if you'll be my wife, I'll spend the rest of my life proving it."

"Oh, Lucas. I love you, too."

Activity swirled around them and Sheriff Garrett's well-trained deputies summoned an ambulance and drove onto the tarmac.

"We'll build a good life together, honey," Lucas said as he helped her toward the gate. "We'll have a passel of kids and all of them will be bright and beautiful, like their mother."

"But...what about—"

"You tell me, princess. Do the circumstances of my birth make a difference to you?"

"Not in the least. I know who and what you are. You're the man I love, Lucas Garrett."

Lucas kissed her, confident that his identity had not been determined by the circumstances of his birth but by the quality of his character. "And that's exactly who I want to be, Princess Honey," he said before he kissed her again.

He was a man who had found the woman of his dreams, and he didn't care that she happened to be a princess. He wouldn't hold it against her.

Epilogue

Dressed in a perfect Dior suit with a stunning diamond pendant around her neck and her hair arranged to cover the bruise on her forehead, Lexie stepped up to the microphones set up in the Destiny airport. On one side of her was her father, King Frederick of St. Novia, wearing his blue uniform and a chestful of medals. On the other side, stood Lucas Garrett.

Flashbulbs exploded. Ramon Acardi was in the front row.

"Is it true, Princess Alexandra, that you're getting married?"

"Yes, Ramon." She couldn't help smiling. Her future with Lucas would be nothing less than perfect. They had decided that after the honeymoon Lucas would continue on as Bluff County Sheriff. They would live in his house and raise saddle horses. The emphasis on that enterprise would not be on bloodlines, however, but on heart, producing the kind of horses people wanted for pleasure and dependability.

She also hoped they would raise a family. Four children, at least.

"What about you, King Frederick? How do you feel about your daughter's plans?" Ramon asked.

Lexie stepped back to allow her father access to the microphone. "The happy couple has my heartiest blessing."

How could he say otherwise after Lucas had saved his

daughter's life and saved St. Novia five million dollars in ransom money? It would've been ungracious in the extreme for Frederick to refuse Lucas any favor after he'd proven himself such a worthy hero.

A prince among men, Lexie thought with a secret smile.

"Is this a love match?" called out another reporter.

Lexie nodded and Lucas beamed as she gazed at her tall, handsome cowboy with his black hair and blue eyes. She loved him more than words could express, cherished the future that stretched out before them with more reasons to be hopeful than there were stars in the sky.

She touched the precious diamond pendant Lucas had given her and smiled up at him with eyes full of love.

"What about the kidnapping?" came another question.

Lexie motioned for Lucas to take his rightful place in front of the microphones. Though he was not accustomed to the spotlight, he spoke clearly and answered every question about the investigation and the ultimate apprehension of Ian Solé aka Agent Paul Browning who was in the hospital, handcuffed to his bed and awaiting trial.

Lucas explained how the corrupt agent had used and abused his position within the Bureau to perpetrate some of the world's most heinous crimes.

"But what about that name?" Acardi asked. "Ian Solé? Do you have any idea what it means, how he chose that intriguing moniker?"

"Browning had a penchant for detail and a fixation with puzzles. As it turns out, the name Ian Solé is an anagram for the name of his sailboat." The vessel upon which Browning had ultimately planned to spend his ill-gotten retirement. Browning's pride and joy: the *Sea Lion*.

"Mr. Garrett—Will," Acardi shouted from the front row. "How do you feel about your son marrying into a royal family? What chance do you give these two, coming from such different worlds?"

Will moved from his position next to Lucas to the microphone. "I'm not worried about my son and his pretty bride," Will declared. "I know they have what it takes to make it."

Lucas put one arm around his father and the other around the woman he loved. "Besides," Lucas added. "As my mother and father proved, the Garrett clan has a history of long and successful marriages."

It was Lexie who ended the press conference with a friendly wave. After saying goodbye to King Frederick and watching him board his private plane, Lucas, Lexie and Will walked out of the terminal and climbed into Lucas's SUV and headed for home.

Seated between Lucas and his father, Lexie sighed and settled back against the seat. The high-country air coming through the window ruffled her hair and filled her senses. "Ah," she sighed contentedly. "A girl could get used to this kind of luxury."

"I'm afraid you'll have to, honey," Lucas said, leaning over to give her a light peck on the cheek. "After all, you are a princess."

The romantic suspense at

HARLEQUIN®
INTRIGUE

just got more intense!

On the precipice between imminent danger and smoldering desire, they are

When your back is against the wall and nothing makes sense, only one man is strong enough to pull you from the brink— and into his loving arms!
Look for all the books in this riveting new promotion:

WOMAN MOST WANTED (#599)
by **Harper Allen**
On sale January 2001

PRIVATE VOWS (#603)
by **Sally Steward**
On sale February 2001

NIGHTTIME GUARDIAN (#607)
by **Amanda Stevens**
On sale March 2001

Available at your favorite retail outlet.

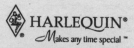

If you enjoyed what you just read,
then we've got an offer you can't resist!

Take 2 bestselling love stories FREE!

Plus get a FREE surprise gift!

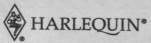

#1 *New York Times* bestselling author

NORA ROBERTS

brings you more of the loyal and loving,
tempestuous and tantalizing Stanislaski family.

Coming in February 2001

The Stanislaski Sisters

Natasha and Rachel

Though raised in the Old World traditions of their
family, fiery Natasha Stanislaski and cool, classy
Rachel Stanislaski are ready for a *new* world of love....

And also available in February 2001 from
Silhouette Special Edition, the newest book in the
heartwarming Stanislaski saga

CONSIDERING KATE

Natasha and Spencer Kimball's daughter Kate turns her
back on old dreams and returns to her hometown, where
she finds the *man* of her dreams.

Available at your favorite retail outlet.

Where love comes alive™

HARLEQUIN®
INTRIGUE
opens the case files on:

TOP SECRET
BABIES

Unwrap the mystery!

January 2001
#597 THE BODYGUARD'S BABY
Debra Webb

February 2001
#601 SAVING HIS SON
Rita Herron

March 2001
#605 THE HUNT FOR HAWKE'S DAUGHTER
Jean Barrett

April 2001
#609 UNDERCOVER BABY
Adrianne Lee

May 2001
#613 CONCEPTION COVER-UP
Karen Lawton Barrett

Follow the clues to your favorite retail outlet.

HARLEQUIN®
Makes any time special ™

Visit us at www.eHarlequin.com